Drizbits Publishing
Orlando Florida, 32811

This book is a work of fiction. Any references to actual people or real places are used fictitiously. Other names, characters, places, and events are products of the author's imagination, and any resemblances to places or persons, living or dead, are entirely coincidental.

Drizbits Publishing Enhanced Illustration
2nd edition
November 2016
ISBN 978-0-9991850-0-1

For information about special discounts for bulk purchases, please contact Willie L. Sheard of Drizbits Publishing at
Willielsheard@Drizbits.com

Thank you for all your support.

I worked on this title for nearly a year prior to its publication date in efforts to tell a story like no other. It's thanks to you that I was able to breathe life into these pages and deliver an ongoing tale of mystery.

"I am what echoes in your mind, what sleeps behind your eyes. I am what drives you, what motivates you . . . I am your all and shall **not** be denied."

Nathaniel

"You shall live abundantly without worry, for I am your protector. Endure the hardships of time and prosper, grow wise with age, and I will reward you with endless bliss."

GateKeeper

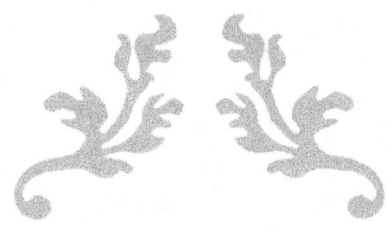

LAMAR AND NATHANIEL

A New Struggle Begins

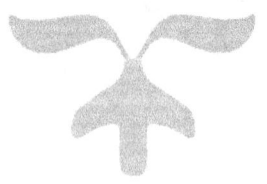

Contents

A Life Long Struggle

A Distant Voice

In the beginning, It was only a voice. A mere grain of sand amongst a mountain, whose influences were equivalent to a single protester drowned out by the masses. It had no shape or substance and lacked the ability of independent thought. It could go nowhere. It could do nothing. It could only exist in the endless void of darkness. An observer of humanity, unable to interfere or enlighten, until the day Lamar heard its voice for the first time.

"...I call onto you, child of this world. Awaken from your endless slumber, see the truths of this world and its cruelty. Succumb to it, immerse yourself in despair, for I shall ease your woes and live once more...."

It spoke, only to have its words land upon heedless ears.

"Child of this world, heed me. You shall be the vessel in which I drink. Grow! Ripen! Fill thyself with knowledge of this world, overflow in despair. That I shall taste life and grow strong!"

Lamar remains fast asleep, comforted between his mother's bosom. He would dream dreams of joy and happiness, for he has yet to experience the woes of life. Still retaining much of his innocence and naivety, Lamar ignores the voice that calls for him as he sleeps ever so peacefully.

A Life Long Struggle

"I shall live within you. Merge thy body and soul and harbor my emptiness. Unify and become my vessel!"

It reached into Lamar's subconscious and pierced through his perceptional reality.

"I shall share the knowledge of man, accept me and prosper...grow fat, greedy, you shall want for naught. Live life as a king! Speak these words, child, and all is yours."

It had begun to merge with Lamar's subconscious, gaining a new shape and form. Carefully it continued to alter Lamar's mind to unify itself without detection.

"Yes, Child of man. Merge, and thy shall be born anew. Man shall rise, and man shall fall, but I shall exist, always. Child of man . . ." It stopped and remained motionless. *"What is this? Something blocking the merger?"*

The air is thickened with murderous intent. It had lost all interest in merging with the child and now wanted only death.

"This child is mine and mine alone! I shall be what devours him!"

The creature then pulls from Lamar's subconscious, spreading itself throughout the entire house.

"Bathe in my despair, for all shall fall before me this day!"

With a single swift strike, It devours all life within the home.

"Tasteless. I had hoped more for this child."

A Life Long Struggle

Despite its incredible display of power, Lamar's body still drew breath while he remained in a state of deep sleep.

"You feeble insolent speck of dust! You dare defy me!"

Just before It could attack again, a slight glow covered Lamar's body, protecting him from Its onslaught. The glow began to shine brighter and brighter until a burst of bright light exploded from his body, pushing It back into the shadows and reviving all surrounding life.

"What is this light...!? No! I MUST have him! Awaken from your slumber, child. I must devour you now!! Come! Come to me!"

It called and beckoned for Lamar to awaken from his slumber, but his childhood innocence allowed him to remain fast asleep while the blast had quickly removed Its presence from existence.

"You are strong child, but I am beyond power. I shall return....I...shall...return...."

The next morning Lamar woke with an abundance of energy, as most eight-year-olds would. His mother had awoken some time before to prepare breakfast. The entire house was filled with the aroma of pancakes, Lamar's favorite meal. After setting the table and washing the dishes, she walked back to their room to wake Lamar. She spoke in a gentle tone, *"Wake up, Lamar. It's time for school."*

Lamar lay in bed, his body fully stretched from corner to corner with a pillow on top of his face. He had stripped himself bare and laid partially wrapped in bedsheets. His mother opened the blinds to shine light into the room as she spoke cheerfully, *"Rise and shine, time to get up. And where are your pajamas! I distinctly remember telling you NOT to undress yourself! You do this every morning, as soon as I leave to fix breakfast you...."*

Lamar rolled over and covered his face with the sheets, "Not now, mommy. I'm still sleeping..." he said as he dozed off once more. His mother replied, *"Wha?! Don't start that early this morning. We both have a long day ahead of us, so let's start it out on a good note. How about you get up like the big boy I know you are and...."*

Lamar pretended to snore, loudly. This continued for a short while until the room suddenly went silent. There were no sounds of footsteps walking away from his bedside nor of any getting closer, just complete silence. Lamar's snoring stopped abruptly, and his eyes popped wide open. He knew what was about to happen next. He slowly peeked over his shoulder and said,

"Mom.....Mommy?? Are you there?"

But there was no reply. The only thought that coursed through his mind was to get up – and fast! He quickly flung the sheets from his face and sprung to his feet only to feel an ominous presence behind him.

".....Mom, I'm..."

Lamar turned around to finish speaking, but his mother's hand was much faster. Her hand was stretched high to the ceiling, fingers spread far apart. Her face was stone cold with a slight humorous yet ominous smile. Before Lamar could respond, she had already smacked him across his face. The impact sent him crashing to the floor. His mother then smiled, tucked both hands on her knees and bent down to Lamar, and spoke lovingly in a soft tone,

A Life Long Struggle

"Good to see you're finally up. That's my big boy. Now, I have breakfast ready, get dressed, then go wash up, and I'll meet you at the table." She then kissed him on his forehead and walked out of the room towards the kitchen. As she walked away, Lamar felt a voice scratch at the back of his mind...

"How dare you hit me...who does she think she is!"

"Who's there?" Lamar said as he looked around himself aimlessly. *"Is someone talking to me.....hello?* Lamar rises to his feet and says, *"Mamma must have got me pretty good. I'm starting to hear things. I better go wash up before she comes back!"*

After breakfast and a long car ride to school, the day was normal. Once they arrived at school, his mother said, *"You know the drill. Be back here, at car pick up at..."* however, Lamar interrupted her before she could finish.

"I know, I know. I'm not a little kid, mom."

"Oh, my little boy has grown up into a man," she replied with a surprised expression as she looked down at Lamar. *"But my little man has forgotten how to wash his face. Come here, let me wipe it for you."*

She licked her thumb and vigorously scrubbed his face, eyebrows, nose, and cheeks. Within seconds all areas of interest had been wiped clean. Lamar struggled to escape, *"Ewww, no mom...Stop it...No...Mom...Ewww...Not with your spit. That's nasty!"*

Lamar jumped out of the car and ran off, wiping his face with the bottom of his shirt. He turned to his mother and waved goodbye as the voice again whispered to him,

"How dare she spit on me! I'm not a spit n chew toy...."

A Life Long Struggle

Lamar's mother's voice chimed in his mind, breaking him away from his thoughts as she waved goodbye, *"Have a good day, Lamar, and remember to be firm. Don't let the other kids bully you. Be confident with your decisions and...."*

"I know, mom. I remember. Attack every obstacle that lay in my path with full knowledge of the outcome ... and ... ummm...thought before action .... I got it, mom! Love you!"

Lamar then ran off to class, eager to start his day; however, this day was different; something had changed. Although he had not heard Its voice, his body had responded naturally to It. Activating a powerful aura that dwelled deep within his subconscious.

This slight change allowed him to hear a second voice that seemed to scratch in the back of his mind with each choice he decided to act upon.

This would continue for the entire day. To decide whether to tie his shoes now or later would trigger feelings of unease. He had never felt such strong feelings before, and yet he didn't know how to explain what it was that he was truly feeling. During lunch, Lamar found himself in an extremely conflicting situation.

"What should I eat?! I really want cookies today, but momma said, "Don't you eat no cookies at school today cause you didn't eat all your breakfast." Humm! No cookies, my butt. Ok! But today is brownie day, so I have to pick between a cookie and a brownie."

"Eat the cookie. No one will know."

"Wha, who said that! Did somebody just say, eat the cookie?" Lamar looked around, but he was the only person

standing at the cookie stand. He looked toward the cashier and asked, *"Lady, which should I get, the cookie or the brownie?"* However, before she could reply, he felt a voice scratch in the back of his mind once more.

"Yes, tell her that you aren't supposed to have cookies today."

The lunch lady replied, *"Well, son, which do you like best?"* Lamar stared at the cookies and brownies for a short while, then proudly replied, *"I like cookies best!"* The lunch lady smiled and replied, *"Okay, then get the cookie."* Lamar's face turned into a frown as he began to confess, *"I'm not sure because my Mommy said—"* but again, the voice scratched,

"Come now, tell the fat lady you can't have cookies."

Lamar paused for a moment, then said, *"On second thought, I'll just have the brownie."* Just as the cashier handed Lamar the brownie, Matthew, his best friend, walked over and said, *"Man, it took you so long to order, and you picked a nasty brownie too. Thought cookies were your favorite?"* Lamar turned towards Matthew holding his brownie, and said, *"They are, but my Mamma said I couldn't have any cookies today since I didn't finish my breakfast."*

"Well, you should've got the cookie then. It's the same thing."

As soon as Matthew said those words, Lamar felt his stomach cringe as the voice spoke to him yet again.

"You are such a bad child to have gone against your mother's words."

Lamar stood frozen with sensations of confusion coursing throughout his mind. Noticing his hesitation, Matthew said, *"Lamar, are you ok, man? You don't look so good."* Matthew *reached out to tap Lamar in an attempt to gain his attention, but* Lamar shoved the brownie into Matthews's hands and shouted, *"Man, why you gotta say stuff like that!?"*

"What'd I do? " Matthew replied with a puzzled expression.

"Know what . . . just forget it. You can have the brownie! I don't want it anymore!" Lamar then walked away in a fury, with his mind in a state of turmoil. Matthew then yelled at him from a distance. *"Thanks for the brownie, and don't forget to come over this weekend to play!"*

Lamar's frustration continued for the entire day. Each choice he acted upon would trigger intense sensations that he couldn't yet understand. Once school had ended, he headed to the child pickup and drop-off area to wait for his mother. He waited and waited until his mind began to have another odd thought that didn't quite belong to him.

"Why is it I have to get picked up by her? She wakes me up by slapping me—should I be listening to someone that hurts me for pleasure? A real mom wouldn't hurt their children like that. Yeah, that's right. She isn't my real mom...I should run away...."

Suddenly a high-pitched squeal redirected his attention, *"Over here! That's my baby! Somebody get him for me! Haayyyy!!"* His mother had been waving at the end of the line, signaling for his attention. Once the cars ahead of her were gone, she pulled up in front of him so he could get in.

A Life Long Struggle

Feeling extremely embarrassed, he walked toward the car, got in, and slid deep in the seat, ensuring no one would see him. But the voice continued to scratch at his mind, inciting an interesting conversation between the three of them.

"How dare she embarrass me like that?!"

Lamar quickly sat up in his seat and said, "What did you say, mom?" *Looking through the rearview mirror, she replied,* "I didn't say a word, honey. Are you ok, baby? I didn't mean to embarrass you." *Lamar smiled and replied,* "It's ok mom, you didn't"

"Like hell you didn't!"

Lamar jumps in his seat as if he were frightened, *"Mom, are you whispering? I can hear you saying something, but I can't hear what you're saying."* His mother adjusted her rearview mirror to see him more clearly, *"Honey, I'm not whispering anything...are you ok?"*

"NO!"

"Yea, I'm ok. I just want to take a nap," Lamar replied. His mother readjusted her mirror then said to Lamar, *"I have to make a quick stop at Supermart. You can rest in the car if you like..."* Lamar agreed even though he knew he would not be able to rest.

After a long afternoon of shopping, dinner and a warm bath was well deserved. At the day's end, fatigue set in, and before long, it was time for bed.

Lamar would cuddle under his mother's arms to sleep a peaceful sleep, just as he'd done many nights before. But It had a different plan. They shared a queen-sized bed, where his mother would spread soft white sheets across them both as her arms wrapped lovingly around his upper body. His back usually faced the walls opposite his mother while his face lay buried within his mother's breast.

Tonight was different. Lamar had been tormented by an unknown presence for much of the day, which had brought him to a new level of mental exhaustion and forced him to sleep abnormally. He pressed his back against his mother's and faced the wall directly. His feet tucked beneath himself as his head rested on top of his arms. It was in this state, where It and Lamar had their first physical encounter. It waited until both were fast asleep. Then again, It called for him.

"Child of man... heed me."

Again and again, It would call out as a cold and unfamiliar presence loomed all around him. Lamar rolled back and forth in his sleep as if to remove the feeling of unfamiliarity from his bedside. Yet, despite all of his efforts, the voice would only become clearer.

"Child of man...heed me."

A force seemed to be pressing him to wake from his slumber for some unknown reason. Increased agitation led him to flop over on his back, his face pointing directly to the ceiling as his eyes slowly opened to a room engulfed in darkness.

"Child of man...Heed me! See me for what I am!"

His eyes glazed over with a blank stare, unaware of the impending danger. Despite Its efforts, Lamar could not see nor hear anything. He reached out for his mother but could not remember the direction in which she had been lying. The room had been swallowed by an endless pool of darkness, a void that had eaten time itself. But this didn't frighten Lamar. No, he simply rolled back over and slowly closed his eyes while drifting back to sleep.

"Child, do ye not see me? Still under the protection of that aura? Clever, you are special. A special one indeed."

However, Lamar could not feel the fear that was brought forth by the pressure of this unknown presence, so he drifted back to sleep with ease while his mother lay wide awake. Her eyes were stretched wide open as goosebumps tread across her arm and down her back.

The next morning, Lamar awoke as he normally did, with an abundance of energy, as most eight-year-olds do. However, he was now curious about the voice. So he started to ask questions and create problems unnecessarily to see if he would hear the voice from yesterday. Before Lamar could leave for school, he had already begun to seek answers to his questions. First, he questioned himself if he should wear black shoes or white shoes even though his mother had laid out his school uniform days prior. Then questioned if he should have milk or apple juice with his breakfast while eating cereal. Afterward, he argued that he should not have to brush his teeth before school since they'd only get dirty during lunchtime. But no matter how hard he tried, the voice would not return.

On the way to school, he sat quietly in the back seat. He remained motionless, in a state of deep thought. He stared out the car window without a single blink of his eyes. His mother had never seen him in such a concentrated state before. She would glance at him from the rearview mirror from time to time and make silly comments as if to trigger some sort of response, but he would only nod his head in approval as he continued to gaze out the window. She continued to reach out to her son, but with each failed attempt, her heart sank deeper into her chest. She began to feel waves of emotions, feelings of sadness, and fear as her thoughts rambled, *"Have I lost my son...is something wrong with him?"*

Just as the pain of uncertainty was about to consume her, Lamar spoke. His words were stale and unsettling, but for a moment, he was himself. He turned to his mother and asked with an expressionless face, *"Mom, how many voices do you have in your head?"*

After he spoke, there was a brief moment of silence. She didn't expect such an odd question from her son. Furthermore, she didn't know how to respond to such a question. She then adjusted the rearview mirror to see if his physical state had changed, only to find that he was staring back at her with the same blank gaze, awaiting her response. She made a quick effort to change the subject, *"Honey, are you wearing your seat belt?"* However, Lamar's expression did not change. He only insisted further, *"When I am awake, I can only hear me when I talk, and no one else. And when I stop talking, I can hear myself in my head. So how come when I sleep I hear something else talking to me...."*

She interrupted him abruptly and spoke calmly, *"Honey, that's just your dreams. You had a bad dream, that's all."*

Lamar sat deeper into the seat, repeating the phrase, *"A bad dream."* He remained still for a short while as he stared at his hands and down to his feet. Then, his expression slowly revived itself. Life seeped into his face, and a slight smile emerged. He then looked up at his mother in the rearview mirror and replied, *"Yep, just a bad dream."*

Once they arrived at school, his mother kissed him on his head and said, *"I love you honey, and have a good day. Okay?"* His reply was the same as it always is with the added, *"I love you too, mommy, and I will."*

After a somewhat brief exchange of words, he appeared to be back to normal. Attending school was always the highlight of his day. His teachers and classmates would praise him daily for being such a good student. There was never an instance where he caused any trouble or fought any of the other children. He would always be the child of reason, the kind of kid that never acts out.

He even had a routine upon classroom entry. First, he entered his classroom. Then he'd put away his lunch pail and hang up his backpack. Afterward, he would always drink from the water fountain just before he sat alongside the other students. However, today was a bit different. Although Lamar looked the same, his mannerisms had changed. He entered the classroom empty-handed; he had left both his lunch pail and backpack in the car with his mother. He didn't even have his daily fountain drink because he had already convinced himself he didn't need it since he had thoroughly brushed his teeth before school.

It didn't take long before his teacher noticed the slight change in Lamar's behavior. He seemed to be agitated with the other students. She would hear Lamar engage in multiple disagreements with the other students and claim that he has another person in his head who helps him make good choices. Before the bell rang for recess, Lamar had become completely detached from the other children. Before long, Lamar found himself swinging on the swing set, all alone with no one to play with.

He began the feel sorry for himself, "Why *don't the other kids* understand me?" he thought to himself. *"How come I'm so different than they are?"*

His mind began to drift off as the world around him ceased to be. He thought harder and harder, in attempts to find the hidden reason behind his difference. But before he could reach a satisfying conclusion, he felt a sharp thump that knocked him from his trance. His vision was redirected to the sand below his feet, where a small girl lay in tears.

She had been in the neighboring swing and fell out because she swung too high. Her face had left an impression in the sand as a stamp would on a sheet of paper. Her tears left tread marks on her sand-filled face as Lamar sat in his swing staring at her.

His first thought was to run over to help the small girl. He would comfort her by saying, *"It's ok, I'm here to help you. Where are you hurt?"* He envisioned himself jumping down from the swing then running over to the girl's aid, *"Here, let me brush off the sand...it may sting a little...no reason to cry. It's ok now."*

He would brush the sand from her face and wipe the tears from her eyes. He saw himself helping her stand to her feet as she smiled kindly at him. He imagined her soft and gentle voice speak out to him in gratitude. Her head would turn slightly as she muttered, "Thank you," just before walking away. But none of this had actually happened. Instead, Lamar was still sitting in the swing staring at the young girl as she wept. He was perplexed. He thought to himself, *"Why is she crying? I'm sure she knew how high she was going and the outcome if she had fallen. So why is she crying? Did she plan this? Does she want me to help her? Why would she hurt herself for attention? I don't understand...should I help her, or should I let her cry like she planned on doing?"*

He remained in the swing and thought to himself. He rambled back and forth with himself arguing, "What course of action should I do next?" Lamar's internal conversation continued with no signs of a conclusion until someone shouted,

"SHE'S BLEEDING!"

Lamar then snapped out of deep thought and jumped up to help the young girl almost instinctively. He began to do exactly what he imagined he would do just before he started to think about it. He and another classmate helped carry the young girl to the clinic where she was treated. Lamar was awarded for his efforts with stickers and many hugs from the other students.

After school was over, Lamar waited for his mother as he normally would. She was always a few minutes early, eagerly awaiting his arrival. On the drive home, Lamar's mother told him how her day was and how she was so proud to receive a call at work about his heroic deeds. She talked on and on for the entire journey home, leaving little room for Lamar to speak. He would just nod and give short responses like "yes ma'am" and "ok." Although it seemed that Lamar was an active audience member in his mother's drive home soliloquy, he drifted in and out of thought, curious about the day's events.

He didn't know why he was unable to help the girl through his own willpower. He wanted to help, but his body wouldn't respond. All he could do was think and analyze the situation, which made him feel helpless in his own skin. As Lamar dwelled on the past incident, his mother continued her day's rant until they finally made it home.

Lamar's routine life continued. He spent much of the day outside playing with his friends and neighbors. Later, he would have dinner followed by a warm bath. Lamar had finally decided to forget the day's events and continue moving in a positive direction, and should a similar incident occur, he would react with

cat-like reflexes. This newfound courage and determination led Lamar to forget all about the voice that scratched in the back of his mind. Until moments before he had fallen asleep.

He laid peacefully under his mother's arms as she embraced him ever so tightly. Entangled between her and layers upon layers of bed sheets sown in threads of gold and white, he could still feel the warmth of her lips where they pressed against his head as she kissed him goodnight. He could hear the melody of her heart as she slept ever so peacefully. Even the tick of the clock seemed as clear as day light, for sleep did not come for him on this night.

He laid awake, staring at the ceiling as the day's events replayed in his mind. He thought to himself until his eyes grew heavy, and he could no longer think clearly. He yawned and stretched about as he slowly drifted off to sleep. But just as sleep blanketed him, again, the voice called out.

"Child of man, heed me."

Something had changed. Lamar could hear the voice as clear as anyone he had heard before. The voice was no longer in the distance but spoke to him as if it stood in his presence.

"I have called for you. I have waited patiently for this moment. Somehow you are protected from me, but I now know how to undo this protection. Come, child of man, I shall open your eyes to this world!"

Lamar began to talk in his sleep, "It's only a bad dream...mommy said so!"

But the voice replied in agitation, "No child, this is no dream."

A Life Long Struggle

Lamar's eyes opened, but he was still partially asleep. He attempted to roll over to regain the sleep he had lost, only to feel as if he were a member in a tug-of-war match. His body swayed back and forth as if his left arm and right leg were being pulled in opposite directions. Still disoriented due to his lack of sleep, Lamar slowly opened his eyes to examine the situation. He noticed something was wrong, and he could not feel his right leg. He turned to face the wall where his leg seemed to be, only to hear his mother cry out, "Grab my hand! LAMAR! Grab my hand!"

Suddenly Lamar felt an overwhelming presence that snapped him from his sleep-like state. He could see his mother's hand reaching out for him, her face twisted with horror and covered in tears. He was surrounded by a dark void that had consumed his right leg and was trying to pull him into the darkness. Realizing this, Lamar began to panic, "*Help me! Mom, help me! Please!*

*"Hold on Lamar, **don't** let go!"*

Lamar begins to kick wildly at the void, hoping the darkness would dissipate somehow, but it only grew larger in size. Lamar's screams woke everyone in the house. Before long, his entire family stood at his bedside, pulling him from the void. Just as they were about to free him, the dark void consumed the whole room, and there was silence. No one could see or hear anything. It was as if the darkness had swallowed the light as well as the sound from the room. A sudden whisper broke the silence, as Lamar heard the voice speak to him once again. He quickly shut his eyes as tight as he could, as the whispering voice spoke clearly to him.

"Your eyes shall open to the world around you, a true judge of your own existence, and no longer bound to the bliss

of ignorance. Remain immune to this world of human nature and you shall live abundantly, but should you succumb to this world's chaos, I shall devour you whole."

Dark Void

Lamar opened his eyes only to see nothing. He stood in a desolate land, shrouded in complete darkness. He was motionless and still, prone to possibility. He remained silent as his eyes scanned the surrounding area in search of light, but none could be found. Lamar then raised his foot slightly in attempts to take one small step forward, but before he could, a voice in the distance cut through the silence and spoke directly to him.

"EM OT EMOCk."

The voice echoed in the darkness, causing Lamar to look in all directions, spinning in place. He then shouted back, "Mommy, is that you . . ." but there was no reply. Lamar continued to speak aloud to the voice, "Turn on the lights mom, I can't see you!" The voice replied, "EM OT EMOCk," *sending chills down Lamar's spine. He paused, then spoke again, "Mom, talk louder...you are too far away for me to hear you!"*

"EM OT EMOCk."

Again the voice in the distance spoke to him, but Lamar wasn't able to understand it. The distance was too great, and the voice had little depth. However, it became apparent that the voice was not friendly. Growing more nervous as time passed and realizing that his mother wasn't on the other end of the voice, Lamar took a single step backward and said, *"Who's there . . . My name is Lamar. What's yours?"* There was a slight pause, then the voice spoke once more.

"EM OT EMOCk."

His heart sped up tenfold. Clinching his chest as the hair on his neck stood tall. Attempting to conceal his fear, Lamar shouted, *"I'm not afraid of you, whoever you are!* His hands trembled as he continued, *"Just because you turned off the lights and put me in a dark room...I'm not afraid! My momma will get you when she finds out you are bullying me, so you had better stop it!*

"EM OT EMOCk!"

The voice deepened as if angered, "EM OT EMOCk!" Lamar could feel the presence of the voice getting closer and closer, "EM OT EMOCk!" Lamar's thoughts rambled as he stood frozen, then there was silence. Lamar stood still, his heart pounding in his chest as his body trembled. No one spoke. Dead silence filled the air, then, just as Lamar began to breathe more calmly, the voice spoke loudly, "EM OT EMOCk!"

Frightened by the approaching voice, Lamar took a deep breath and quickly stretched both arms out to either side, reaching for anything to grasp on to. His arms spread full length as his fingers extended, twirling in the darkness. He searched on his left and right, then in front and behind him. Growing more anxious by the second, he spoke aloud to the voice, *"Boy, are you gonna get it when my mamma gets here, Mister! She gonna bop you one good, just you wait!"*

A Life Long Struggle

Lamar then kneeled down towards the floor, hoping to find something he could grab hold of. With his anxiety building, Lamar continued to speak, *"I'm gonna open the door when I find it and call her, and she will come get me, and she's gonna beat you good!"*

Despite all of his efforts, there was nothing to grab hold of. He had truly been surrounded by darkness. Realizing this, Lamar felt a sharp pain course through his body. He suddenly felt heavy. He squatted down and placed his head between his knees, then pressed his hands firmly against his ears. Then, in a sudden outburst of anger and sadness, Lamar shouted out, *"I can't find anything in here! Mamma, where are you!"*

His eyes teared with grief, *"I hate you,"* Lamar shouted, pounding on the floor. He punched and smacked the floor as hard as he could while he screamed as loud as he could. But unknown to him, a thick liquid was forming underneath his feet. It grew thicker and thicker the more Lamar hit the floor's surface, collecting undetected. The substance slowly made its way up Lamar's body until he felt the cold and slimy substance near his stomach and back.

Leaping up, he shouted, *"Momma, stuff is crawling on me! Ma help me, please!"* Clawing and pulling at the sticky substance, Lamar struggled to free himself. But the substance seemed to be alive! It pulled back and slithered from area to area as if it was trying to avoid being pulled away. Lamar shouted, *"They're everywhere! Get 'em off! Get 'em off!"*

Intense sensations of longing and fear began to overwhelm him and spew from his body only to be absorbed by the oily substance, like leaches. Lamar's thoughts ran rampant in his mind. He thought, "*I gotta get 'em off me! Rub them off...my arms, my legs! Brush this stuff off me! Get off me!*"

As his emotions intensified, the land began to shift beneath his feet as if to carry him over vast distances in an instant. He could hear this world call out to him. He could feel his body begin to change as his flesh burned and his blood boiled. Lamar thought to himself, "*I must escape. I have to RUN!*"

An immense sense of urgency took over as Lamar tried to flee and free himself from this prison. Tearing the substance from his body, he lets out an ear ringing yell. The substance fell to the floor and vanished, blending with the void. Lamar, now free of the substance, stammered forward in pain, then shouted out,

"*Mommy, I'm ready to go . . . Right now please....*"

He staggered forward, struggling with each step. His feet felt heavy and still, "*What the heck is this,*" he said, looking to his feet. The floor was covered in that thick and sticky oil-like liquid. He tried to pull the substance from his feet, but it wouldn't budge. He then tried to run, but the substance clung to his feet, causing him to fall flat on his face. Quickly pushing himself into the pushup position, now face to face with this odd substance, he thought, "*What is this stuff?*" *He lowered his face closer to smell it, but it was odorless.* "*I can't move covered in this!*" Lamar said. "*I have to stand to my feet and keep moving. Momma told me to be strong, never let anybody bully me! I have to get out of here, and this sticky stuff won't hold me back!*"

He struggled to stand. The substance stretch like bubble gum, making it increasingly difficult for him. He struggled and squirmed. He screamed and yelled until he stood to his feet. Feeling extremely exhausted, he cleaned the remaining substances from his body. Although Lamar hadn't noticed it, the substance had

already begun to drain his energy. His motions lagged as if his entire body had slowed down while his mind sped up. Lamar, now freed from the substance, continued to search for an exit.

Now let's go! It's time to get out of here," he said to himself. Although he had freed himself of the substance, the floor remained covered in it. Lamar struggled with each step as he talked to himself aloud, *"ughh...I can barely move my feet. What ... Is ... going ... on here."* Fatigue had begun to set in as the substance continued to sap the energy from him. *"This stuff on the ground is super sticky, like man! I gotta get out of here,"* Lamar said to himself.

"EM OT EMOCk"

The voice had returned, and it was closer than it was before. Lamar shouted, *"Oh no! I gotta go NOW! Go go go go go! Come on body, we gotta go! Move! He's coming! He's coming!"*

"EM OT EMOCk"

His breathing intensified as his heart rate increased; he entered a state of severe panic with no form of relief. His body had frozen, but his mind was free. His feet were trapped, but his eyes could see. He could go no further; he had reached his peak. He screamed out for help . . . but none would see.

"STOP!!!" Lamar yelled with his arms stretched wide! *"Whoever you are...where ever you are. Stop, this is not funny anymore!"*

Tears fell from his face as he closed his eyes tightly and began to plea, *"I'm just a kid...I'm not a big boy yet. I'm just a kid!"*

A Life Long Struggle

He then opened his eyes and glanced down towards his feet, where his tears had landed. The land seeped of an oil-like substance that had begun to slither its way up his body once more. Lamar's struggles had suddenly stopped; his tears could no longer fall. This substance that slowed his movements had siphoned away his will, his hope, and his determination to escape.

Just as Lamar reached the verge of giving up, a voice spoke to him, clearly, *"Finished already?"* The voice resonated within Lamar's mind causing him to cry out furiously.

"It's the voice! The bad voice in my head!?"

"Did you forget, already?" The voice then replied, *"Allow me to remind you. Should you fall prey to this world of man, I shall devour you!"* Instead of feeling hopeless, life seemed to ignite *within* Lamar as he shouted back at the voice.

*"I will **not** be trapped by a voice! Hear that Voice! You will not keep me here in this place!"*

He thrashed about, flailing his body in efforts to free himself. His body started to respond, and with each thrust, each struggle, he began to free himself. As Lamar continued to struggle, the voice continued to speak to him.

Child of man, have you not learned anything? Then struggle...yes...struggle and hope...."

Desperation became hope as Lamar's mobility slowly returned. In realizing that he could possibly have a chance to escape, Lamar lets out a powerful outburst, filled with hope, vigor, and energy.

"I...CAN...DO IT!!!"

A Life Long Struggle

The voice continued to taunt Lamar, "Show me, child of man. Show me...and ripen before me."

Just as Lamar had reached a point of total mobility, he burst free from the substance that confined him. However, the substance reacted to the sudden eruption of energy and quickly engulfed Lamar's entire body, with a powerful surge of dark energy.

Lamar was now completely confined in a cocoon. He remained motionless, weak, and helpless, blanketed in darkness as the substance constricted him as it drained away all of his energy. Lamar had been completely consumed by the hopelessness of the dark void as the voice echoed around him.

"Do you understand now, child of man? Your struggles are futile. Why do you continue to suffer? Do you enjoy this feeling of hopelessness, of agony? Give in to this world, succumb to it, indulge yourself, and the pain will subside."

Light and Wisdom

Suddenly, a flash of bright white light gleamed across the horizon, shattering all darkness. Still trapped in a cocoon, Lamar was unable to see what was happening around him, but he could feel the heat from the extraordinary light. Unable to free himself, Lamar shouted, *"Ahhh! What is this light?! It's so bright and hot! What's going on in here?!"*

A massive shock wave of sound, followed the sudden blast of light, which vaporized all surrounding substances, freeing Lamar from his prison. The substance that confined Lamar was instantly disintegrated, and Lamar fell from darkness into a world of infinite light. Surprised about the sudden change of events just mere moments after being devoured by darkness, Lamar shouted, "Woo, my God," as he covered his ears and clenched his eyes shut in anticipation of what was to come next.

However, nothing happened. Everything was completely silent. Confused, he began to talk to himself, *"What is going on around me? First, it was dark and sticky, now it's really bright...and...and I can't feel the ground anymore!?"* Lamar curled up in a ball with his head buried between his knees. Using his right hand, he felt around him where he thought the ground would be, but there was nothing there. He retracted his hand and thought to himself, *"Maybe if I open my eyes really quickly, I can see what's going on."* Using his other hand, Lamar again felt for the floor, hoping that he'd find something on the other side. But again, there was nothing. Lamar pulled himself into a tighter ball clenching his eyes even tighter. He sat for a moment, then spoke aloud, *"I'm gonna open my eyes...just for a second. Just for a second. Okay, on three. Here I go."* Bracing himself for the worst, he continued, *"...ok...ok...here I go...1...2..3!"*

Lamar quickly opened his eyes only to see a brilliant world of light. He panicked and shouted out, *"Holy crap! There's no floor!"*

Releasing himself from his ball, his arms and legs extended completely as if he were falling from great heights, *"Ohh! Ohh, I'm gonna fall," he shouted.* He began to flap his arms and kick his legs in all directions, trying to balance himself. After a short while, his arms and legs grew heavy, *"Oh no...I'm getting tired,"* Lamar shouted. *"Is this even working?"* His thoughts ran a mile a minute, but his body was unable to continue. Exhausted from flailing around, he spoke in a tired and unsure tone, "Ok, I'm gonna stop now....ok...ok... here I go...."

Lamar stopped moving. He had curled back up into a ball, hoping that he would not fall to his doom.

"Don't fall, don't fall, don't fall."

Despite his uncertainty, he did not fall. Instead, he slowly freed himself from his ball-like state and shouted, *"Holy crap, I can fly! Mamma, I think I'm Batman!"*

All feelings of hopelessness and agony faded. Before he could realize it, Lamar had begun to bask in the warmth of the light. He floated in a state of bliss, allowing his body to absorb the light that this new place was emitting. Soon after, his mind was calm and a bit more rational. His eyes now opened, he thought to himself, "It's time to find the exit." Spreading his fingers far apart, Lamar began to use his hands to probe his surroundings. He maneuvered his body as if he were flying, using his arms like wings and his feet as a rudder.

"This place IS really bright," he thought to himself. "But where is it coming from? I feel like I have searched every inch of this place, but I have yet to discover the source of this light. Nor have I touched or seen a single wall."

Lamar stopped his search and stood upright. He continued to think to himself, "I'm starting to feel like there aren't any barriers in this place! Hmmm, now what should I do? If this place is truly void and completely empty, then although I believe I can see in all directions, I cannot. And although I feel as if I can travel in all directions, I cannot. Hmph, I really should be worried, but for some reason, I'm not. I wonder why that is…."

Lamar again stood in a world of nothingness, but instead of darkness surrounding him, he had been immersed in a world of comforting light. A world of bliss and serenity. He had no such feelings as pain or fear, nor could he recall how these emotions felt. He instantly became utterly ignorant of all negativity and accompanied feelings. However, this significantly increased his curiosity. He remained deep in thought as he continued to ramble on to himself,

"No matter how far I search, I cannot find anyone else. It is so bright and spacious; I can no longer tell if I'm even moving. Everything looks and feels the same. But yet different. I have never felt calmer than I am right now. I have never felt less worried than how I am right now. I wonder…have I changed since I arrived in this place. I feel the same, and yet different. I have memories of a different self, another different than the one I am now . . . This place is changing me somehow...I know I am the only one here, but I don't care. There aren't any walls, ceilings, or floors, yet I don't care. I am trapped in this place, but still, I don't care...."

Lamar continued to think about his situation, all while basking in the marvelous light. Then, a sudden thought crossed Lamar's mind that piqued his curiosity more than ever, "I wonder . . . if my state of mind has altered vastly, in such a short time, then what has become of my physical appearance?"

Without any physical effort, that single thought manifested itself into a single sheet of reflective material that appeared before him. Surprised, Lamar thought aloud, "Ha, look at that. It seems that, where ever this place is, it responds to my thoughts. Interesting. Hmm, I don't look like me. My skin is as bright as this place . . . where . . . are my eyes, my nose, my mouth, and ears? Strange, all of my facial attributes are gone. Did I die? Hmm, all I have now is space and time. Come, ole inner voice of mine, I shall wait for thee."

Lamar only grew more curious by the second. He floated in this endless abyss while deep in thought. He wrestled with all previous questions he had until there were none to be questioned. He thought, "What is time?" But quickly drew an answer to his own question. He answered, "Time seems to be irrelevant, just a construct to incubate unformed actions."

As Lamar regressed deeper in thought, he reached a point of internal conflict. He compared his newly found bliss to the previous feelings of hopelessness and concluded that this current void was the same as the previous void.

A Life Long Struggle

"To be completely overwhelmed with intense feelings of pain and fear, followed by a surge of wishful possibility, then regret can only result. Regret with emotions of hopelessness, where no willpower can exist. In a sense, the same can be said for a blissful existence. To have little concerns, oblivious to problematic issues, to live a life of complete happiness is the same as a life without hope. Two sides of the same coin. Which means this world is the same as a dark and empty void...."

His last thought brought him to terms with his situation. He was trapped, and whether it be a world of fear and hopelessness or a world of blissful joy, the fact remained that he could not escape. It was this thought that brought forth that familiar voice, *"You have been stripped of all emotion, and yet you remain idle in this void. Must you be reminded again? Should you lose yourself in this world of man, I shall devour you whole."*

Lamar's curiosity peaked once again as he replied, *"I've been waiting for you, ole voice of mine."* Lamar then repositioned himself, making himself comfortable, then he continued to speak with the voice. *"You say that if I lose myself, I shall be devoured? But humans cannot change; they can only adapt to new information. I have learned this much through this journey of two voids. So now let me ask you something, ye ole voice of mine. If one cannot change, then how does one lose one's self? Mustn't he be lost at birth? This makes your pursuit of me futile, doesn't it?"*

Although Lamar had been stripped of emotion, his character remained intact. His natural rationality and curiosity balanced equally with his emotions absent, allowing him to seek out questions in a place where none needed to be asked. Their conversation began to shape the reality of the void until only voices could be heard. There was no color, no light, no signs of life, only voices as their conversation continued.

A Life Long Struggle

The voice answered, *"In the world of man, to lose one's self is the same regardless of how the loss is achieved. Rather one succumbs to riches, fame, power or is born into misery. The loss is equivalent. Change is unnecessary."*

Lamar then replied, *"How then, do you explain my ability to hear your voice? I was unable to hear you for some time now. Yet here we are, speaking as if we were old friends. If no change is necessary, are you saying I have simply lost some of myself due to an adaption of information?!"*

"Precisely," The voice replied, *"NOW do you understand? It is inevitable, I will consume you, and you shall cease to be."*

There was a short pause, then Lamar replied, *"Then why go through all this effort to alter my perception of reality? The truth is, you have no control over how I perceive things. All you can do is give information and watch how it unfolds."*

"Is this a challenge, child of man?" The creature said with a slight hint of curiosity in his tone. *"You have already fallen. The proof of this is your acknowledgment of my existence."*

Lamar quickly insulted the voice in a humorous tone, *"If I have truly lost and have fallen far from recovery, then why is it you have no form. You are an enigma, incomplete at best. My words are all that binds you. Should I refuse to acknowledge your existence, YOU shall cease to be."*

Furious with Lamar's ego, the voice shouts, *"Then challenge me, BOY! You claim that I am powerless, that I can only watch without interference. Then show me your conviction! Show me your will to survive... to live... or I shall devour you here and now!"*

A Life Long Struggle

Lamar, now equally frustrated as the voice, spoke in an infuriated tone, *"You do not scare me…but I'm no fool. I have gained tremendous enlightenment while trapped within this domain, and I have yet to comprehend your agenda. You claim to possess the ability to consume me, but yet we converse. You have the ability to alter my perception, and yet you leave it intact. You hold no power, creature."*

The voice, now in a state of rage, spoke with ill intent, *"Hear me, BOY. I grow weary of this conversation. Return to the world of man! But know this, I shall forever be near. Should the day come where you lose yourself to that world of man, I shall be there to consume you. Body and soul."*

The void had begun to breakdown and lose its integrity as both light and dark mix. The voice forced Lamar from its domain, extracting all acquired knowledge while doing so. Lamar's subconscious faded from the void returning to his body as the journey of the two voids would forever be a distant memory as his mind reverts back to a childlike state. And again, there was nothing.

In the far corners of Lamar's mind, the voice spoke in an enlightened tone, *"You have intrigued me, child of man. But, should the day come, where you lose yourself to that world of man, I shall consume you, body and soul."*

As Lamar's subconscious returned to his body, he could feel a welcoming presence that hovered around him. Although he remained unconscious, he could still feel drops of warm liquid fall onto his face while a heavenly voice cried out to him. He slowly opened his eyes, but he could not see. He followed the voice with his head and eagerly reached out to close the gap between them.

A Life Long Struggle

At first, he could only see shades of colors as his mind adjusted to the sudden change. His eyes began to water as his vision returned. He struggled to open them entirely until his mother's hand caressed his forehead. His eyes sprung open once again, but there was no void to look upon—only the loving face of his mother who stood before him, as tears fell from her face.

"Welcome back, son," she said with a smile. Overfilled with joy, she hugged and squeezed him as tight as she possibly could. Her voice crackled with emotion, "*I thought I had lost you,*" she shouted. "*You weren't breathing, and your heart had stopped . . . I didn't know what to do! But you're back now, and everything is going to be okay!*"

She released him from her grasp and stared into his eyes. She quickly noticed that something had changed. He was not the same boy from before. Her face looked confused as she asked, "*Lamar, are you ok. You seem different somehow, are you feeling alright?*"

Lamar replied while rubbing his eyes, "*Mom, I remember being in a hard place. Somewhere that I couldn't leave. I felt sad and hopeless. I think I died...then I was in a happy place, but it was too happy. I had time to think, so I did. For a really, really long time. But I wasn't happy there either.*"

Lamar's mother's heart pounded harder with every word that he spoke. She wanted to comfort him, but she felt her son wasn't the same child she remembered. She interrupted him from speaking and just held him tightly. Lamar began to cry silently, then he spoke in a soft tone,

Mommy, don't let me lose.... Nathaniel will devour me if I do.

One Stubborn Child

Vanessa looked down towards Lamar with a confused expression on her face. *"Who is Nathaniel,"* She asked. Lamar looked up at her, and just as he was about to speak, Vanessa noticed that his pupils were fully dilated. His mouth closed tight as he sat up straight, unable to see her clearly as if he had suddenly gone blind. Vanessa then placed her right hand on her forehead for a brief moment. Then put it on Lamar's head to compare his temperature to hers. But he seemed okay. No fever or any tell-tell signs of a cold or flu. She kissed Lamar on the top of his head and repeated her question, *"Honey, who is Nathaniel?"*

Again Lamar did not respond. A hollow and blank stare had blanketed his face. His eyes wandered the room as he thought to himself, *"I feel different somehow. My hands...my feet...I feel different. Am I really home?. . Nothing is as I remembered it to be. This room is so lively. I hadn't noticed before...The walls aren't a dull white as I remember; instead, they are covered by wood paneling. Shades of black and brown patterns that mimic the bark of many trees. A forest of trees, whose tops tower beyond the heavens! And the floor...it's made of marble!? Ha, I thought it to be painted white, in a dull luster. But it glimmers of marble! Even the air has a different smell – It's like a sweet women's perfume. A sea of aroma and I sit at the bottom basking in its reverence."*

Lamar's eyes continued to scan the room as if he had never been there before. His mother began to worry. No matter what she said to him, his eyes still wandered the room. She then shouted out, "LAMAR LOOK!" His eyes shifted in her direction, and with a surprised expression, they doubled in size.

Lamar had not stopped analyzing his surrounding but paused briefly as his eyes landed upon his mother's face. He gazed upon her as he thought to himself, *"Oh my, she's not old! I imagined her to be similar to an old wicked witch, but astonishingly enough, she's younger than I expected! Her skin is soft to the touch, and her eyes are the same as mine. She has long dark hair...and...what?"*

Lamar squinted his eyes as if to see in the distance. His mouth opened slightly as his thoughts continued to flow faster than his actions. He thought to himself, *"Is she speaking to me? Her eyes are watery...her posture is unnatural. Has she been crying? This newfound perception of mine isn't working in my favor right now. I don't know what to do. Right now, everything around me is new to me. I must relearn everything, and I must do it quickly."*

All of Lamar's senses flooded his mind with constant information. His interpretation of the world became stale to emotion and blossomed with rationality. His mind drifted as his face contained a blank stare while he concentrated on deciphering all the newly acquired information. He noticed that his mother spoke, her mouth moved, but he couldn't hear any of her words. She then embraced him tightly as his mind remained in a state of awe.

A Life Long Struggle

"I cannot remember a hug from her feeling so good," he thought to himself. *"She's nice and warm. I can truly feel how much she cares for me."* Then, a sudden jerking motion caused him to redirect his attention to his mother once more. *"What….I can feel her body vibrating…she must be speaking to me. I'm sorry mom. For some reason, I can't hear you right now. I believe my body is in a state of extended shock. I'm sorry, but all I can do right now is think."*

Vanessa then releases him from her embrace. She stares at him for a short while, then kisses him on his forehead once more. Her eyes began to water as tears fell from her face. She then muttered something, but Lamar was still unable to hear it.

"Wait…maybe I'm not in a state of shock," Lamar thought to himself. *"I can see, and I have some control of my motor skills . . . I know that I have changed in some strange way. But maybe…if I focus…."* Lamar then looked to his feet and tried to wiggle his toes. Just as he moved them slightly, sound fragments vibrated his eardrum like the chime of a bell in the distance. *"Yes, I'm not in a state of shock,"* Lamar thought to himself. *"It must be some side effect. Something happened to me. Something that I can't remember, but for now…I must focus."*

As Lamar attempted to regain control over his senses, Samantha, his younger cousin, burst into the room. Along with Simeon, his uncle, and the second youngest of his mother's siblings. He could see their immense state of panic, but he continued to concentrate. He could see everyone's attempts to talk to him, but to no avail, "I must concentrate," he thought to himself. His eyes became more and more colorless and dull as his concentration deepened. His body turned as malleable as a lump of clay while his arms and legs dangled as his mother held him.

A Life Long Struggle

As Vanessa desperately tries to hold herself back from a total meltdown, her brother Simeon insists on arguing with her. He tugged on her shoulder and demanded her attention.

"I told you! We should have called for an ambulance!" Simeon explained.

"Really?!" Vanessa shouted back, pulling away from him, *"And what would we say happened to him? He was sucked in the wall by a demon,"* she exclaimed as she held Lamar closely. *"Or how about, "Well, officer, after we were spat out from the WALL—"* She then cuts her eyes at Simeon in disapproval.

"Ok, I get it!" Simeon replied, *"But what will happen if he doesn't get better . . . what if he doesn't wake up completely. What then!?"*

Vanessa looked down at Lamar, his eyes still dilated. She rubs his head then says, "I guess explaining a sick child is better than a dead— …. well….go get the phone…."

Simeon ran out of the room with Samantha tagging behind him. Although she tried her hardest to hold back as much as she could, the thought of losing her only child caused Vanessa to overflow with tears. Just as hope faded from sight, she felt Lamar tug at the bottom corner of her shirt. He lifted up his head as his eyes slowly shifted back to reality. Lamar was slowly learning how to control his new ability. Still deep in thought, his mind rambled on, *"I can hear them! I can hear them now!"*

His eyes had regained their luster, and he had finally gained control over his newfound ability of perception. However, before he could speak, he noticed his mother's composure and aura had changed dramatically. He watched as his mother's arm flung back, stretching at full mass. Her fingers were spread apart as if she was reaching out to swat a fly from midair. Lamar then thought to himself, *"What is she reaching for... is there something on the ceiling?"*

As Lamar glanced toward the ceiling, his mother's hand swung downward with great force, crashing into Lamar's face. His eyes widened as his jaw dropped. His face went numb as the pain spread across his cheek as if millions of sharp pins danced on his face, causing him to cry out.

"Awe mom, what was that for!! That hurt!" Lamar shouted while holding his face. His eyes began to water, and his face declared a state of confusion.

Vanessa cried out, *"Oh my goodness! My baby!"* just as Simeon burst into the room, holding the phone in hand. *"What's going on?"* Simeon asked. Vanessa quickly replied, *"Hang up the phone Sim. Everything is alright."*

Lamar, still holding his face, began to cry. His mother then comforts him by kissing him on top of his forehead. She gazed into his eyes with joy and relief. "Wait a minute," Simeon said, still holding the phone. "What...how the hell you know he's ok?" Although Simeon stood just inches away, Vanessa didn't hear him. *"Nessa.....Nessa! You hear me talking to you?!"* Simeon exclaimed.

"Everything is alright," chanted Vanessa. *"I truly thought I had lost my only child. But everything is going to be ok."* She continued to ignore Simeon's plea and continued to confront Lamar while tears fell from her face. She wiped her face with her hands, smiled, then leaned down to whisper something in Lamar's ear. Her words sent goosebumps through his body as she spoke with a devilish tone, *"The next time I call for you, it had better not take three attempts for you to respond...I won't be so gentle the next time."*

A Life Long Struggle

Although she spoke with a gentle smile, Lamar felt the truth behind her words. A feeling of harmful intent seeped from her harmless smile as she reassured Lamar not to respond slowly the next time she called. He responded quickly, placing his hand across his head like a soldier would solute his superior officer, *"Yes ma'am!"*

Lamar then peered over his mother's shoulder, staring at his uncle in the background while Samantha stood at his heels. He then spoke with a cheerful smile, *"Hey, uncle Sim."*

Glancing back at Lamar, Simeon replied with a puzzled expression, *"How you feeling?".*

Placing his chin on his mother's shoulder, Lamar quickly replied, *"I'm alright, a little sleepy though."*

Simeon walked over toward Lamar, placing his hand on top of his head, *"Are you sure,"* Simeon inquired as he slouched over, looking Lamar square in his eyes. But before he could reply to Simeon's question a second time, Vanessa jerked Lamar away from Simeon as she turned around abruptly and said, *"Yea, he's sure!"* Her eyes began to tear up as she calmly demanded that he not mettle any further. *"Let my son rest,"* Vanessa implored as she sat Lamar on the bedside.

"Mom," Lamar said as he rubbed his eyes, *"I'm not really sleepy."*

Vanessa turned towards him, then spoke quickly, *"No, I don't want to hear it. Lamar, you look exhausted, and no matter how you think you feel, it's still bedtime. And bedtime means it's time to rest."* Ignoring Simeon's presence, Vanessa preps Lamar for bed once more. Watching as Vanessa tucks Lamar in bed for the night, Simeon mutters, *"Alright then, I'll go tell Daddy and num that everything is ok."* Vanessa replied abruptly, *"Yeah, you go do that!"*

Simeon walked out of the room in disapproval, slamming the door behind him. *"Finally, some peace and quiet,"* Vanessa said as she climbed into bed. *"Please be ok,"* she said as her eyes grew heavy. She wrapped her arms around Lamar and began to doze off. *"Lord, please watch over my son."* She said as her eyes closed slowly. The room grew quiet as both Lamar and his mother slept, allowing Helen to enter undetected. She hovered over the two sleeping bodies holding a vial of unknown liquid. Dipping her finger into the liquid, she marked both of their heads and recited a short mantra.

Lamar's eyes opened for a brief moment looking directly at Helen, causing her to step back slightly. His eyes closed, and he muttered, *"Go away . . . Helen."* She covered her mouth in suspense, then stumbled out of the room.

A short while later, Lamar woke from his slumber. He had slept peacefully. There weren't any feelings of unease, mentally or physically, in any way. Instead, he felt revived, better. He leaped from the bed and ran to find his mother. He had one question that needed to be answered. Eager to have his answer, he bolted towards the living room. Upon entry, he noticed that everyone had been waiting for him. His Uncle, Simeon, who stood over six feet tall, towering above everyone in the family. Two of his aunts, Falisha, the second oldest of his aunts, and Kayla, the youngest of the trio. His younger cousin Samantha and her older sister Demetria were also present, along with both of his grandparents. He had gone unnoticed by everyone as he walked into the center of the living room and asked, *"Where's my Mommy?"*

There was a brief silence, then his grandmother spoke in a gentle tone, "Baby, are you alright?"

"Yeah Granny, I'm fine," Lamar replied.

She glanced down at Lamar, smiled, then said, *"You sure?"*

Lamar smiled back and replied, *"Yeah Granny. I'm sure. I just need to find Momma."* As their conversation continued, Lamar's grandfather noticed something peculiar. Interrupting their conversation, his grandfather asked, *"What you need her for?"* Lamar quickly said, *"I gotta know if today is…."* Interrupting him again, his grandfather said, *"Come over here. Boy let me have a look at cha."*

Lamar walked over to his grandfather, fearful that he had done something wrong. *"Hold ya head up,"* his grandfather said, examining Lamar's eyes. *"Helen, come ova here,"* his grandfather insisted, *"Has his eyes always been this color?"* Helen walked over and looked down into Lamar's eyes. As they began to perform a minor analysis of his wellbeing, Vanessa walked into the house.

The sound of the door closing behind her alerted Lamar, and he dashed to greet her while shouting, *"Momma! I need to ask you something!!"* He jumped up and down, excited for her reply.

"Somebody is feeling better, I see," his mother replied. *"What is it you need to know?"*

"What day is today?"

Before she could answer, her father shouted, *"Vanessa! Come on in here so we can talk…"*

"Okay daddy!" Vanessa replied. After placing the groceries on the table, she walked over towards her parents with Lamar right

behind her. As they entered the living room, Helen, Vanessa's mother, insisted Vanessa peer into Lamar's eyes. *"What do you see, Nassa,"* Helen asked.

After quickly inspecting Lamar's eyes, Vanessa looked at her mother and said, *"His eyes are different …."* But before she could finish, Lamar interrupted her and asked, *"Momma, what day is it?"*

Lamar seemed to be uninterested in the adult's ongoing conversation.

"It's Saturday," Vanessa replied.

Lamar's face brightened with joy, *"What time is it?"* Lamar added. He could barely contain himself as he waited for her response. His mother looked over at the grandmother clock that hung on the wall and said, *"Go ahead Lamar, It's after three."* He turned and ran to his room, anxious for the day's events. Simeon, seeming upset, shouted, *"Nassa, why are you letting him go outside after all this mess?"*

Vanessa cuts her eyes in his direction and shouts angrily, *"Look here Sim! Until you have kids of your own, don't tell me how to raise my son!"* Just as she lashed out at Simeon, her father interrupts, *"Well, I'm ya daddy, and I don't think he should be goin outside after all this here."*

"Daddy, don't make me keep him in the house," she implored. *"I'm worried too, but I need to know he's okay."*

Her father continued, *"The boy eyes done change, who knows what else done changed in him. So if you gonna let em go, you better watch em close."*

A Life Long Struggle

Lamar ran through the house, darting towards the front door with his shoes in his hands and socks on his feet. He slid across the tile near the living room while hurrying to the door, then stopped abruptly to put on his shoes and tie his laces. He scampered to the front door, swung it open, and turned to shout, *"I'm going down the street to Matthew's house, and I'll be back later."* Vanessa tried to see him off but could only get a glimpse of his crimson eyes as he closed the door behind him.

Filled with excitement, Lamar ran down to Matthew's house, knocked on the door and shouted, *"Can Matt come out to play?!"* The door swung open, and Matthew stood in the doorway, blocking its entry. He folded his arms across his chest, and with an excited expression, he shouted, *"What took you so long?"* Lamar replied, *"Man, I was super tired. I was sleeping all day long."*

Lamar's eyes suddenly teared up as he began to yawn as if he had just woke up from a deep sleep. He wiped the water from his eyes as Matthew stared at him awkwardly.

"What happened to your eyes?" Matthew asked.

"I don't know," Lamar replied as he struggled to wipe his face clean. *"My mamma num kept talkin about em, but my eyes not bothering me at all."*

"Ohh," Matthew replied nonchalantly as he continued to stare. *"They look cool to me,"* Matthew blurted out, breaking away from the awkward moment. Lamar then shoves Matthew aside as he walked into the house. *"Hey Matt, let's play Tanks on the Atari,"* Lamar said as he searched the living room for the console. *"You cheated last time we played, so I deserve a rematch."* Matthew turned around to face Lamar, then replied calmly, *"Nah, I didn't cheat, you just suck."*

A Life Long Struggle

Lamar's eyes widened with surprise as he gasped for air. "Whatever, you always cheat! Just like when we played kickball." Matthew interrupted Lamar and shouted, *"I didn't cheat last time!"* Lamar suddenly paused, then took a dramatic deep breath and said, "Really . . . you didn't cheat! YOU *called for a substitute and had your big brother Keith kick for you. Remember!"*

A slight smile gleamed across Matthew's face. *"That IS in the rules!"* He said nonchalantly.

"Not when he isn't IN the game already," Lamar replied angrily.

Matthew then turned around with his back to Lamar and muttered, *"You always complaining and whining when you lose. Like a lil baby."* Lamar stomps the floor in rage and shouts, *"OKAY THEN, REMATCH!"*

Matthew swung around to face Lamar again. His face glowed with a smile that stretched the width of his face, "Ok, when you lose this time, don't cry like a little baby." Lamar desperately tried to keep calm as he replied, *"Funny, ok then. If my team win, you gotta call me king of kickball."*

"Yeah right, as if that will ever happen," Matthew muttered. *"And if I win, you gotta say, you cheated every time I asked you about a game."*

" *Deal,"* Lamar shouted as he gritted his teeth in anger. *"And we keeping the same team as last time MINUS Keith,"* Lamar added.

"OK. Ok. Let's go get everybody, so I can beat you....I mean, so we can start."

"Ha! So funny that I forgot to laugh."

A Life Long Struggle

Lamar and Matthew ran off together. They went door to door, collecting all the children from their previous game. Once all the players had been collected, they stood in the center of the street, making preparations to start the game.

Matthew stood in the center of the group as the game's coordinator. Using his fingers, he began to map out the players for each team.

"Alright, let's make sure everyone is here. Let's see; Leon, Lonnie, and Trey, all three brothers are here. The sisters Demetria and Samantha are here. Tamond is here, my sister Maryanne is here, Mark is here. Oh, Simeon AND Donte are both here, Okay! Darrel and . . . we're missing somebody! Lamar! We're missing one person...anybody seen Lamar?"

Suddenly, Lamar comes running from the neighboring street, through a path that had been created by all of the neighborhood children.

"Willie is coming! He's just getting ready," Lamar shouted as he ran over.

Matthew faced the group then said, "Ok yall, since me and Lamar got everybody, we're gonna be the captains. The teams are gonna be the same as last time. It's me, Samantha, Mark, Trey, Darrel, and Donte versus the rest of yall, and Willie gonna be the all-time pitcher. Alright then, we got the teams, so now we just have to decide who kicks first."

Lamar dug into his pockets, pulled out a coin, and said, *"I already got a quarter,"* He then placed it on his thumb and flipped it into the air. *"Go Matt, call it in the air. . . ."* Matthew quickly shouted, "Heads," as Lamar caught the coin and opened his hand to see which side was face up.

A Life Long Struggle

"Nope, tails, we kick first!" shouted Lamar. Willie then took his place at the pitcher's mound marked by a circle drawn in the center of the street in pink chalk.

The kickball game finally started. Lamar stepped to the plate as the first kicker for his team. With his first attempt, he was able to make it to second base. The start of the game was filled with the screams and yells of all the players. Just as the ball was tossed back to the pitcher, Lamar dashed from second base to third without being caught. He stomped on third base and, in a roar of excitement, shouted, *"Alright yall! I'm on third base now!"*

Matthew began to taunt Lamar by accusing him of cheating, but he was overly excited and was able to brush off Matthew's comments. Lamar shouted, *"Let Sim kick so we can get a quick and easy home run."*

Donte replied, *"No the hell! Yall let him kick, and his ass will be out in a flash."* Simeon ran to the plate as the next kicker while pointing at Donte, *"See all that shit you talking Donte? Alright. Watch this kick!"*

Simeon and Donte were the oldest of the bunch, Simeon being 19 years old and just one year behind Donte. Regardless of age, they were natural rivals. Always looking for ways to challenge each other, and the kickball game was another way for them to test the other's limits. Simeon stepped to the plate, a crushed soda can — and pointed to the sky, marking the presumed distance of his kick with his finger. Donte kneeled down as low as he could, poised and ready for anything.

Willie rolled a fastball directly toward Simeon. With a big grin on his face, he shouted out, *"Home run!"* He made a quick step forward towards the speeding ball and kicked with all his might! But he slipped, losing all his momentum. His kick, lacking in power and direction, spun in place after bouncing just a few short feet away. He stood there baffled with his mouth wide open as Donte took off running at full speed. He and Lamar had both sprinted toward home base. Once Simeon had recovered from the momentary displacement, he too took off running, but toward first base.

Donte, being faster than them both, scooped up the ball and flung it towards Simeon all in one motion. Simeon jumped as high as he could to evade the oncoming ball. But Donte had anticipated his jump and had aimed for his head instead of his body. The ball struck Simeon near his lower thigh in midair, causing him to come crashing down to the street pavement. Donte then caught the ball as it bounced back after colliding with Simeon. He turned to scan the area in search of Lamar. But he was just a few steps from home plate. Donte, now out of time, took a pitcher's stance and, with all his might, flung the ball toward home base.

Lamar continued to run at full speed, only focusing on the home plate. His vision had begun to tunnel as nothing else mattered but the home plate. He took a leap to mark his victory as his right foot firmly landed on the soda can, marking home base. Then with his hands above his head, he turned slightly left, facing first base where Simeon had ran to. But before he could plant his left foot on the ground, Donte's speeding ball crashed into the center of his face. A solid hit!

Everyone shouted, *"Ohhhh!"*

Lamar's body was swept off his feet due to the unexpected impact. His body flipped into the air and slid across the pavement before coming to a complete stop. Both teams ran over to him to ensure he was ok. Donte, the first to arrive, helped Lamar to his feet and said, *"Hey man, are you alright?"*

Lamar quickly jumped to his feet and dusted himself off. With his face covered with minor cuts and scrapes, he replied, *"Yeah. Man I'm good. Let's finish the game."*

Lamar's team gathered in the outfield, being that Simeon was their third out. Despite Lamar's injuries during the incident, the game would continue as if it had not happened. The ending score left Lamar's team as the victors.

With victory in toe and crowned King of Kickball, Lamar decided to join the older kids in a game of Man Hunt, being that it was close to nightfall, and he felt undefeatable. Although he and Matthew had volunteered to play with the older kids, Simeon wasn't too eager to allow them to play such a dangerous game. So, before the start of the game, he pulled Lamar aside for a brief conversation.

"Now Lamar, I know you tough and all, but this game can get dangerous. I don't want your mamma bitchin' to me if you get hurt. If you plan on playing with us, you can't be a cry baby. You understand?"

"Yea, I got it. Besides, if me and Matt are gonna be on the same team, nobody can beat us, especially when we work together."

"That's not exactly how this game works. But, since this is your first time playing with us, let me lay down the rules of the game."

"OK."

"It's like Hide and Seek. There's a base, and there's an IT, but instead of the IT being one person, it's a team of people. And instead of being tagged or frozen . . . you get beat up and then

brought back to the base. We call that BEING CAUGHT, but only if the IT team gets you back to base....got it so far?"

"Yea... it's like jail and tag put together."

"Yea . . . Ok good. But the most important part is that you get the entire neighborhood to hide in. So that's five streets, and you can hide anywhere except for the house where the base is. However, being that you are my nephew, you can run home at any time you feel scared . . . Still wanna play?"

Lamar paused for a short while, looked over at some of the older kids, then said, "Do *yall be hitting hard?"*

"No, if you get caught and give up right away, you can't get hit. But if you try to run before or after you get back to base, then we can take you by force."

"Me and Matt will be on the same team, right?"

"Yep, and the same rules that apply for him apply for you."

"Alright, then let's play."

"Alright, it's about thirty of us in total. Yall can play for fun, so yall don't count. If yall get scared, then go home, okay?"

"Alright."

After the rules were explained to Lamar and Matthew, they were again explained to the rest of the players with emphasis on the young newbies. Simeon and Donte then gathered up all the players and divided them into two teams. Donte's team were the runners, and Simeon's team were the ITs. Lamar and Matthew were scared. Neither of them had played with the big kids before, but neither of them wanted to alert the other of their fear.

Matthew peered over at Lamar as they waited for the game to start and said,

"Lamar, do your face still hurt from earlier?"

"What?!"

"I'm only asking because your eyes are back to normal...guess you just needed to be bashed in the face with a ball."

"Yea, whatever! You the one that's gonna get bashed this time cuz I'm not gonna get caught!"

"I bet you get caught before I do!"

Simeon interrupted their conversation and said, *"Alright yall, it should be dark enough by now. On the count of three, RUN and the game will start! We will give you till the count of 60 to find a hiding place. Once we blow the horn, yall can try to make it back to base. Alright! 1........2.........3!"*

Lamar and Matthew ran off in the same direction. Running behind all the older kids, they found a small berry bush with a tiny opening that they could crawl into. Once inside, they sat opposite each other, confident they wouldn't be found. Shortly after, they heard the sound of a horn indicating that the game had started. They were suddenly faced with two options; either stay in their hiding spot until the game was over or try to make it back to the base without being caught. Matthew had begun to speak before Lamar could gather his thoughts, *"Let's go, I think we can make it,"* Matthew said.

"What?! No, let's stay here. Give them time to catch the other people first."

Matthew replied, "*Stop being a scardy cat! They probably not even looking for us. We ARE playing for fun, remember.*"

"*Yea…..well….you go first then.*"

"*Why I gotta go first?!*"

"*Cuz, it was your idea…your idea means you go first.*"

Just as Matthew positioned himself to leave the cover of the bush, he heard a group of people running in their direction. Matthew quickly turned to Lamar and whispered,"*Shhh, they coming!*" It was a three-on-one battle. The 'It' team had pursued a runner, and they stampeded in the direction of Lamar and Matthew's hiding place. The other team tackled the runner, knocking him down to the ground. "*I got him,*" he replied after pinning the runner to the cold grassy floor. Then another member of their team shouted out, "*Give up already! We've been chasing you for two blocks. You are not going to get away!*" But before the team could gather over the captured runner, he escaped, breaking the hold of his captor. He bolted in the direction of Lamar and Matthew then attempted to jump over the bush where they had been hiding. However, the third member and furthest away, had picked up a sizable rock and flung it at the fleeing runner.

The rock flew like a homing missile, knocking the fleeing runner from mid-jump. He fell into the bush where Lamar and Matthew were hiding. Two members of the 'It' team quickly caught up to him and beat him into submission. Their hiding place now exposed, Matthew took off running at full speed with Lamar behind him.

"*Two more of them are coming your way!*" A voice in the distance had alerted more team members, and four more sprouted in their path. Matthew shouted, "*We gotta split up. Meet me at my house in the back yard!"* Matthew turned left and Lamar right. Looking back, he noticed Matthew had been caught! He could hear his best friend yell out for help, but he continued to run.

He ran until he lost his sense of direction. He ducked behind a car in a nearby house to catch his breath. Lamar sat, terrified of this crazy game. His thoughts rambled as he realized what he'd gotten himself into. Lamar took a deep breath as he readied himself, but before he could move, he heard someone whisper, *"Gotcha."* The third member of the It team had followed him. Lamar tried to run as fast as he could, but the older kid was much faster than he was. Lamar quickly yelled, *"I give up, you got me,"* but the older kid replied, *"No little kid that plays with the big boys is gonna get out of an ass whipping that easily!"* He pushed Lamar to the ground and started kicking and punching him mercilessly.

Lamar began to kick and scream for help, but no one would come to his aid. The older kid held Lamar by his ankle as he punched Lamar as hard as he could until Lamar landed a solid kick in the center of his attacker's face.

Lamar tried to crawl to his feet and attempt to run, but the older kid cornered him yet again. Lamar stood to his feet, his mouth bleeding and his body aching. He balled his fists tightly and readied himself for battle. *"You think that just because you're bigger, you can bully me*?!" yelled Lamar.

"Damn straight," the older kid replied. Then he punched Lamar in the stomach and pushed him to the ground, *"Get up, you little shit,"* the older kid replied.

Lamar rolled on his back, trying to recover from his loss of breath, only to be kicked while he lay in agony. He struggled to stand to his feet, enduring the barrage of punches and kicks the

older child delivered until he was finally able to stand and distance himself slightly from the older child. His slouched-over demeanor and loss of breath made the older child smile.

"Now stay still, brat. And take it like a big boy," just as the older kid tried to strike Lamar one last time, a voice spoke to him, *"DUCK!"*

Lamar quickly dropped to the ground and covered his head as his Uncle Simeon leaped over his head and punched the older kid, knocking him to the ground. Then, taking a second step towards Lamar's attacker, Simeon landed a solid kick that caused Lamar's attacker to levitate up from the ground. *"Go home Lamar! The game's over,"* Simeon replied as he monitored Lamar's attacker.

Scared and frightened, he dashed for home. His legs were like noodles due to the fear of being cornered again, his shoes flung from his feet and caused his knees to buckle. His body flew through the air and came crashing down face first, and slid across the street, leaving a trail of dust behind him. Lamar then quickly jumped to his feet after a smooth roll-like recovery and continued his journey home. He ran through prickly bushes and vines. He jumped small ditches and took every path he could remember in order to make it home as quickly as possible.

Just as he began to slow down due to exhaustion, he heard his mother call out to him, *"Lamar! It's time to come home!"* She had been calling him for some time now. Lamar smiled as he ran faster and faster. Before long, Lamar stood in front of the driveway. His face, hands, and clothing were colored with grass, blood, and dirt stains. He brushed himself off and walked toward to front door.

"I'm home mom," Lamar said, panting from exhaustion.

A Life Long Struggle

"Oh my lord! What happened to you?!" Vanessa shouted, *"Why are you covered from head to toe in filth!?"* Lamar paused for a moment, then quickly replied nonchalantly, *"I fell."*

Vanessa stared at him in disbelief then replied sarcastically, *"You fell."* Lamar looked directly into her eyes and responded in a serious tone, *"I fell a lot."*

Again Vanessa paused, as a slight smile decorated her face, *"Well, get inside and clean yourself up. It's time to eat. I've been standing out here calling you for the longest!"*

"I'm sorry mom," Lamar blurted out.

Vanessa reached over and grabbed Lamar by the hand, gently pulling him closer, *"Come here, let me have a look at you first,"* she said, wiping some of the dirt from his face.

Jerking back suddenly, Lamar said, "I'm alright ma," as he quickly brushed himself down. *"I'll meet you at the table. I want to clean myself tonight."*

Vanessa stared at him awkwardly after his reply. At first glance, she seemed confused as to why Lamar managed to be so dirty. He was covered in mud, grass fell from his hair, dirt covered his face, and his clothes were torn. After she gave Lamar a good look over, her body trembled as she giggled slightly. She could barely hold her composure as she scolded him for being so careless. Then, while pointing her hand towards the bathroom, she said,

"Ok, go clean yourself up. And don't take all night. Dinner will be ready soon."

Although she hadn't shown it, Vanessa was relieved to see that Lamar had a typical day playing with his friends. She thought to herself, *"I'm happy to welcome home a dirty and scraped up child rather than no child at all . . . Everything IS going to be okay."*

After a few moments of being left alone, Vanessa peeked into the bathroom to check on Lamar. He had already started his bath. He ran warm water and tested the temperature of the water before he entered. Once he was sure the water had reached a suitable temperature, he jumped in, submerging himself without a second thought. It was only after he was completely submerged that he realized he had made a big mistake. Pain surged through his body from the many cuts and scrapes he received from the numerous encounters with grass and gravel. The pain caused him to screak out in agony, but surprisingly, Lamar didn't call out for help. Instead, he covered his mouth to endure the pain and continued to bathe himself, carefully wiping each cut and scrape.

Before emerging from the bathroom, he covered all his cuts and bruises with band-aids to ensure he was all patched up. Once he emerged from his steamy bath, he put away his dirty clothing and made his way to the dinner table. He sat in his usual place next to his mother. The dinner table consisted of the entire family, his mother, grandmother, grandfather, his three aunts, four uncle, and two cousins. He was the last to reach the dinner table and was greeted with blank stares. There was complete silence as Lamar sat at the table, and immediately he became curious. He thought to himself, "Why is everyone staring at me?" Just as his thoughts concluded, everyone burst into laughter.

Lamar's entire face, along with both legs and arms, were littered with bandages. He had placed bandages on every cut and scrape he had received from his efforts to run home. He had bandages on his nose and cheeks, some near the neck, and more above his eyebrow. To make matters worse, he had planted a huge bandage smack-dab in the center of his forehead, where the kickball had hit him. The entire family began targeting them all with crude remarks as if he had marked hit points on each one of his Band-Aids. The first comment thrown was from his youngest cousin Samantha, whom he'd often addressed as Kia.

"What happened to your face...did you lose a fight with the lawnmower!?"

"Kia, that's not funny...."

"You're the one covered in band-aids like a crazy person!"

"Well, your face is covered with ugly, but you don't see me laughing at you."

Samantha and Lamar continued to bicker back and forth. Although they were the closest of relatives and the best of friends, this fact could easily be overlooked once a fight brewed up amongst the two of them. Lamar knew just what button to push to ignite Samantha's rage. She was nearly two years younger than Lamar but had already begun to show signs of self-consciousness. Lamar would use this to his advantage. Even though she was a better trash talker, Lamar had a secret weapon up his sleeve. Samantha continued the assault, gaining momentum by the second, *"Look at you. I'm sure you let some fat kid sit on you and beat you up."*

"No, that's not what happened!"

"So what happened, Band-Aid Face?"

"I fell."

"You fell?"

"I did, and don't call me Band-Aid face!"

A Life Long Struggle

"Aww, poor baby is about to cry! Look at the poor Band-Aid Baby!"

Samantha proceeded to gather input from other family members at the table. She inserted them into her shenanigans against Lamar, and due to the many bandages that covered his face, they all sided with her. Lamar sat at the end of the table in a daze of sadness. He watched as the members of his family laughed at his efforts to take better care of himself. He started to feel alone and distant from those around him. The pit of his stomach clenched as his throat felt dry, then Nathaniel spoke,

"They don't love you . . . they can't love someone that they cannot begin to understand."

Nathaniel's voice resonated within Lamar's mind. He responded to Lamar's confusion and rapid flux of emotion.

"I feel what you feel. Give in to the anger, allow it to take charge, and I will ensure they will never tease you again. You can feel it...the difference. You have changed. You have power now. Speak it, and I shall teach you to use it here and now."

Lamar sat completely still while he and Nathaniel conversed. He didn't move, blink, or breathe. His entire body remained motionless with one slight alteration. His eyes had changed color once more, but not to that of crimson. Despite how small and suddle the change, it didn't go unnoticed by Samantha. She then demanded a response to her insults as well as an explanation as to why Lamar's eyes changed color.

"Hey Band-Aid boy, why are you so quiet? I know you hear me talking to you! And what's with your eyes . . . you keep getting uglier and uglier by the second!"

Lamar didn't respond verbally, but he did hear Samantha's remarks. His eyes quickly turned in her direction and followed her every movement. Lamar's expressionless face frightened Samantha and froze her still. She had been paralyzed from his gaze. Her body started to tremble as fear glossed over her face. In this short amount of time, Lamar could feel the fear seeping from Samantha's body flow into his, like water into sand.

"Do you feel it . . . can you taste her fear? It feeds us . . . It can also sustain us if you give into it...give in...to me... I can take them away, along with the pain they cause. I know this IS what you desire, after all, I am . . ."

Before Nathaniel could finish, Lamar blurts out, *"NO, you're the ugly one!"*

Lamar pushed Nathaniel to the edge of his mind silencing him with just a single thought. His eyes slowly reverted back to their normal state, and Samantha's fear dissipated. Lamar had reverted back to himself, displaying an enormous smile. He reached into his cargo pants and pulled out his secret weapon. He faced Samantha confidently and spoke firmly,

"The only thing uglier than THIS is THIS!"

Lamar held a small mirror in his left hand and a larger mirror in his right. Both pointed directly at Samantha. Lamar had predicted that he would be teased at the dinner table and had tucked away his secret weapon just in case of an emergency. He had forgotten about it at first, but once he felt the fear that Samantha released, he wanted to do something, and that's when he remembered his secret weapon. Lamar thought to himself,

"My family does love me...and this is how we display it. We make each other mad, and sometimes we make others sad, but no

matter what, this is my family, and I love them. We are who we are, and I would never change that no matter what."

The entire dining room was as lively as ever on this night. They all laughed together, fought with one another, and more importantly, they all ate together.

However, amidst all the joy and laughter, Nathaniel had learned a great deal about Lamar. And he spoke to him once more. As Lamar played at the dinner table, Samantha could see his eyes had changed to their original color and had not changed back since his outburst.

"I applaud you, child. You continue to defy me despite my efforts. I have caused you much pain… why not give in? Anger is easy…..relax….and all shall flow red as vast as the ocean is deep! I shall have you, child of man. Ye shall know the full depths of this world, and ye shall drown within it. Heed me child…tonight…I shall come for you. We shall merge and become one. Ready thy self or perish."

The Merger Begins

Nathaniel's last words resonated throughout Lamar's being. He thought to himself, *"What did Nathaniel mean when he said we shall merge and become one...ready thy self or parish. And what is a merger? Is he already a part of me? Inside me, or is he hiding around here somewhere?"* Lamar began to display signs of paranoia. He scanned the dinner table and the living room for anything seeming out of place. As each member finished eating and removed themselves from the dinner table, he would briefly check to see if Nathaniel had been hiding among them somehow. Lamar thought to himself, *"Just calm down, no reason to be afraid of some old voice."*

"Boy you alright?" Asked Lamar's Grandfather. He had finished eating and now hovered above Lamar with his dirty dishes in hand, awaiting a response.

"Yeah granddaddy, I'm alright. Just thinking," Lamar responded with his head tilted towards the floor.

"Well, don't think too hard son," his grandfather added with a slight smile. *"You might find yourself to be an old man in a young man's body."* Lamar lifted his head slightly, smiled, and said, *"Okay granddaddy."*

A Life Long Struggle

His grandfather then kneeled down just a bit, *then he spoke in a whisper, "Besides, if you think too much, that ole' Kia will always be a step ahead of ya! And we can't have that, right?!"* Lamar lifted his head and nodded in agreeance.

"That's right Granddad," he said, rubbing his hands together as if he had just devised a diabolical plan.

"That's the spirit!" His grandfather shouted as he patted Lamar on his back, *"We guys can't let the women in this family push us around. We have to stand together and be—"*

Just before Lamar's grandfather could finish, Helen, Lamar's grandmother, interrupted their conversation. *"Mark Junior! What you filling that boy head up with?"* With her hands on her hips and dressed in her nightgown, she positioned herself in front of them both as she stood in disapproval.

"Aww, come on now Helen. This here is a man's conversation." Mark said as he stood upright.

"Mmmhmm," Helen replied as she reached for his dirty dishes, *"so it's a senseless conversation then,"* she added as she scowled at Mark.

"Gon ni Helen. This don't got none to do with you, just me and my grandson."

She took the dishes to the kitchen, then as she returned, she muttered calmly, *"Well, yall boys don't stay up too late. I know there's so much to talk about at this hour."*

"Alright Helen," Mark replied sarcastically. He waited for Helen to leave the dining area before he spoke to Lamar. Once she had gone, he placed his hand on his head and spoke calmly, *"I'm off to bed now Lamar, and remember . . . it's okay to think about*

your life but not too much. Don't allow your life to pass you over cuz it will if you let it. And remember, too much of anything, is bad for you. So lift ya head up from time to time and peak from behind them clouds of yours." Lamar had never heard his grandfather speak in such a way. His face lit up with joy as he shouted, "Alright, good night Granddaddy!"

After the festivities of dinner were over, Lamar sat at the dinner table, staring into his empty plate. Normally, he would scurry from the dinner table to avoid helping his mother with the dishes. But this night was different. He was the last to leave and had begun collecting the remaining dishes from the table. With his arms filled with dirty dishes, he staggered to the kitchen. He carried half-emptied cups, dirty forks, knives, and plates, all stacked in the most inefficient way possible. His mother stood near the sink, filling it with clean water. She had begun aligning the dishes in their proper fashion before she noticed Lamar staggering to the kitchen.

She quickly braced Lamar, preventing him from dropping all that he brought into the kitchen. *"Be careful honey,"* Vanessa said as she safely dismembered the tower of plates and glasses. After avoiding a catastrophic mess, Lamar placed the remaining dishes on the counter and spoke in a most humbling voice, *"Do you need help cleaning the dishes?"*

Vanessa chuckled then said, "Oh, you are offering to help me tonight? You must have really fell hard today." Lamar shrugged his shoulders then replied in a saddened voice, "Not funny mom." Vanessa then wiped her hands on her apron and replied. "Aww, I'm sorry baby. I didn't mean to upset you. It's just odd that you would ask to help me with the dishes, when most nights you'd run off and pretend to sleep."

A Life Long Struggle

Lamar nodded his head and looked to the floor, then said, *"Well Mom, the truth is I want to ask you something, and I'm getting older now, so it's time that I learn how to take care of myself."* While Lamar continued to speak, she reached for the dishes he had brought to the kitchen and began to arrange them near the sink. She then pulled a short ladder from under the cabinet sink and signaled Lamar to come to help her do the dishes. Lamar continued, *"I've changed a little bit Mom. I don't see things the way I used to, but it's hard to explain. Like today we played kickball...."*

Vanessa interrupted him briefly and said, *"Baby I'm listening to you, but you have to dry the dishes if you're gonna help me. Let's not be in here all night, okay."* Lamar picked up the drying cloth and started drying the cleaned dishes as his story continued.

"We played kickball, and it was my team versus Matt's team. And everything that could go wrong went wrong! I got kicked in the face with the ball. That's why I have this big Band-Aid right here," Lamar pointed at the center of his forehead, where the largest bandage sat. *"Then I fell and scraped up my hands and knees,"* again Lamar pointed at other Band-Aids while he continued to speak. *"The whole game, I was the only one getting hurt. Mamma, I even tripped over my own shoes!"*

"Seems like you had a long day," Vanessa replied as she wiped her hands on her apron once again. *"Wait mom. There's more for me to tell you,"* Lamar said as he used his hands to signify that his story wasn't complete. *"After the game of kickball, we played Man Hunt...."*

"WHAT!!" Vanessa shouted as she turned to face Lamar directly. Her composure changed dramatically as she waited for his response.

"No...I asked Sim if me and Matt could play..."

Vanessa's rage caused her voice to heighten, "He let yall play with them rough kids from around the corner?!"

"No...wait...that's not the point. Just listen."

Vanessa took a deep breath, pulled the stopper from the sink abruptly and smiled then said, *"Ok, but we gonna come back to that part later. Go ahead and continue your story."*

Lamar continued as he put away the stepping stool, *"I was kinda scared to play with the older kids...."* Vanessa interrupted and said, *"Yeah! They ARE twice your size. I don't understand—"*

"Mom!"

"I'm sorry...I'm listening."

"When the games started, me and Matt ran and ran till we found a bush we could hide in, over by where Donte live. At first, when we got in it, I didn't know that it was a sticker bush. It had thorns that cut me on my face and arms and my legs. That's not the bad part. When we was about to leave and try to get back to the base, we seen one of the boys get caught by the other team!" Vanessa crossed her arms and leaned against the sink.

"So yall were the Runners, I take it?"

"Yea. The boy tried to run again, after he was caught, but he fell in the bush that we was hiding in!"

"Oh my Lord!" Vanessa shouted as she sprung from the sink, her face in shock as she stood with anticipation of what had happened next.

"*Then me and Matt took off running! But he got caught when we separated.*"

"*Why did yall seperate?!*"

"*It was his idea...I don't know why we split up. But when they caught him, I wanted to go back and help, but he was screaming for me to keep running. I could tell them boys was hurting him because I never heard him scream so loud. He was saying all kinds of stuff like, GO, and GET OFF ME, in between his screaming. I heard him say, STOP THAT'S MY FINGER...YOU WILL BREAK IT... Then that's when I heard him scream so loud. I could hear him as I ran away.*"

Vanessa's face twisted with agony, "I get the idea...what happened next?" she said, motioning him to pass that part quickly.

"*After that, I ran and ran and ran until I got lost. I had found a car in somebody's yard, so I hid behind it. But that's not the bad part. One of the guys that caught Matt had followed me. He tried to sneak up on me, but I ran!*" Vanessa again interrupted him, signaling him to leave the kitchen.

"*See, this is why I don't want you out there—*"

Lamar jumped ahead of her and said, "*Mamma, I'm not done yet.*"

She replied, "*Ok, go ahead...but I need to sit down for the rest of your story. Let's go brush our teeth first. Then you tell me more.*" They walked down the hallway toward the bathroom; midway there, his mother asked, "How have you been feeling, and give me an honest answer."

"What do you mean?" Lamar replied.

A Life Long Struggle

This short exchange of words bloomed into a conversation of its own.

"You are my son and the only child I have. So I know when something isn't quite right. But I want you to talk to me. If something is going on in your life, I want you to come to me and tell me about it."

"I'm okay Momma."

"I'm serious Lamar. You have been acting unusual, and it's starting to worry me."

They both entered the bathroom. Lamar stood on the toilet to reach his toothbrush that sat on the bathroom sink. He then rinsed it off, spread on his favorite toothpaste, and began to brush his teeth while actively listening to his mother's concerns. She continued to speak while brushing her teeth.

"It started with that night you had fallen behind the bed. I could have sworn that you were being pulled into the wall! It was odd –the lights wouldn't turn on, and you didn't make any noise at first. And the thing that bothered me most is when I started to pull you. . . . I felt something pull back!" She then looked down at Lamar and asked, *"Do you remember any of this?"*

"No," Lamar replied calmly.

She looked away as she continued, *"When we finally got you back from behind the bed. . . . or whatever…, you were freezing cold. Your pulse was shallow, and your skin was so pale. I didn't know what to do! Mamma and I prayed and prayed because that was all we could do for you. Then all of a sudden, you got so hot, you were burning up! Your skin changed in color, and you started to sweat. You were sticky and nasty."*

"Eww!"

"But I held you anyway. Daddy brought me some cold hand towels to wipe your face with and keep your temperature even. I fed you soup when you were cold and dried you when you were hot."

Lamar rinsed his mouth with warm water and proceeded to wash his face. As his mother continued to talk, he reached for a towel that hung on the wall across from the toilet. *"I had no idea I did all that in my sleep,"* he said with his eyes wide open with suspense.

Vanessa replied, *"Baby, you died that night."*

Lamar dropped the towel as Nathaniel's words pierced his mind, *"We shall merge and become one. Ready thy self or perish."*

"I what?!" Lamar said abruptly.

His mother had finished brushing her teeth. She dried her face and glanced down towards Lamar and further explained. *"Your heart stopped. I held you in my arms as your lifeless body laid in my lap like a rag doll".* Vanessa motioned her hands to mimic how lifeless his body was. *"Your arms flung to the floor and legs stretched flat. You took one last deep breath . . . . Then all signs of life VANISHED from you. I screamed and cried out, 'Somebody help me, my son . . . my son!' but you just lay there, lifeless. I froze! My world had stopped. All I could do was hold you close. I thought I had lost you. But that didn't stop me. I performed CPR, breathing into your mouth and pumping the air out of your chest, like this with my hands,"* Vanessa clenched her hands together to demonstrate what she had done, *then continued. "But the more I pressed on . . ., the more I tried . . ., the more hopeless I felt. All I could see was your lifeless body, arms dangling from the bed as I pressed on your chest. Your little feet were stretching across the bed, falling every time I breathe into your mouth . . . it was like living a nightmare I couldn't wake from."*

Lamar stood in the doorway of the bathroom, head hung low as his thoughts rambled on, *"Does Nathaniel really have the ability to devour me whole?"* He thought to himself. *"Should I tell her about him, about Nathaniel, or should I—"* Vanessa then held Lamar's hand, breaking his concentration as she escorted him to their bedroom. Then, speaking in a more cheerful tone, she continued.

"Then, a miracle happened! You began to breathe on your own, and all of your color returned, most of it anyway." She smiled as she continued, *"you even felt lighter. I was so relieved that I couldn't stop crying. I held you until you finally woke up, and when you did, you had beautiful crimson eyes."* Peering down at Lamar, she said, *"But all I could see was my little boy."*

They entered their room, and Vanessa sat down on the bed next to Lamar and kissed him on his forehead. She stood up, walked over to the dresser, and brought back new bandages and Neosporin. She gently removed the old bandages Lamar had used to dress his wounds and added new ones with the applied ointment as she continued her explanation.

"And before that night, you had already started acting slightly different. Do you remember when you helped that little girl that fell off the swing? I was so proud of you that day. But what I didn't tell you was that her mother called along with another teacher. They both said that you sat in the swing and watched her fall. That you stared at her with a devilish grin as she lay in the sand

crying. That you didn't intervene until enough blood could be seen by another student. To be honest, I didn't think much of it because it wasn't your problem to begin with. At the time, I was more concerned about how did two adults see this happen, and yet they did nothing."

She paused for a moment, glanced down at Lamar and said, *"Baby, what I'm trying to say is, I'm here for you no matter what you are going through. I am worried, but we can get through it together."*

Lamar looked up at Vanessa, his eyes watery and voice crackling due to sadness. He tried to clear his throat before he spoke but he felt even more sadness. Unable to speak clearly, Lamar stood to his feet, faced his mother, and slowly lifted up his shirt.

His mother's eyes widened in terror, then she burst into tears, shielding her eyes from Lamar's body. He then turned around, his shirt over his head to display his back to her.

His body was covered in thick blotch-like bruises where he had been kicked and punched brutally by the larger child. There were two blotches near his neck and collar bones, another pair on his left ribcage, a massive bruise that covered his entire right side of his body from mid ribcage to lower stomach. And his back was dotted in bruised where he had been punched multiple times by the larger child.

Pulling down his shirt and wiping his tears away, Lamar began to speak, "Mommy, I have changed. I am different now." His first words struck Vanessa's heart with sharp pain. Clinching her hands together in agony, she listened silently as each word tore at her heart.

A Life Long Struggle

"I have been acting strange for a few days now. But it wasn't until I woke, I mean really woke up, that I understood this change. Mamma, I see the world differently through a new set of eyes. I feel...new...or altered in some way. I have access to words and ideas that I can't explain, that I . . . never had before. When I first woke up, it was hard for me to move, remember? You had to slap me in order for me to come to. But before that, it was like I had been reborn. I could see for the first time, feel new sensations . . . Look," Lamar held his chest where one of the many bruises lay, *"This is where he kicked me...but it didn't hurt."* Pointing at another bruise, *"This is where I was punched; however, that too didn't hurt! BUT when I came home and was laughed at, in that short time, it hurt."* Clinching his chest where his heart would be, *"It hurt more than any kick or any punch I had ever felt . . . The scary thing is, Mamma, I didn't feel pain from this hurt. I felt anger. I felt rage. I felt . . . like I wasn't me. Like I was becoming something else. Something I don't want to be. That's why I wanted to talk to you. I wanted to tell you about my day. I wanna tell you that . . . Mamma I'm scared of what's happening to me."*

Vanessa leaped from the bed and hugged him tightly. As her tears fell onto his head, she spoke in a seemingly inaudible tone, *"I'm so sorry baby. I didn't know what you were going through these last few days. I didn't know what to do. Just know Mommy's here, and I will always be here to protect you!"* She then knelt down to his eye level, wiped the tears from her face, and spoke mercilessly, *"I will punish that kid who did this to you. I will find him, and he will get what he deserves!"*

Lamar looked at her, smiled, and replied, *"It's ok, Uncle Sim already got him. When he was kicking me on the ground, uncle Sim flew in, and BAM! Punched that guy so hard that he flew back like ten feet! That's how I got away. Uncle Sim beat up that guy for me."*

Feeling a bit at ease, Vanessa stood to her feet and said, *"Well, I think you had enough adventure for today. It's time to go to bed."*

Lamar suddenly jumped back and said, *"I don't want to sleep in here. Can we please sleep in the living room?"*

This peculiar request incited a bit of curiosity within Vanessa's mind. She desperately wanted to inquire as to why a change in location was needed. But given today's events along with those that preceded them, she thought it wise not to pry, at least not tonight. She looked toward Lamar and spoke calmly.

"Ok, Lamar. We can sleep on the couch tonight. But just for tonight, okay?"

Lamar, now filled with joy, sprung from the bed and replied, "Okay!" She then took the sheets and comforter from their bed and proceeded to the living room with Lamar prancing behind her with pillows in hand. She spread the blanket across the sofa as Lamar placed the pillows, from the bed, on the head of the sofa. She then knelt down along the side of the sofa, clasped her hands together, and signaled Lamar to join her. Lamar knelt next to her, and without a moment's thought, he began to pray aloud.

"Our Father, who art in Heaven, hallowed be Thy name. Thy Kingdom come, Thy will be done, on Earth as it is in Heaven. Give us this day our daily bread. And forgive us our trespasses, as we forgive those who trespass against us—" Lamar paused. Vanessa raised her head slowly as she watched Lamar curiously. He looked over at her and said, "Mom, let's not say this tonight." Her face twisted with confusion, but before she could respond, Lamar continued to speak, "These are empty words that we recite. Can I make a new prayer, something that comes from my heart and soul? One that I feel to be true, from deep within?"

Once he finished speaking, his mother simply bowed her head, smiled, then replied, "Go ahead, son." Lamar began to speak, and his words astounded Vanessa.

"Dear Heavenly Father,

We come before you with bowed heads and humbled hearts. Our minds troubled and actions wavering, we ask that you relieve us of these conditions and walk with us through this journey of life. Keep us strong and unfolding, clear of conscious, and sturdy. Gift us the ability to walk a path expelling all evils from our inner selves. Watch over us and protect us from those who wish harm upon us. And us that we not wish harm upon others. Let us see this world without tainted eyes, allow us to sleep peacefully, and that we not suffer greatly. Give us comfort in times of need and stand with us in times of desperation. And to all battles, we cannot fight alone, give us knowledge to seek help from those who can. And this we pray.

Amen"

As Lamar lifted his head to stand to his feet, his eyes displayed a slight shimmer just before they faded back into their natural state. His mother kissed him on top of his head then proceeded to rest for the night. She slept on the inside, closest to the back of the sofa where you would normally rest your head, while he slept outside closest to the sofa's edge. Her arms wrapped around him as his back faced her. Lamar had fallen asleep first, being that the day's journey had depleted much of his energy. Vanessa would fall asleep shortly after, mentally drained due to the day's incidents.

As the time neared twilight, Nathaniel emerged from the shadows. He, still formless, had waited patiently for the opportune moment to approach. He collected himself near the far corner of the living room as he watched silently. *"The time has come, child,"* Nathaniel said as he vanished then reappeared at Lamar's side. He stood over the sofa as a beast posed to kill its prey. There was a brief pause of silence, and with a single thought, Nathaniel froze time still, then he spoke aloud in a language unknown to man,

"I, The Enigma Nathaniel, shall open the gate of merger. Unify the firstborn, the bestower of Nathaniel . . . come, become one and live anew!"

The floor beneath the sofa opened, and a pool of shadows took its place. Nathaniel stood before Lamar, removing his body from his mother's grasp with his mysterious power, and had begun to sink his feet into the pool of darkness. Nathaniel spoke one final time.

"The shadows shall be the medium in which we merge. Total darkness surround, hand to hand, and arm and feet. You sleep as one but will awaken as we! By my name, merge thy being with me!"

Nathaniel then entered Lamar's body as he stood in the pool of shadows, using it as a medium between himself and Lamar. He spoke," *I shall live within this child and consume his soul until he is no more!"* Nathaniel stepped from the pool of darkness, using Lamar as his new vessel. He stood on the surface of Lamar's home for the first time. He looked upon himself, ensuring that he had complete control over Lamar's body. Nathaniel took a second step, then a third, but quickly realized something was wrong.

Lamar's body began to quiver, then a sudden blast of energy expelled Nathaniel from Lamar's body, flinging him across the room and crashing into a far wall. Nathaniel quickly stood to his feet and watched a new creature emerge from within Lamar. Angered by what had happened, the enraged Nathaniel shouted in an unknown tongue,

"How dare you! This is MY vessel! MINE and mine alone. I shall rip you from all existence!"

A Fight for Survival

The shockwave from the blast shook the Earth violently as it repelled Nathaniel from Lamar's body. As time remained still, the glow from the blast condensed onto itself, and a new creature was formed. It blazed golden in color, as bright as the sun, just before dimming into a crimson red. It steamed as vapors sprang from its body as if the air itself was fleeing from its presence. It stood calmly, its outer shell vibrating as still water would during a downpour. Nathaniel collected himself and spoke in a fury, *"Who are you, to interrupt my merger with MY vessel?!"* the creature remained silent. Nathaniel continued, *"Speak . . . or face oblivion!"* The creature remained motionless, oblivious to Nathaniel's threats.

Suddenly its outer exterior began to solidify, dulling in color, as another blast burst from its body. The creature let out a painful roar accompanied by the sounds of breaking bones and burning flesh. The room temperature spiked as this creature let out yet another burst of energy. It stumbled forward, planting a hoof firmly on the living room floor to maintain its balance while shaking the entire home by doing so. Its body slouched over in agony as the creature sprouted razor-sharp wing-like appendages from its back. Again the creature sent forth a burst of energy as its form continued to alter. Several arm-like structures forcefully sprouted from its left side and from its right, causing the creature to let out a horrifying bellow that froze Nathaniel still. Multiple heads emerged from its apex, each resembling ancient beasts as they fought for dominion over the creature's body. It thrashed about while it continued to grow in size, aging all that it touched and turning it to ash.

Nathaniel watched while the creature's body morphed before him, as he remained helpless due to the gravity produced by the creature's shockwaves. In fear that his vessel, Lamar, would be killed, Nathaniel placed a barrier around him and the entire home, protecting all that dwelled within. *"This creature must be stopped. I will not allow such a primitive creature – one who cannot control its own form – to foil my merge! This shall end NOW!"*

Just as the creature released its final blast, it slowly stood upright, repositioning itself. Surrounded in a circle of ash, it peered towards the heavens. Its chest enlarged then collapsed as if it had taken a deep breath. Nathaniel quickly lunged at the creature with the intent to kill, having temporarily altered his composition to a substance harder than diamonds. He was poised over the creature, ready to slice it in two. Just as he was about to deliver the finishing blow, the shockwaves from the earlier blasts had receded and crashed into the creature, pummeling Nathaniel to the floor. This force, now consistent, repeatedly crashed into the creature, changing its form with each pulse, until it stood calmly before Nathaniel. Its exterior was no longer a vibrant crimson but had morphed to a dull bronze. Its appendages had all receded into its being until it appeared to be in a more humanoid form.

Nathaniel, now formless, positioned himself before the creature analyzing its composition. Nathaniel then created a sphere-like appendage, hovered it over Lamar's body and said, *"Speak creature, for I am the enigma Nathaniel, and you have interrupted my merger with this, MY vessel."* The creature peered over toward Lamar's body as Nathaniel's appendage hovered above him, then turned back towards Nathaniel. The creature remained speechless while glaring at Lamar's body. Nathaniel's fury boiled over as he demanded an explanation, *"Why are you interrupting my merger, nameless one? Do you wish for oblivion?"* Again the creature remained silent. It stood facing Nathaniel as if it were paralyzed. Nathaniel then changed the form of his appendage to that of a blade. The blade-like appendage sailed toward the creature and stabbed it from behind. "I shall send you to the abyss, creature!" shouted Nathaniel as he thrusts his appendage deeper into the creature's blindside.

Moments after Nathaniel witnessed himself skewer the creature, he felt something strike him, sending him flying across the room with great force and pinning him to the wall. He cried out, *"What is this trickery! I am The Enigma NATHANIEL! Release me!"* Letting out a dark and ominous aura, Nathaniel escaped the creature's grasp as it stood motionless. It had defended itself effortlessly.

The creature had spawned a tail, which mimicked that of a prehistoric scorpion's tail. It retracted itself and lay at the creature's feet while a second tail wrapped around Nathaniel's sword-like appendage, stopping it from penetrating its body.

The creature turned toward Nathaniel and spoke, but his tongue did not reach Nathaniel. Seeming perplexed, the creature spoke again but in a different language. Yet again, his speech was inaudible to Nathaniel. The creature then waved his hand to manifest a reflective material to see himself. It began to change its form. His color darkened to that of Nathaniel's while he coated himself in an exoskeleton that complemented its massive tail. It examined itself, then spoke audibly to Nathaniel, *"Ah, yes...this form should suffice. It's been quite some time since I have looked like this. What do you think of it, Nathaniel The Enigma?"*

Nathaniel summoned his appendage with a simple gesture. By reshaping itself into its original sphere form, the appendage freed itself then merged back with Nathaniel's body. Once whole again, Nathaniel spoke and an interesting conversation ensued.

"What are you called, and why are you interrupting my merger? Speak quickly, or I shall display my power and release my wrath upon you."

"Come now Nathaniel, calm thy self."

"There is no calm only rage. You have disturbed my merger! I have waited for this time. I have toiled for days in this child's mind plucking at the threads of his innocence. Embodying meager children, to ripen this vessel. This merger is the fruit of my labor, and you, a nameless interloper, have intervened. I shall not be calmed tilts' my rage has been satisfied."

The creature turned to Nathaniel, lowering his second tail and dispelling the reflective material in effort to continue their conversation.

"Let us not be savages, Nathaniel. I find it discomforting, bickering like mere humans. Nevertheless, we shall speak; should our exchange of words cease to amuse us, then one shall perish."

"You speak as if you know me, nameless one! Your presence is no longer welcome. Vanish from here, Nameless, and I shall spare you."

The creature took a step forward in Nathaniel's direction and said, *"I have been called many names, by many creatures, but* never, *Nameless. Amusing.*" The creature continued to walk toward Nathaniel as he spoke, "*You, Nathaniel are equally amusing as this form I have taken. Like you, this primitive and crude form keeps me . . . entertained. So let us continue to entertain each other.*"

Nathaniel's rage overflowed, "*Yes, let us talk. Entertain me, Nameless!*" His body started to solidify as he took a form similar to the Nameless creature. Becoming more and more intrigued by Nathaniel's actions, the creature taunts him, "*Come now, Nathaniel...The Enigma...let us converse.*" Then, with a burst of energy, the beings clashed, bursting through the roof of the house into the open sky. The world trembled as the two being continued their destructive conversation. Nathaniel was able to fend off the creature's advances for a short while, before being knocked back to the ground.

The creature landed on top of Nathaniel with both of its tails aimed at his head while rocks and debris flew into the air. The creature spoke, "*Come now, Nathaniel. I stand between you and a successful merger . . . you must do better!*" The creature then flung Nathaniel into the air. However, Nathaniel was able to latch onto one of the creature's tails, dragging them both into a dark void.

There Nathaniel was able to take a new form to combat the creature. Covered in a shell-like armor, resembling a pangolin, wings that scaled twice his body size, and armed with claws and fangs, Nathaniel's new humanoid form stood firm, awaiting the approaching creature. The nameless creature quickly recovered from Nathaniel's maneuver then spoke to him from a distance.

"*So this is your void. Come Nathaniel, gather your strength and face—*" before the creature could finish, Nathaniel had closed the vast distance between them and attacked the creature directly.

A Life Long Struggle

The battle began to turn violent as Nathaniel started his onslaught by tearing off one of the creature's tails, then using it to impale the creature, pinning it to the floor of the void.

"Now heed me, nameless creature. Tell me, why have you interrupted my merger?" Before the creature could respond, Nathaniel cut off the creature's second tail and tossed it aside. "Answer me," shouted Nathaniel. "Where did you come from, Nameless?"

"I am not nameless," the creature said abruptly, while absorbing the tail that had impaled him. The creature began to glow as he pulled himself from the void's floor. It then spoke viciously, *"I have been called many names throughout the eras, but no creature alive has referred to me as nameless."* Nathaniel jumped back, readying himself for the creature's counter-attack. Springing from the void's floor, the creature rushed towards Nathaniel as he braced himself for the counter-attack. But to Nathaniel's surprise, the creature simply flew past him to retrieve its severed tail.

It picked up his limb and reattached it to itself. *"Nathaniel, The Enigma . . . you have begun to amuse me, a great deal. So to display my gratitude, I shall answer one of your inquiries."* In the blink of an eye, the creature lunged at Nathaniel and forced its hand through his chest. *"I interrupted your merger because you WILL NOT merge with that child."* Then the creature pulled itself from Nathaniel's chest then swatted him like a fly with the once severed tail. Nathaniel flew across the void with astonishing speed. The creature then caught Nathaniel by his left wing and flung him to the floor of the void, ripping the wing from Nathaniel's body.

Just before his body could land firmly on the floor, the creature appeared below him and tore off the second wing, then again skewered Nathaniel with its tail, dislodging them both from the void. As the creature held both of Nathaniel's wings in its hands, they began to be absorbed. *"I am the entity that repelled you from Lamar's mind during your first merger,"* the creature said as it ripped off Nathaniel's right arm and absorbed it. *"I am the being that glows behind Lamar's eyes,"* the creature said as it tore away Nathaniel's left leg. *"I am what stands between you and this child. You will not have him!"* Nathaniel's body, now free from the void, reverted back to a formless state.

The weakened Nathaniel spoke softly, *"I cannot hold a form in this world for long . . . due to my nature as an . . . enigma. But you, nameless one, you have held this from for quite some time now . . . tell me how . . . does it feel?"* The creature's body began to lose its integrity. Just as the creature showed signs of weakness, Nathaniel quickly reformed himself and kicked the creature's head clear from its body. He then reached into the cavity and attempted to merge with the creature.

"Who are you?! Tell me all!" Nathaniel shouted. *"I wish to know your purpose and to what reason brought you here!"* As Nathaniel probed the headless creature for answers, wings erupted from the headless body's back and stabbed Nathaniel. Then, using the same energy that shaped him, the creature's wings pinned Nathaniel to the wall, causing Nathaniel to cry out in agony.

"Release me, nameless CREATURE!"

"I have torn away your arm and leg. Stripped you of mobility, and yet you refuse to make a sound. But this . . . this hurts you, doesn't it, Nathaniel!

A Life Long Struggle

"I shall rip you to bits!"

"Now, now. Calm yourself, Nathaniel." The creature said as its wings grew in length. "Allow me to speak to you face to face," the creature added as its body turned in search of its severed head. Human humor ha! Now, where did you kick it . . . . . ahh . . . there it is."

The creature kept Nathaniel pinned to the wall, with its wings acting as nails while emitting a steady flow of compressed energy. It then picked up the battered head and molded it onto itself.

"Now Nathaniel, where were we. You had kicked off my head—and thought you could get answers from my soul. If you had questions, why not ask? We are simply conversing, are we not?"

"Do not jest with me, creature!"

"I do not jest . . . nor do I lie. As I said before, should this conversation fail to amuse, one will die. Surely you see the difference in our abilities . . . However, I am enjoying this little talk. It's been too long since I've talked. And you have so much to say . . . I believe you have asked two questions. If my memory serves me well, the first was – 'Why have you interrupted my merger?' And the second was, 'Where did you come from?' I've answered both questions... have I not? Thus your left leg and right arm shall serve as payment. BUT . . . I took your wings because on two separate occasions you interrupted me from speaking . . . and I so hate that."

"Ha! And you do not jest, you say. Yet here we are. On the precipice of conversation . . . and yet you believe to have the upper hand. I shall share this with you, creature . . . our abilities

complement our being, as do our limitations. And yours, nameless one, shines bright."

Nathaniel's composure changed dramatically. As he spoke, he began to absorb all heat from the room. The creature had not noticed what Nathaniel had started to do. As the heat drained from the room, a thick cold fog condensed on the floor. It thickened until it felt like a snowy block of ice. The creature, after feeling the decrease in temperature, looked to its feet to see what Nathaniel had done.

Surprised by Nathaniel's unorthodox approach, it refocused its attention back toward Nathaniel and plunged its wings deeper into Nathaniel's being. *"You clever, clever creature,"* it said in an aggravated tone.

Nathaniel replied, "As life is born, it burns bright. A crimson red equally bright to that of the sun. But will soon dull to that of a lusterless bronze. That is how I would explain your existence. One that meddles in the realm of life, aging all that it touches. That is the nature of your being."

The creature attempted to pull away from Nathaniel as he continued to absorb the heat from the room, growing colder as the heat dissipated. Nathaniel then shouted in a demonic rage. *"You will not escape me, creature!"* Nathaniel then saps the heat from the creature's wings, freezing them in place within his being.

"You have taken my wings – allow me to return the favor!" Nathaniel then shatters the creature's frozen wings as it lets out a terrifying roar! "HURTS, DOESN'T IT, NAMELESS ONE!" Nathaniel shouted. Freed from the creature's grasp, Nathaniel pulled the remaining wing fragments from his being. *"I believe this is the end of our conversation,"* said Nathaniel. The creature, still in agony,

swung its tail at Nathaniel, hoping to finish him off with one massive blow. However, Nathaniel had dropped the temperature to that of Infinite zero, a constant and never-ending decreasing temperature. Ensuring the creature would have little to no mobility. Nathaniel stopped the creature's tail with ease and shattering it upon contact. Nathaniel, instead of finishing off the creature, spoke calmly.

"This conversation is at its conclusion . . . tell me nameless one . . . is there more to your existence? You claim to be the guardian of this child, his protector, and yet you have lost this simple word exchange . . . what more of you is there? You once declared that I, Nathaniel, would not have this child – how could you make such an absurd claim? Hmmm . . . you do not jest, so indulge me, nameless one. You are one who's power lie with vigor, youth . . . and . . . TIME. Have you bound yourself to this child . . . or is it?"

The creature's body began to burn bright crimson once more as it tried to heat itself. Nathaniel, being overwhelming surprised, spoke joyously, *"No, you aren't bound to this child . . . you are bound to . . . the entire family! You are their protector!"* Just as Nathaniel figured out the creature's purpose, it erupted in black flames, clearing the room of ice and raising the temperature to a more suitable level.

"Yes! I am the guardian of this family. It is as you say, specter, but this changes nothing. I will not allow you to have this child. He is under my protection. Yield!"

Wager

"Yield?! The lowly, nameless Guardian, beckons me to yield?! I shall do NO such thing! Guardian of this child, creature of heat and time, I, Nathaniel, challenge you! Guard thyself, for I command living frost that consumes all things! Prepare! Your demise is nigh!"

The two creatures stood poised, facing one another. Nathaniel covered himself in a living frost that continuously absorbed the surrounding heat. While the creature blazed crimson, encasing itself in a pulsating aura. "You continue to test me, Nathaniel," the creature said with a confident melody. "Come, let us conclude this conversation. I do enjoy tragedies such as this. A confident enigma tries to take from the tree of life only to be cut down by its guardian. Such is a great story, wouldn't you agree, Nathaniel?"

"I have no further use of your knowledge, Guardian. Let us end the old conversation and start anew. Which one of us is the stronger, you or I?!"

Nathaniel lunged at the creature, altering his shape to that of man in the process. At the end of his advance, Nathaniel hurled a right hook towards the creature. However, it was blocked by the creature's previously shattered tail. Nathaniel followed his first attack with a right kick to the creature's abdomen, causing the creature to shield itself with its battered wings. Then Nathaniel followed his kick with a powerful downward left hook he intended to be the final blow, but the creature jumped away, causing Nathaniel's punch to crash towards the floor, instantly freezing it solid.

*"You are no Guardian!" Nathaniel said as he glanced at the creature. "Look," Nathaniel added as he pointed at Lamar. "This child lay on the floor surrounded by my living frost. Had my barrier not protected him, he would be dead already. A dead child is of no use to either of us! No, you are **not** a guardian....you are a gatekeeper. A lowly gatekeeper!"*

The creature quickly flew across the room to counterattack. However, just as the creature landed in front of Nathaniel, its form altered as well. By retaining its armor-plating and crimson color, the creature also took the form of man to combat Nathaniel in close quarters. The creature flung a left hook as its first blow, but Nathaniel blocked it with a jumping knee and then countered with a downward punch, only to be blocked by the creature's newly formed tail.

Each blow produced an immense amount of energy that caused time to flow inconsistently—forcing it forward one second with every clash.

After the creature had blocked Nathaniel's last attack, it landed a solid kick near Nathaniel's neck, sending him crashing to the floor. But Nathaniel was able to cushion his fall using his frost. But before Nathaniel could react, the creature coiled up its tail and leaped towards the ceiling. Then, by using his tail as a spring, the creature bounced from the ceiling and stomped down on Nathaniel's head, forcing a mist of frost to spew into the air.

The creature shouted, *"You may be satisfied with the knowledge of me, but I am not done with you, Nathaniel!"*

As the mist cleared, the creature noticed that Nathaniel had protected himself using his paddle-like tail. Nathaniel quickly grabbed hold of the creature's legs and flung him to the floor, *"I care not for your interests, Gatekeeper. For you shall never know of me."*

"Really now." The creature said as it suddenly vanished and reappeared within inches of Nathaniel's face. In an instant, the creature covered Nathaniel's face with the palm of his hand and, with a powerful thrust, flung him to the floor!

As he landed, the creature used his tail to wrap around Nathaniel's legs, then he picked him up and flung him to the floor once more. Frost leaped from the floor as the creature followed up a swift kick to Nathaniel's stomach, which sent him speeding towards the ceiling. But instead of colliding with the ceiling, Nathaniel phased through it, watching the creature as he vanished.

"Not good enough," Nathaniel said as he reappeared behind the creature and used his tail to swat him to the frozen floor like a fly.

As the creature lay flat, smothered by the substantial weight of Nathaniel's tail, he glanced over in Lamar's direction. Their fight had caused time to start and stop many times over. As time slowly passed, Lamar had turned to face them as if he were watching. He laid on the floor with his torso twisted as if he were trying to pick himself up. His eyes were wide open, in a suspended

state of surprise. Noticing this, the creature spoke, *"Wait Nathaniel, Look!"* Nathaniel slowly raised his tail, *"Do you concede Gatekeeper!?"*

The creature replied, *"I never concede . . . but look, there!"*

Using his tail to point at Lamar, Nathaniel looked behind him. Lamar's eyes were wide open, having seen all events that had taken place. Nathaniel spoke, *"He cannot see us through the veil of time, Gatekeeper – you know this as well as I."*

The creature responded, *"You are as wise as a fool. He need not see us, only be aware of us, Imbecile."*

"Should this happen, it would only serve as a mere nuisance. Merging with that child would be more difficult . . . But what would happen to you, Gatekeeper." The creature then sat on the icy floor, his legs crossed as his tail lay across his lap.

"That is not your business, Nathaniel." The creature crossed his arms as if deep in thought, *"But we face a dilemma . . . we don't have time to continue this conversation nor complete the challenge you proposed. But there is another way we can continue our—"*

"I do not care for this conversation nor our challenge. All I want is my merger! I care little if this feeble child can see me. I will simply merge with him by force!"

"Do not test me, Nathaniel. I have indulged our chat thus far, do not feel as if YOU are the superior being here."

"I am superior. The proof is nigh." Nathaniel turned to face Lamar and began to walk in his direction. *"You cower in the face of this child. But he cannot see us, nor can he hear us. We live outside*

of his reality. Even now, we stand at the edge of his time, moving faster than light, millions of times over. Yet you still cower before this little face."

"Nathaniel, do not jest. Do not take another step towards that child or I—"

"Will do what, Gatekeeper?! What will you do?! What can you do?"

"I shall say this only once. If you touch that child, I shall strip you of your form and return you to the shapeless enigma. Painfully."

Nathaniel continued to walk over towards Lamar as he remained frozen in time. He lowered himself to Lamar's eye level. Then turned toward the creature and spoke, *"I am the superior one here."*

"No, you are not." The creature replied.

"I propose . . . a wager." Nathaniel said as his tail lifted into the air and smashed into the floor. *"To the victor goes the spoils, and the lesser shall perish."* Again his tail rose and crashed upon the floor. *"I shall utilize **all** my power to strip this child of his innocents and plunge him into darkness, and you, nameless. You shall try to stop me using all of your power."* Nathaniel then stared into Lamar's eyes as his tail rose and smashed into the floor again. *"The superior being will repel the lesser and drain him of his power. Once in this weakened state, the stronger of us can do away with the lesser."* Nathaniel moved closer towards Lamar as the creature spoke abruptly.

"I like the way you think, Nathaniel The Enigma. However." The creature slowly stood to his feet as he continued to speak. *"I*

detest any other being tainting this family. So do not touch the boy during this wager."

"I shall do no such thing! As I said, I shall do all in my power to have this child; that includes touch and even taste."

"Then, I shall burn away every appendage of yours, that even gets close to this child!"

"Then let us start this wager!"

Nathaniel suddenly attempted to plant his hand firmly on Lamar's head, but before he could, the creature stopped him with a crimson blast, different from any Nathaniel had seen before. The blast struck Nathaniel tearing away all his limbs, disintegrating them instantly.

Nathaniel let out a painful screech, then reverted back into his formless state but not before expelling an aura of his own. Nathaniel's energy crashed into the creature commanding it to revert to its most primitive form.

The creature roared in agony as he thrashed about. *"Damn you, Nathaniel,"* the creature said as it fell to the floor. But to Nathaniel's surprise, the creature didn't change much. His color changed to a dark black, resembling one's shadow. Wings sprouted from his shoulders and draped across his back like an old ragged cloak. Horns grew from its head which, at just the right angle, appeared to be an old and tattered wrangler's hat. The creature stood before Lamar as Nathaniel's protective barrier was dispelled. As Nathaniel faded into the shadows, his hold over time was undone. All that was damaged had been restored, and time had begun again.

A Life Long Struggle

Lamar sat up on the floor, rubbing his eyes. Unable to see clearly, he crawled around on the floor—one hand rubbing his eyes while the other reached out for the furniture. *"My eyes are really burning, like really really burning. I can't even open them! I must have fell on the floor last night or something. I will never sleep out here again. My eyes are on fire, and it's cold as snowman balls, geese! And I can't find the darn sofa. Just how far did I roll when I hit the floor!?"*

Crawling along the frozen floor, Lamar had stumbled into the pool of shadows that Nathaniel had used for their merger. "What is this stuff, bubblegum?!" Lamar said once he entered the pool of shadows. Nathaniel and the creature watched the child struggle. Delighted by the turn of events, Nathaniel manifested himself into the pool. His voice echoed through the house, *"Still . . . still thyself child."* The shadows, which are now a part of Nathaniel, leaped from the pool and clung to Lamar's body, entering his nose and mouth to ensure a successful merger.

The creature had not expected Nathaniel to attempt a merger in open time. Surprised by Nathaniel's actions, the creature watched out of curiosity. He watched as Lamar fought back relentlessly. He thrashed about while holding his breath and clenching his mouth shut, preventing Nathaniel from entering his body.

"How unfortunate."

Then, with a swift wave of his hand, the creature dematerialized and rejoined with Lamar. The creature was able to force Nathaniel from Lamar's body effortlessly, *"Calm thyself, child. You are in no danger."* Responding almost instinctively, Lamar suddenly stopped struggling. He sat still, frozen with his arms stretched wide as if he were holding up a large object. His eyes, mouth, and ears were dripping with black shadow sludge as the two beings battled within him.

Lamar's previous struggle against the shadows had knocked him against the sofa where his mother was sleeping. She, a fairly deep sleeper, had rolled over, seemingly unaware of the current events. Vanessa reached behind herself to see if her son remained asleep, but he no longer laid next to her. She sprung forward in fear that she had knocked Lamar to the floor. Vanessa turned abruptly, only to find Lamar on the floor with some sort of black sludge oozing from his eyes, ears, and mouth. Her heart sunk within her chest. Horrified by what she saw, she was unable to scream. Instead, her heart danced about as she spoke softly, *"La . . . maa, son. What are you doing . . . let's not play like this. Mommy doesn't like it."*

Hearing his mother's voice, Lamar's head turned slightly in her direction. Then, with his arms stretched about and the black substance leaking from his eyes and mouth, Lamar tried to call out to her, "Mommy? "

Vanessa screamed! Her body was in complete disarray and horrified. She sat back on the sofa, pulling in her legs and clinching the sheets, *"Oh my Lord, get up from the floor, Lamar! Get up, get up, get up!"*

At this time, the creature was able to drive Nathaniel from Lamar's body fully, while all the remaining shadows suddenly vanished. Once expelled from Lamar's body, the creatures again stood on the edge of time as Lamar's mother swept him from the floor. "Just what the hell is going on!" Vanessa cried out as she leaped back into the sofa, cradling Lamar in her arms.

A Life Long Struggle

Amused by the sudden change of events, the mysterious creatures began to talk amongst themselves, unaware that Lamar could now hear and understand their conversation.

"You are fast Gatekeeper, but you will have to be faster next time."

"This wager of yours, I accept. The life of this child, for a bit of entertainment. Yes—"

"Oh no, Gatekeeper. Your life as well! I shall continue to drain your energy, and should you weaken, I shall strike you down!"

"Ohh, Nathaniel. Do not be so foolish. Your life energy is not unlimited, and it too will decline. However, I will not wait until you're in a weakened state. I shall come after you, with intent to erase you from existence, with EVERY attempt you make at Lamar's life. You should be on guard. Remember, I am this child's protector, and you are the intruder."

Try as you must, Gatekeeper. Let us see who shall be the last being standing!

Lamar was able to hear their conversation completely. However, instead of displaying signs of fear or disarray, he spoke calmly to the creatures. "Who is my protector? Show yourself!" Lamar squinted his eyes, scanning the living room, "Come out," he whispered while attempting not to alert his frightened mother.

"Go, Gatekeeper," said Nathaniel in a humorous tone. *"Show yourself to the child. It seems he is quite the stubborn one. To have heard us **and** understood us without fear. There is more to this child . . . this family . . . that you have not to reveal. Yes . . . I shall enjoy ripping them from you."*

A Life Long Struggle

As Lamar's mother squeezed him tightly, her face in tears, time again slowed. And in the distance, a voice spoke, *"Child, look here, into the distance, where the floor and corner collide. Look. Hard. And you shall see what you desire. Knowledge is but a construct in which time is born, but its misuse can conceive a deadly offspring. Look upon me, child. See your Guardian, see what awaits you after life seeps from your body."*

The voice turned silent as the sound of thunder shook the house knocking the pictures from the walls and causing Lamar's mother to shriek in fear. She then barriers her head in Lamar's back as she squeezes him tight. His head fixed, staring in the distant corner. A sudden BURST of lightning collided with the roof of the home, causing all the lights to go out. Lamar's mother cried out, *"Somebody help, turn the lights back on,"* as Lamar continued to stare at the corner. He hadn't moved nor blinked. He just stared into the distance. Again lightning crashed down upon the house, but this time a shadow formed after the burst. The temperature in the home had risen several degrees as the shadows began to outline an unfamiliar shape. Now intensely focused, all of Lamar's senses heightened. He was unable to hear, feel, taste, or smell. He had unknowingly focused all of his senses on sight. There was a sudden silent flash of light, and then Lamar saw The Gatekeeper for the first time.

He stood tall. His head nearly touched the ceiling. He was as dark as a shadow cast in moonlight. Without any facial features, the creature peered towards Lamar, looking over his shoulder as a dark and ragged cloak drenched over his back. He wore a dark straw hat, his hands resembled claws, and under his cloak hid a massive scorpion-like tail that had slightly moved from view.

A Life Long Struggle

Looking down at the creature's feet, Lamar noticed that its shadow was different in color. It appeared darker than the standing figure, and its shape didn't quite match. Lamar felt as if he had seen this figure somewhere before, so he refocused his attention solely on the creature's shadow.

For a moment, the shadow seemed normal, but in a sudden jerking motion, the shadow moved slightly as a voice spoke, "Fear me." The shadow leaped from the floor, reshaping itself in the process. "You are mine, child of man," said the shadow as it sprung forward.

Lamar could not evade the approaching creature, but a sudden gust of wind sliced the creature in half.

"Do not test me, Nathaniel!" shouted The Gatekeeper as an unknown force flowed throughout the house.

After swiftly spinning itself around, The Gatekeeper flung away the two halves of Nathaniel with one hand then reached out towards Lamar with the other. Suddenly lightning **crashed** into the house once more, shaking it at its foundation. Lamar clenched his eyes shut as fear gripped him tight.

Suddenly, the lights flickered back on, and the two creatures vanished.

Good Boy

The storm cleared as fast as it came. Vanessa's cries for help alerted everyone in the house, and they rushed to her aid. She held Lamar tightly with her head buried within his back as he gazed into the distance. Vanessa's father burst into the living room and spoke in an angered tone, "What the hell is going on in here, Vanessa!" She replied, "Daddy, there's something on the floor! It possessed my son. Something is after him!" Mark stood to the right of the sofa near the hallway's entrance. He glanced at the floor left of the sofa, where Vanessa and Lamar were sleeping. *"There ain't shit down there girl,"* he said, pointing to the floor with an open hand. *"You making all this ruckus for nothing. We in here trying to sleep, and all I hear is you screaming like a lil girl. You outta know by now that you're too old for all this."*

Vanessa shouted back as she wiped her tears away, *"I'm telling you the truth. I was asleep until I felt a bump, like something had hit the sofa. Then I rolled over to see Lamar on the floor. Something had pulled him to the floor and—"*

"Nall, he wasn't pulled to the floor. Your big ass knock him to the floor! I just don't understand why the two of yall, in here sleeping on the couch, when you have a nice big bed in that room down the hall!"

Vanessa sat up straight as she continued to hold Lamar. *She spoke in a serious and unwavering tone, "I wasn't screaming because he was knocked to the floor. It was because of what I saw when I found him there."*

Acknowledging Vanessa's change in posture, Mark faced her directly, *"Well, tell me what you saw,"* he said with a puzzled expression.

She released Lamar, placing him on the opposite end of the sofa. By tucking her feet beneath her as she sat in the sofa, she recreated what she saw then spoke, *"He was kneeling on his knees . . . his hands were up like he was begging for something."* She then propped her arms upward, tilting her face towards the ceiling. *"Then . . . then I . . . I saw . . ."*

"What the hell did you see, Nessa," Mark said impatiently.

Tears began to roll down her face as she dropped her hands then covered her eyes, *"His eyes were completely black and some sort of black . . . STUFF . . . it was going IN him. Then it forced its way into his mouth and down his throat . . . in his eyes and ears!! Lamar was trying to fight it at first, but he just sat there, motionless. I tried to call him. I shouted out for him! I didn't know what else to do!"*

As she continued her story, Mark looked at Lamar to check his response as her story continued. But he didn't show any signs of disapproval. He sat on the end of the couch with a blank stare as his mother continued to recall the night's events.

"I called out for him . . . then he turned to me and said, 'Mom...ma' with the black stuff oozing from his face." Mark immediately interrupted her, *"Wait a minute, didn't you just say*

the black ooze was coming out of his body, but before you said it was going into his body. Which is it?"

"It was both," Vanessa shouted. "First, I saw it force its way inside of him, and then after I called his name, for some reason, it started coming out of him." She paused abruptly, took a deep breath, and said, "It gets weirder! After it dripped from his face, it kind of collected in his lap. Then like a snake, it slithered to the floor and POOF! It was gone."

"Poof," Mark said nonchalantly while staring at her awkwardly.

"Don't look at me like I'm crazy," she replied. "I know what I saw. Ask Lamar, he will tell you!"

Mark glanced over at Lamar again, but he still looked as if he were glazed over. "I would ask him, but this child looks preoccupied at the moment. I don't know what happened in here, but I can tell that you believe your story." He paused briefly then spoke gently, "Nassa, I love you, but I don't wanna wake up after 12 o'clock in the morning, tryin to piece together what happened to you moments prior." Vanessa tried to interrupt, but Mark continued to talk as if she hadn't said a thing.

"It's quite a few of us that live in this house, and I don't wanna hear crazy stories from ya brothers and sisters. Especially that Amanda, her ass is the gossip queen. She talk so damn much! I wanna just slap her sometimes, even when she ain't talkin. That damn girl just . . . on and on and on about nothing! I mean nothing! I can't take her adding more dim-witted shit to her list of things to talk about. So please, sleep in the room. I pushed everybody back in theirs before I came in here, so no one else knows what you told me except Lamar, and I'd like to keep it that way. Okay?"

Vanessa took a deep breath and sunk back into the sofa, *"Alright Daddy,"* she replied. *"I won't tell anybody else what happened."*

Satisfied with her reply Mark began to walk away, *"We can talk more tomorra. Till then, get you some rest,"* he said as he exited the Livingroom.

Once her father was out of view, Vanessa draped Lamar with a blanket and spoke to him in a soothing voice, *"It's all over now. Let's go to bed."* With all his senses still focused on sight, Lamar couldn't hear anything his mother said. He watched as her lips moved, and once they had stopped, he simply smiled and replied, *okay.*

He continued to watch his mother as she folded the sheets, occasionally looking back to where he saw the creatures. With his senses still in disarray, Lamar simply mimicked what he saw his mother do. As she folded the large comforter, he folded the smaller sheets. He struggled, flopping the corners and rolling the center until he had created a ball instead of a folded sheet. His mother chuckled as she watched him struggle vigorously. Once he had finished, Lamar stuck the tightly raveled sheet under his arm then stood facing the corner where he last saw the creatures. As his senses returned from their heightened state, Lamar thought to himself,

"That creature . . . the one called Gatekeeper. He felt familiar to me somehow. Nathaniel scares me a lot but The Gatekeeper . . . he feels . . . safe. But the way he cut his shadow . . . no the way he cut Nathaniel – is he stronger than Nathaniel!? And just what is a Gatekeeper anyway? What gate is he guarding . . .

A Life Long Struggle

me? But I'm no gate . . . I'm Lamar...I'm me. There must be some reason—"

As his feelings grew clearer, his mother's voice pierced his thoughts. *"Lamar come on, let's go,"* she said as she held out her hand. *"It's time for bed."* Adjusting his folded masterpiece, switching it from his left armpit to his right, Lamar grabbed hold of his mother's hand and walked with her down the hall to their room. Just before they entered, Vanessa looked down at Lamar and said, *"I know you don't want to sleep in here tonight, but it's better in here than it is out there. I won't question you about what happened tonight, but you have to be brave."* Looking up at his mother, he interrupted her and said in a calm yet fearless voice, *"Mamma, I'm not scared anymore. I have a protector, and he's a Gatekeeper too."* Lamar then walked into the room, jumped into the bed, and began to unravel the sheet that he'd folded. He stood in the bed's center as he flailed the sheet open and attempted to spread it across the bed. His mother walked over and tucked the corners of the sheets under the mattress until they were evenly distributed across the bed.

Then she flung the comforter across the bed in one swoop. It unfolded perfectly in mid-air just before landing gracefully on top of Lamar and blanketing the entire bed.

Lamar, jumping with the comforter drenched over his head, flopped down and lay happily across the mattress. Then, his mother shouted, *"Here comes the tickle monster!"* She slid under the covers and tickled him until his eyes started to water from laughter. *"Okay, okay, mom, you win – it's bedtime now . . . okay, okay, oh-kay,"* Lamar rolled over in a ball to protect himself for his mother, the tickle monster.

After she stopped playing with him, Lamar rolled back over, peeked from under the covers, and said, *"Mom I'm getting older now, and I know that things are a bit tight . . . but I'd like to sleep in my own bed."*

"What makes you say that?" Vanessa asked as she stood to her feet.

"Well, I am getting older, and I want to be able to . . . sleep on my own, especially when—"

Vanessa interrupted him while placing her hands on her hips, *"When what"* she implored.

"When I have bad dreams," Lamar said, struggling to emerge from beneath the bedding.

"Do you think something as small as a bad dream is going to pull us apart?" Vanessa said irritably. "I'm not afraid of your dreams, Lamar."

Sitting up and forcefully removing the comforter, he replied, *"Mom, I heard you scream tonight."* Vanessa shook her head in disagreement, then sat on the edge of the bed next to him and calmly replied, *"What happened tonight was no dream."*

"That's what I mean," Lamar said, using his hand to display excitement. *"Remember when I said I was changing? Well, it's not just a feeling anymore."*

Vanessa's heart began the beat heavily, *"What exactly are you saying, Lamar. Are you seeing ghosts?"*

"No," Lamar replied while redirecting his attention towards the floor.

"Do you think this house is haunted?" she asked with deep concern underlining the tone of her voice.

"No," he said quietly.

"Well, what do you mean?" Vanessa asked, questioning his posture. *"Better yet, why don't you tell me what happened tonight?"*

Lamar turned towards her, his face more serious than ever as he began to speak, *"If I tell you . . . you gotta promise me that you won't get scared or scream again."*

Vanessa froze. Lamar's sudden change in demeanor intensified their conversation, causing Vanessa to hesitate. She paused slightly, balling her fists tightly as a single bead of sweat rolled down her cheek. *"Okay. I'm ready to hear what happened,"* Vanessa said cautiously.

Lamar, looked deep into his mother's eyes. He could sense the fear in her heart. He sat up in the bed with a serious look in his eyes, took a deep breath, and said, *"A **monster** came for me tonight. He tried to merge with me."* Lamar paused as he continued to look at his mother. Her face grew more and more scared with each word he spoke. But he continued, *"His name is Nathaniel . . . and . . . he--"* Lamar began to feel uneasy the more he spoke.

Suddenly his face brightened, and the look of seriousness vanished as he continued his story in a new vibrant melody. *"He took all my toys and ate all of the food we had in the house. You tried to stop him, but he hit you like that boy did me. You were crying, really badly. I tried to help you, but I wasn't strong enough. Then I fell to the floor and woke up. But when I did, I couldn't stop crying. I heard you scream at me, but when I tried to wipe my face, I only made it dirtier! I was so scared mommy! That's why I wanna sleep in my own bed. So I won't worry you when I have bad dreams."*

His mother's face straightened with signs of confusion, *"What about the black stuff that was coming from your face! It's was dark and thick like blood and oil? What happened to that part?"* Lamar remained silent as his feet dangled from the edge of the bed. *"I saw it jump up and cover you!"*

Lamar turned his head sideways like a confused dog then said, *"Mommy, you had a bad dream just like me! Yup, it IS time to sleep in different beds because we are both having bad dreams now!!"*

With a brilliant smile on his face, Lamar crawled to the head of the bed, fluffed his pillow, and laid down. His mother, feeling confused, stood at their bedside. *"Honey, are you sure it was only a nightmare? Are you positive something supernatural didn't happen?"*

Lamar replied in an exhausted tone, *"Good night, mommy. I love you."*

Lamar then wrapped himself tightly in the sheets and dozed off. However, his mother had not been convinced by his childish story. She watched over him until he entered a state of deep sleep. Once he had cast off, she stood at her parents' door to consult with her mother. She knocked on the door then spoke through it as though her mother stood in front of her.

"Maa, I need your help. I believe that there is something following my son and is trying to hurt him. I don't know what it is

that stalks him or why, but I'm sure it's not good. Can you pray with me tonight?"

The door crept open, and her mother stood at its entrance. She was wrapped in a crisp white, outdated gown with creased corners and hanging tassels. She spoke in a dull but sweet tone, *"Vanessa, it's after 3 in the morning. What's bothering you, honey?"*

"I know it's late, mamma," Vanessa replied. *But I need to talk to you. Just for a few minutes, then pray with me."*

Helen walked out into the hallway closing her room door behind her. *"Go ahead, Nessa. I'm listening,"* Helen said as she held a bottle of blessing oil.

"Ma, I believe that Lamar is possessed," she said without hesitating.

"Possessed?!" Helen replied, shocked by Vanessa's confidence. *"By what . . . a ghost?"*

Vanessa stopped to think, and said, "No, something far more powerful."

Helen popped open the bottle of oil then marked herself, *"By what then . . . a demon?"* Helen asked as she marked Vanessa's forehead.

"Maybe," Vanessa said, shrugging her shoulders.

"What do you mean, maybe?" Helen asked, reaching down to grab hold of Vanessa's hand. *"What exactly happened tonight?"* Helen gazed deep into Vanessa's eyes as she continued to talk, *"Junior told me that you were spouting some foolishness. About something oozing out or inside Lamar — or something or another.*

We heard you screaming too. But we thought it was a simple nightmare. Had you not rambled on for so long, we wouldn't have come out to check on you. So, tell me what is going on?"

Vanessa covered Helen's hand with both of hers and said, *"Mamma, I saw something leap from the shadows and almost smother Lamar to death! It looked like . . . old dry blood – but it moved like water. It was thick and clumpy and smelled like rotten pig meat. It covered his eyes, nose, mouth, and his ears—then, for some reason, is stopped. Like it had died. I called out to him, but I was so scared. Before I knew it, the stuff . . . the blood . . . was coming out of him! It was so disgusting! To top all of that . . . Lamar had turned to me, covered in blood, and spoke – he called to me. That's when I screamed out loud as hard as I could!"*

"Oh my lord!" Helen said in a soft yet frightened voice. She had removed her hand from between Vanessa's hands and took two steps back, away from her, placing her freed hand on her chest. Vanessa continued, *"I know it's hard to believe but--"*

Helen quickly interrupted her, *"What did it look like, the demon . . . did you see it?"* Helen spoke quickly, insisting that Vanessa respond swiftly.

"What?! Ma, have you heard me? I said Lamar was possessed. How can I see it if it is inside of him?"

Helen's face turned stale and emotionless as she placed both hands on each of Vanessa's shoulders, *"You said that it jumped onto Lamar, right? Well, what did it look like? Think, tell me exactly what you saw."* Vanessa took a few steps away from her mother. She paced back and forth with one arm crossed and the other planted under her chin. She turned towards her mother and used her hands to give her words life as she spoke.

"It looked like . . . a blob . . . or . . . some sort of shadow."

Taking a step in Vanessa's direction, Helen replied, *"What did Lamar say about this? Did he mention how the creature looked . . . or its name?"* A sudden and strange sensation ran through Vanessa's body.

"A name?" Vanessa said while trying to contain herself. *"What do* **you** *mean . . . do you know what's going on here, ma?"*

Helen placed the cork back onto the bottle of blessing oil, pushing it in tightly, *"This family has a dark past—well, let's say: Our family is protected but at a cost."*

Vanessa's frustration began to boil over, *"At what cost!"* she shouted, demanding answers. *"Tell me! This is* **my** *son we are talking about, YOUR grandson!"*

"You don't need to know any more than you already do. You wanted me to pray with you, right? So let's pray."

Vanessa paused as a strange sensation coursed her mind. Suddenly she spoke aloud, "No wait, you asked about a name . . . Lamar mentioned a name. But I don't know who it is." The conversation shifted as tension filled the air.

"What was the name?" Helen asked. *"Speak it softly and wholly,"* Helen said, motioning her hands slowly.

"Nathaniel," Vanessa recited calmly.

Again there was a brief pause. Helen took a step back as if she were deep in thought. *"Nathaniel . . . no that's not the name, but it could be . . ."* Vanessa stomped her bare foot onto the floor, *"Mom! Tell me what's going on here!"* She demanded.

A Life Long Struggle

"This creature is our family's protector. As long as Lamar has not seen or spoken to this creature, he is in no danger. He, most likely, is just having a bad dream."

"How do you know," Vanessa replied. *"I'm convinced that what I saw was nothing good. So how are you so confident?"* Helen paused then whispered to herself, *"Because . . . I must be. This creature took your broth—"* She lifted her head high and spoke aloud, *"Vanessa do as I say. Now let us pray."*

Helen grabbed hold of Vanessa's hand and walked with her into the room where Lamar slept. Dissatisfied with her answer, Vanessa followed without saying a word. They both knelt down and began to pray with Helen leading. As they continued, their combined bodies casted a shadow along the floor, and from that shadow, Nathaniel appeared. He watched as the women bowed their heads and uttered their thoughts to the heavens.

"Once, I sat between worlds, just to exist. Until this child unknowingly formed me, he gave me freedom and birthed Nathaniel unto this world. I shall repay that deed with unification. I shall have this child's soul. But I must first dispel this formidable presence from his being. The Gatekeeper. He had not shown himself until now. Why?"

Nathaniel watched on as the two women prayed over Lamar's bedside. As they did, a dark aura began to rise slowly from his body. Unable to be seen by the human eye, the substance collected itself over Lamar's body. Nathaniel suddenly took his Humanoid form, preparing to defend himself. He stood at the ready, but the substance did not attack. Curious enough, Nathaniel spoke to the mysterious fog.

A Life Long Struggle

"*Hear me, creature, who are you? Are you The Gatekeeper . . . or maybe you are many? Speak!*" By the time Nathaniel had finished, the substance had fully condensed over Lamar. It took the form of a faceless human torso whose arms stretch the total length of the bed. It had ignored Nathaniel's presence and continued to watch as Vanessa and Helen pray.

"*Do not ignore me, creature,*" shouted Nathaniel. "Why have you come in such a feeble form? Have you no knowledge of me – Nathaniel The Enigma!"

The creature continued to watch over the family as their prayers were nearly complete. Nathaniel continued his attempts at communication with the creature.

"*I grow impatient. I no longer care who or what you are. This child is mine, and I shall have him now.*" Nathaniel then stepped from the shadows with the intent to take Lamar for himself.

"*I shall have him, on this night . . . yes!*"

Nathaniel took his first step toward the family, but the figure that hovered above their bedside reacted swiftly. Its color glowed crimson, and spikes sprouted from its spine and elbows. Nathaniel took a second step and the figure redirected its attention at him, causing Nathaniel to stop his advance. "*Interesting,*" Nathaniel thought to himself. He lifted his foot in preparation for the next step, but the substance spoke before Nathaniel could plant his foot firmly on the floor below.

"*Do not proceed any further, Nathaniel The Enigma.*"

Nathaniel held his body in mid-step as he spoke to the creature that hovered over the bedside. *"So it is you, Gatekeeper! Just when things were getting interesting!"*

"Do not take another step; should you value that appendage."

"Hmm, this form of yours, what is it? How did you acquire it?"

"Go back from which you came, Nathaniel. I am in no mood for pleasantries."

"Good. Neither am I!"

Nathaniel firmly stomped down on the floor with enough force to split the home in two. However, The Gatekeeper severed Nathaniel's foot twice. Once at its base, causing the power to disperse and again diagonally, to silence any would-be sound.

Unable to maintain his balance Nathaniel fell to the floor as The Gatekeeper plunged a spike towards his head. However, Nathaniel quickly dematerialized to avoid The Gatekeeper's attack. Reforming himself two steps backward, Nathaniel spoke, *"Such power, Gatekeeper. Much more than our last encounter. Come now, Gatekeeper. Tell me, is this the power of a bounded creature!? Tell me, Gatekeeper! Are you bound by pr—"*

Before Nathaniel could finish and before The Gatekeeper could respond, Vanessa and Helen spoke in unison, "Amen."

The Gatekeeper's body unleashed a burst of energy that shot throughout the entire home. Into every room and every corridor. The Gatekeeper vanished while purifying the house and taking Nathaniel along with him. As their bodies disintegrated, they engaged in a final conversation,

"Begone, Nathaniel."

"Just temporarily. Tomorrow brings promise, Gatekeeper."

"We shall see."

"Yes...We shall."

As the presence of both Nathaniel and The Gatekeeper vanished, Vanessa and Helen stood to their feet and took a deep breath. *"It feels a lot better in here,"* said Vanessa. *"I don't know how you do it, mamma, but when you pray, everything seems so much . . . cleaner."*

Helen smiled and spoke softly, *"That's a family secret, one you will learn but not tonight. Go on and get some rest. We can talk more later. And one more thing. I'm not sure what was said, but if Lamar wasn't fully truthful with you, I'm sure he has his reasons. He's young and naive, but above that, he's a good boy. That in itself is enough to overlook what was said. Anyway, goodnight Vanessa. See you in the morning."*

Helen walked away as Vanessa thought about the night's events. She peered down, looking at Lamar sleeping peacefully and thought to herself, *"A good boy . . . yea, my son is good. I know he's hiding something from me, but he is a good kid, so maybe I shouldn't worry too much. That's right, I trust my son, and I trust this family, so I must trust that everything will be OK without question. Everything will be fine. And to ensure that, I had better buy a new bed. After all, he won't stay young forever! I've sheltered him long enough. It's time to let him find his own way ... his own identity."* After a session of internal thought, Vanessa spoke aloud,

"Alright Vanessa, time for bed! Tomorrow is a new day. Sleep off the old and awake anew!" She turned off the lights, climbed into bed next to Lamar, and kissed him on his forehead. *"This is the last night we sleep next to one another. The last night of your sheltered innocence, a new world awaits you in the morning."*

Vanessa then rolled over on her back and stared at the ceiling. Her eyes heavy and her mind worried, she spoke softly as she drifted off to sleep, *"Lord, please watch over my son for the rest of his days. Keep him safe from harm . . . and give him the strength to endure all hardships . . . may his body age gracefully . . . and . . . his mind . . . sturdy . . . as he grows into . . . adulthood . . . strengthen his will . . . and ...all...manner...of...power...given too . . . . Amen."*

Just before Vanessa had dozed off completely, she opened her eyes slightly and saw the shadow of a man standing at her bedside. He stood tall, covered in a long dark trench coat and dark straw hat. Her vision a blur, she closed her eyes and moments later reopened them. The man was walking away, his back to her. He peered over his shoulder and spoke, *"Your will, be done,"* then vanished. Too sleepy to differ real from not, she closed her eyes and drifted into a deep and pleasant sleep.

It wouldn't be until two days later that Vanessa would see a significant change in Lamar. She woke well-rested like the many days prior. She turned to her side, flopping her arm across the bed, searching for Lamar. She probed until her hand landed on a lump where Lamar had slept. As she pressed down, the bump slinked into the bed, revealing itself to be a mass of tangle sheeting. The worried mother sprung to her feet and shouted out, *"Lamar!"* Her heart pounding, she dashed from the room and slipped on a random piece of clothing carelessly tossed to the floor. She gracefully caught hold of the doorway wall, which separated their room from the hallway. Her lightning-fast reflexes prevented her from crashing to the floor. *"Almost broke my neck worrying about this child! Lamar, where are you?"* She shouted angrily.

The bathroom door cracked open, and the sound of running water broke the silence. *"I'm taking a bath,"* replied Lamar. Surprised that he had already woke up by himself, Vanessa stood upright and walked over to the bathroom door and said, *"Why on earth are you taking a bath at this time of day?"*

"To wash off the old me and start fresh," Lamar replied. *"Besides, you woke up late. I had to make breakfast on my own."* Vanessa then pushed the door open, but Lamar pushed back. *"No, keep the door closed. I'm naked!"* Lamar said in a high-pitched tone.

Vanessa replied, *"Boy, you don't have nothing I ain't seen already."* Lamar pushed the door closed.

"I'm a growing boy. I need my privacy."

Vanessa grabs the doorknob, *"What? Did you just gain a new sense of privacy overnight?"* Lamar quickly locked the door

"Mom!" he shouted as he walked back to the bath.

"Don't mom me. Open this door."

"No," Lamar replied. *"The other night, you agreed to get me a new bed because I'm growing up, right? Well, this is part of growing up too. I'll be out soon. I'm almost finished. If you want breakfast, I left the box of cereal on the table and a glass of iced milk for you."*

A Life Long Struggle

Vanessa stood speechless near the edge of the door. She took a step back slowly then walked towards the dinner table, where Lamar placed her bowl of cereal and glass of milk. She smiled slightly and thought, *"Such a big change in such a short amount of time."* She said as tears rolled down her face.

Moments later, Lamar had finished bathing, brushed his teeth, and was dressed, all without leaving the bathroom. He looked in the mirror one final time to check to see if he did everything right. Then after giving himself a thumbs up of approval, he proudly emerged from the bathroom dressed and ready to go. He trotted into the dining room, where his mother sat fully clothed and eating the cereal he had left out for her.

He spoke joyously, "I guess I'm making you breakfast now."

Vanessa glanced over, scanned his choice in clothing, and said, "You can make breakfast, but I'll still have to dress you." She stood up, placed the spoon back into the cereal bowl, walked over to Lamar, and adjusted his clothing.

"No! Maaa, this is how I like it!" Lamar replied as he readjusted his wardrobe.

"Your shirt needs to be tucked in. Your collar needs to be folded down flat, and look at these jeans, all wrinkled!" Vanessa said while pointing at his attire. *"Green and brown doesn't match . . . and you are wearing sandals? Oh noo. No child of mine is going to school looking like a hag!"*

Well, I like it. Lamar replied. *"I picked it out myself, and I'm happy with it and how it looks."* Lamar hopped back, untucking his shirt. *"I have to learn how to be in-da-pen-dent."*

A Life Long Struggle

Vanessa took her bowl from the table and placed it in the sink upside down. *"I can't deal with you this morning!* She said as she grabbed her keys off the table, placing them in her pocket. *"If you want to walk around looking tacky, then you go ahead!* Vanessa then walked to the door and signaled to Lamar, *"Come on, let's go before we are both late."*

Lamar stood still. His body swayed back and forth as if he were concealing a hidden secret. *"Umm . . . mom . . . I'm catching the bus to school today."* Vanessa replied in a worried tone, *"No, you are not! That's out of the question!"*

"Why not?!" Lamar said as he walked outside and pointed to the corner of the street. *"The bus stop is at the corner of the street, in front of Matthew's house. All the kids who I play with every day all go to the same bus stop, and it's right there."* Lamar said as he gestured calmly. *"You can just drop me off and not have to worry about me being late for school."* Lamar turned to Vanessa and spoke more convincingly, *"Mom, I don't want to be the only one that is having his mother dropping him off like a little kid. I want to start riding the bus like the other kids. Besides, it's the last week of school before the break."*

Vanessa could see that Lamar really wanted to act more independently. Feeling excited and a bit worried, Vanessa replied, *"OK, OK. You can ride the bus, BUT I'm driving you to the bus stop."* Lamar's face brightened with excitement.

"Deal!" he shouted as he ran off to the car. *"The last one to the car is a rotten egg,"* he shouted out as he neared the car door.

Both Lamar and Vanessa dashed to the car with the door slamming behind them. Lamar reached the car first, being that

A Life Long Struggle

Vanessa stopped to lock the house door behind her. She unlocked the car doors, and before she could seat herself, Lamar had jumped into the front seat instead of the back. He reached for his seatbelt, fastened it, and placed his backpack on the car floor. With his feet dangling off the seat, he started humming a song of his own creation. Vanessa looked over, smiled, and started the car. She was thrilled that her son was eager to grow up but also terrified of the possibilities. She pulled from the driveway and slowly crept up to the bus stop. Once there, she parked the car turned to Lamar, and opened her mouth to speak, but Lamar shouted out, "BUS!"

He quickly unfastened his seatbelt, grabbed his backpack from the floor, and dashed from the car towards the bus. Vanessa's heart cringed as she watched her son run away from her. Her eyes began to water as thoughts of him being injured floated through her mind. She rolled down the window with tears in her eyes and shouted, "I LOVE YOU," but Lamar was too far to hear. He climbed up the steps of the bus, entered, and the door slammed shut, taking him away. She sobbed for a moment, started the car, sobbed a bit more, then started her lonely drive to work.

Meanwhile, Lamar sat in the back of the bus with all his friends, talking about what they were going to do once school was over. The school day flew by without any incidents. Lamar had completely deviated from his usual self and had become a new person. He no longer functioned in a routinely manner, which allowed him to see the world as it is while making sound judgments and decisions. Time continued to stroll by as the end of the school week marked the start of summer break and the beginning of Lamar's true life.

Lamar stood at the bus stop waiting for his bus as a familiar voice called out to him, *"Hey, is that you, Lamar?! Boy, your mamma is about to have a fit if she don't find her baby boy at the child pick-up area."*

Lamar turned around to seek out the voice. It was his best friend, Mathew. Once he had identified the voice, Lamar quickly replied, *"I see somebody's happy to be out of school.* Lamar turned to face Matthew, grinning from ear to ear. "Oh, was that a joke just then? I'm sorry . . . it was so funny I forgot to laugh, Ha!" Just as the two began to exchange recycled witty comments, their bus pulled up.

"All aboard!" The driver said as the doors slid open. Lamar was the first to enter, only to be tripped by Matthew. "Alright, funny guy," Lamar said as he caught himself from falling. Matthew acted as if he hadn't done anything wrong. *"You know what, Matt, if you weren't my friend, I'd kick your butt."*

"You— beat me? Oh boy! Now that's how you tell a joke," Matthew replied sarcastically. Lamar ran to the back of the bus and sat in his newly found favorite seat. As Matthew sat in the seat across from him, Lamar said, *"Don't act like you don't remember the time I had to come save you from Bronterius.* However, Lamar's comment didn't faze Matthew. He simply nodded and replied, *"Oh, don't bring that up! I had to save you from Autraya!"*

"That's because I don't fight girls! And you know I don't. So stop bringing that up all the time," Lamar shouted.

Matthew replied as he laughed out loud, "See! Ha! I told you. Now look who's acting like a lil baby!" Lamar turned away and faced the window, *"Aww, come on, little baby! Coochie coochie coo."*

A Life Long Struggle

Lamar pinched Matthew's cheeks, causing his face to brighten in pain. Matthew swatted away Lamar's hand and shouted, *"Come on, man, stop playing!"* By the time Lamar and Matthew had stopped bickering, they were nearly home. Suddenly Matthew shouted, "Today's game will be Frisbee!" Overhearing Matthew's outburst Leon, Lonnie, Trey, and Mark all pop up from their seats. The group of kids huddled in the back of the bus like a football team just before a decisive play. However, Lamar was nowhere to be found.

The bus jerked, causing everyone to take their respective seats. As Matthew and the other kids talked of the adventure that awaited them, Lamar stared out the window in awe. This being his first week riding the bus home, he sat quietly, enjoying what the journey had to offer. His eyes brightened as his senses heightened, lengthening the bus ride home. Amazed by much of what he saw, he wasn't able to snap from his enhanced state until Matthew tugged at his shoulder and spoke, *"Hey man, it's time to get off."* Lamar turned towards Matthew, his face stale as his eyes gleaned in the sunlight. Matthew jumped backward, away from Lamar in fear. Seconds later, Lamar stood to his feet and emotion-filled his face once more. He smiled and said. "Alright, let's go!"

As they walked to the front of the bus, Matthew asked, *"Hey man, are you alright?"* Lamar replied, "Yeah," and continued onward. They exited the bus, but as they walked down the stairs, Matthew asked again, *"You sure you're ok?"*

"Yea, I'm sure," Lamar replied.

The two boys exited the bus and began their short journey home. Once the bus was out of sight, Matthew stopped walking. He stood in the middle of the street with his head hung low. Once

Lamar realized Matthew had stopped cold, he looked back at him and said, "Are YOU ok?" Matthew responded angrily, "I thought we were friends!" Confused by his blunt statement, Lamar replied, *"We are best friends!"*

"Then why are you lying to me?" Matthew shouted as he shoved Lamar in the chest. *"I saw how you looked on the bus . . . man, that was scary. Tell me what's going on."*

There was a momentary pause – then Lamar spoke, *"It's hard to explain, but because you are my best friend, I'll tell you. But you have to promise me that you will NEVER tell anyone as long as you live."* Again there was silence as the young men stared at one another. Matthew opened his mouth to speak, but before he could reply, Lamar said, *"I'm just playing with you Matt. I'm ok, just ready to beat yall at Frisbee!"* Matthew's mouth dropped as Lamar ran off, shouting at him in the distance, *"Meet me at my house once you put down your backpack and hurry up. Don't let Leon num beat you there!"'*

Lamar darted off down the street towards his house, wondering if he should tell Matthew what was going on or leave him in the dark. "I don't know what chaos Nathaniel could bring down onto my friends if I allow them to get too close."

Bad Enigma

Lamar stopped running once he reached the entrance of his driveway. Looking back in the direction where Matthew had stood, images of Nathaniel and The Gatekeeper flashed in his mind. Lamar quickly clenched his eyes tightly to clear the visions from his thoughts.

"I can't tell anyone what's going on...if I do...it would only end badly for them," Lamar thought to himself. *"I don't want to drag anyone else into this mess I've created. I would hate for my best friend to go through something like what happened with my momma. So until I know exactly what's happening, I have to keep this to myself...even if it means being the bad guy."*

Once he collected his thoughts, he took a deep breath and marched into the house. He greeted everyone with a smile as he put away his backpack and changed his clothes.

Before taking off for the day's events, he stopped in the bathroom to relieve himself. Afterward, he washed his hands and peered into the mirror. "Pull yourself together," he said to himself while smacking the sides of his face with both hands, *"Get it together."* Once his pep talk was over, he splashed a bit of water onto his face to clear his thoughts. He then reached for a towel to dry his face and peered into the mirror one last time.

But to his surprise, a dark figure stood behind him in the mirror's reflection. He froze with his eyes locked on the figure. It then moved slightly as if to acknowledge its presence. But Lamar was not afraid. He repositioned himself firmly and spoke calmly to the figure without shifting his eyes, *"I do not fear you, creature. Whether you be Nathaniel or Gatekeeper, I will not run, and you shall not harm me. Understood?"* His eyes burned bright as his words caused the figure to speak directly to his mind.

"I have grown stronger, child. You have dubbed me Nathaniel The Enigma and given me much strength. So much so I stand in your presence. I shall not harm you physically, this time. But gratitude is due. No harm shall come to you by another's hand, if not by my own doing. I shall pluck all that is innocent from your being and gift you with knowledge till you see this world as the hell that it is. Careful child, should you falter and succumb to this world, I shall devour you."

Lamar took his eyes off of the figure and continued to dry his face as he spoke, *"And The Gatekeeper?"*

There was silence. Lamar removed the towel from his eyes and peered back into the mirror in search of the creature, but it had vanished. Lamar then put the towel away and stepped down from the sink.

He paused before exiting the bathroom, waiting for the creature to speak once more, but nothing happened. He turned off the bathroom lights and headed towards the front door. But just as his hands gripped the knob, Nathaniel's voice spoke to him, *"Should you fall, not even The Gatekeeper will save you from me."*

A Life Long Struggle

"*Begone from my mind, Nathaniel,*" Lamar replied as he flung the door open, dispelling Nathaniel from his inner thoughts.

His face held various emotions of anger, fear, and concern as he walked outside. But they quickly faded once he heard Matthew's voice in the distance, "*Hey, let's go!*" Lamar snapped back to his youthful self and raced down the driveway to meet everyone. He gave Matthew a high five, then spoke in an energetic tone, "*Alright, it looks like everyone is here! What should we play today?*"

"*I thought we all said we were gonna play Frisbee,*" Matthew responded.

"*We are!*" Lamar replied peculiarly. "*I mean, what kind of Frisbee game are we playing?*"

Leon looked at his brothers Lonnie and Trey and blurted out, "*Let's play Free-For-All!*" His brothers nodded their heads and spoke in unison, "*Yea, let's play.*" Matthew replied, "*Yea sounds good to me. It's not like we have even teams anyway.*" Matthew paused then spoke again, "*Yea, let's do it . . . but let's change the rules!*" Suddenly Lonnie blurted out, "*you always changing the rules! Why we can't just play a normal game without you trying to make the game harder!?*" Matthew glared at Lonnie as if he were about to punch him in the face, then calmly said, "*Shut up, Lonnie.*" Before Matthew could hear Lonnie's reply, his two brothers intervened and began to yell at Matthew in unison. His face began to redden as he started yelling back at the trio as loud as he could.

Annoyed by the noise, Lamar jumped in between them with his arms acting as a separation bar. "*Calm down, yall. It's not that serious. We don't have to change the rules of the game if we don't want to. Matthew was just giving us a new idea – and if we wanted to play, then we could."* Lamar looked over his shoulder at Matthew and said, *"Isn't that right, Matt?"* He turned away without saying a word crossing his arms across his chest. *"See, Matt agrees with me. So how about we play a normal game of Free-For-All, and whoever gets five points first wins. Everybody okay with that?"*

Matthew pointed his finger at Lonnie and his brothers and said just what he felt, *"Man Lamar, you always try to fix everything like you a superhero. I don't see why they **always** have to get their way all the time."*

"Let them have their way this time, and you can next time." Matthew turned around with a smile on his face and said,

"Okay, but I wanna be first to throw the Frisbee!"

Trey quickly stopped Matthew from being the starter by saying, *"Everybody put your foot in! I'm the counter!"* *"Ugh!"* Matthew let out a disapproving sound as he stomped his feet.

They formed a circle with their feet as Trey counted to see who would start the game. He used his finger and touched each foot one by one as he recited a song, *"Eenie meany miny mo. Catch a tiger by its toe. If it hollers, let em go – My mommy told me to pick the very best one, and you are not it!"* Trey lands on Matthew, and he blurts out, *"Man shit!"* He stepped back and watched painfully as Trey continued to count. When he finished, Leon was the last standing. Matthew shouted, *"Figures one of yall would be it!"*

"Stop complaining," Leon said abruptly. *"All I'm doing is throwing the Frisbee to start the game, no big deal."* Matthew shrugged his shoulders and walked away.

Trey handed Leon the Frisbee after he retrieved it from its hiding spot. Leon shouted, *"Okay, yall know the rules! Everybody gotta stay moving for the whole game! We going down to Matthew's house and back. Whoever has the most points once we get back wins! And each catch is worth only one point this time, so Matt, you can't make up numbers before you throw it!"* Matthew remained silent.

Leon gripped the Frisbee tightly, then with all his might, he flung it in the air. The disk flew up straight as it soared through the sky with a stampede of children following behind it. Matthew, being faster than everyone else, jumped ahead and caught the Frisbee, gaining the first point. As he gripped the Frisbee tightly in preparation for his throw, everyone breezed by him as if they were running a relay race. He waited a few extra moments, creating more distance for his throw.

Matthew then clenched the Frisbee to his chest and spun around twice as if he were throwing an Olympic disk. He released the Frisbee, and it shot straight for the group of kids. It hovered just below chest level as it sped towards Lamar. He braced himself for the catch. His knees slightly bent while his arms stretched straight out, similar to a home base catcher. Just as the Frisbee reached his fingertips, Leon slid in front of him and nabbed it all while tearing his jeans in the process.

"That was my point!" Lamar shouted.

"Well, you gotta be faster than that to get a point. Better get the next one!" Leon replied. Lamar ran in the direction of the other kids as Leon shouted, *"Here it comes!"*

As Lamar ran, he noticed that everyone else was acting weird. He thought to himself, *"Why is Lonnie jumping up and down? That's odd. And why did Trey cover his eyes? We still playing Frisbee, right? What...why is Matt running towards me? Or is he running towards Leon . . . what's going on behind me?"* Lamar then turns around, in mid-sprint, only to see the Frisbee spinning inches away from his face. His only thought was, *"Aww man, not again!"*

The Frisbee struck Lamar in the center of his face causing his feet to tangle as he tumbled to the pavement. Matthew ran over, scooped up the Frisbee, and shouted out, *"My point!"* He then glanced down at Lamar as he rolled back and forth, holding his nose. Matthew knelt down on the pavement and helped Lamar sit upright. His hands and elbows were scraped. His nose bled as he desperately tried to hold back his tears. *"He's ok yall, he just scraped up his hands and stuff,"* Matthew said aloud. He then tugged at the bottom of his shirt and used it to wipe the blood from Lamar's nose. He leaned closer and whispered to Lamar, *"Don't worry man. I'm gonna get 'em for ya. Just keep playing, and I'll do the rest. You'll see."*

Matthew rose to his feet with a devilish grin as he stared at Leon and said, *"As soon as Lamar is ready, we going back in the other direction. And just to let yall know, I'm still winning!"* Lamar stood to his feet and dusted himself off, wiping the blood from his hands and elbows onto his pants.

"Alright, I'm ready!" he shouted as he took off in the opposite direction. Before anyone else could react, Matthew tossed the Frisbee to Lamar, allowing him to gain one point. Lamar then allowed Matthew to run past him, and he quickly threw the Frisbee back, allowing Matthew to gain another point.

"That's not fair!" shouted Trey.

"Yall cheating!" shouted Leon.

Meanwhile, Lonnie ran as fast as he could to catch up. Once he caught up to Matthew, Lonnie held him and shouted to his brothers, *"Come on you guys! Catch up! I got him…."* Matthew struggled to escape Lonnie's grasp, rocking him back and forth, twisting and spinning until Lonnie's hand accidentally struck Matthew in the stomach, forcing him to drop the Frisbee.

Both Trey and Leon had caught up and passed the struggling duo. Lonnie quickly dove for the fumbled Frisbee, but Matthew kicked it just as he was about to land on top of it. The Frisbee rolled and bounced away as Matthew shouted, *"Lamar, get the Frisbee!"*

Trey, being the slowest, stopped running and shouted, *"I got it!"* Lamar and Leon raced towards the Frisbee as everyone shouted at Trey.

"NO! DON'T YOU TOUCH IT!"

Just before they reached Trey, Leon tripped over his untied shoelace, causing him to fall face-first on the pavement, but not before grabbing ahold of Lamar, causing them both to come crashing down. The Frisbee rolled into the gutter, where Trey simply walked over and picked it up. Overjoyed, he shouted out, **"POINT!!"** then flung the Frisbee as hard as he could without looking to see where he tossed it.

Leon shouted, *"No! You gotta wait till we're open before you throw it, dumbass!"* Then Lonnie added, *"Why would you just throw it without looking!?"*

The Frisbee soared straight up, then moments later, it began to fall. The boys watched anxiously, wondering where the Frisbee would land and if someone could catch it. Matthew shouted, *"Here it comes!"* No one stood up, and no one tried to catch it. They all watched as the Frisbee fell from the sky. Leon shouted, *"Move!* That thing is gonna hit you!" The Frisbee wasn't merely falling, but it was falling as if someone had stamped it with *return to sender.*

Just as the Frisbee was about the crash down on Trey, a strange and ominous wind knocked the Frisbee off course and into the neighboring yard.

Trey covered his mouth and said, *"Oops...."*

"Aint no damn oops!" Leon responded, *"Now go get it!"*

"No! Do you see where it went?!... it's in Mr. Jenkin's yard! If you want it, you go get it!" Their bickering continued as Lamar and Matthew watched from a distance.

"Trey, you always messing everything up!"

"It ain't my fault the wind blew. It's not like I can control the weather!"

"You can control how you throw a Frisbee – could've just threw it right and not all crazy like."

"I can throw it however I want to. You ain't my daddy, and you ain't the oldest. So shut cha face!"

Just as their argument reached its peak, someone spoke in an angered tone that brought everyone to a cold stop. *"Who in the hell hit my car with this damn Frisbee?"* Mr. Jenkins had been watching them play the entire time and held their Frisbee as he stood next to his car.

"You know damn well nobody ain't hit your car!" shouted Matthew. He stood to his feet, brushing himself off. "You always taking our stuff and making up lies. Why don't you have some kids of your own and lie on them!"

Lamar ran over to Matthew and tried to quiet him. "Shh! Be quiet, man. Don't talk to him like that."

Matthew looked at Lamar and said, "He's always taking our toys and making up lies to our parents. I've gotten in enough trouble because of him and his lies. So if I'm gonna get in trouble anyway, I might as well say how I feel, right?"

Before Lamar could think about what Matthew had said, Mr. Jenkins shouted out, "You damn kids ain't getting this Frisbee back. Every day yall rip and run up and down the street. I have to hear yall screaming and yelling all damn day. Well, not today. I want peace and quiet! Go play at the park somewhere!" Mr. Jenkins then locked the Frisbee inside his car and walked back into his house, slamming the door behind him.

"Now what?" Matthew shouted, staring at Trey in disapproval.

"Don't yall look at me like this is my fault. Cuz it's not," Trey replied as he crossed his arms and shook his head. "See, this is why I hate playin with yall . . . Be mad all you want – I'm goin in the house!" Trey walked away from the group with his head hung low.

"Do yall think we was too mean to my brother?" Leon said as he watched Trey run home.

"NOPE!" Matthew shouted.

A Life Long Struggle

"I'm not the one to point fingers, but it IS his fault," Lamar added. *"Well, since we don't have a Frisbee anymore, let's go to the park."*

Leon's face brightened up as he spoke aloud, *"Yea, the park is a good idea! Let's go before my brother come back."*

Just as they decided to go to the park, Lonnie interrupted their conversation with a smile that could brighten the gloomiest room. *"Wait!"* he shouted. *"Aww crap,"* Leon said, shaking his head. *"I know that look on his face – yall step back, here comes an award-winning dumb idea."* Lonnie stood in front of the group, smiling while his body twist-n-turned joyously.

"I have an idea," Lonnie said with a smirk, *"And you are gonna...like it,"* he added. They looked at each other, then looked back at Lonnie and spoke in unison,

"Tell us already!"

Trying desperately to sound intelligent, Lonnie spoke, *"Well, gentlemen, as I've heard, you three are intending to go on a venture to journey to the park. Correct? Be that the case, Mother doesn't allow two of the three brothers to go it alone. THEREFORE! I deduct that we you-ta-lize all of the ree-sources at home to keep our fun alive. Furthermore—"*

"What the HELL are you talking about?!" Matthew shouted as he interrupted Lonnie's speech.

Lonnie quickly pulled a concealed soda can from behind his back and held it up above his head as if he had found water in the desert. The can was completely flat, due to being run over by many cars. It was circular in shape and didn't have any jagged edges.

"What . . . is that, Lonnie," Matthew said sarcastically.

"I told you he was about to say something really dumb," added Leon.

Lamar then tapped Leon on the shoulder, *"You guys really can't go to the park alone?"*

"No," Leon replied. *"Our Mom wants us to stick together whenever we go somewhere far. She thinks it's safer that way."*

Lamar nodded his head, "Oh, I see," he replied. *"Well, what should we do then? We can't go to the park, and we don't have our Frisbee. Any ideas?"*

Matthew turned his back towards Mr. Jenkin's house and said, *"I don't know what to do, but I'm kinda hungry. Lamar, member when we played Manhunt with Simeon num?"* Lamar replied with a slight nod of his head. *"Well, when we got separated, I noticed that the tree behind Mrs. McDougal's house got oranges now. And, they low enough for us to pick them right off . . . Let's go get some."*

Leon clapped his hands together and shouted, "Yeah, that's a good idea. Let's go!"

As the others continued to talk about the orange tree, Lonnie stood outside the group. *"What about my idea?"* he asked while still holding the soda can above his head.

The group paused as they all turned to look at Lonnie. Matthew took a step forward, then in unison, they all replied, *"That's stupid."*

Lonnie felt a deep pain strike his chest. His heart sank like a ship that had been hit by a cannon in open water. His head hung low as he lifted up his shirt and stuffed the flat soda can in his back pocket.

The group took off running for the orange tree, with Lonnie lagging behind. Once there, they picked as many oranges as they could carry, filling their pockets and turning their shirts into holsters to carry more. After they had picked more than they could carry, they pranced back to Lamar's house, where they sat at the end of the driveway, eating their fill.

"This was a good idea Matt."

Lamar said as he bit down into his pealed Orange. *"I told you,"* Matthew replied with his mouth full of half-eaten oranges. *"My idea is much better than Lonnie's idea to throw an old can around."*

"Hahaha . . . yea, much better than that," Lamar replied while pealing yet another orange. Matthew glances over at Lamar's stack of oranges as they sat in the gutter, *"How many did you get Lamar?"* he asked while comparing their piles.

Analyzing his collection of large oranges, he replied, *"I got . . . 1, 2, 3 . . . 5 . . . 6...7. Yeah, I got 7 of 'em. "What about you, Matt? How many did you pick?"*

"I got 5, but I got a bunch of small ones in my pocket," Matthew replied without thinking while he peered down towards the brothers. *"I wonder if they got as many as we got,"* he said aloud with a puzzled expression.

"Ask 'em how many they got then," Lamar said as he began to peel another Orange. Matthew refocused his attention back onto his partially eaten Orange, *"I tried before, but for some reason, they don't talk much when they eat."*

"Really?!" Lamar replied with a surprised expression. *"I eat and talk all the time. Everyone in my family can do it . . . it's easy."*

"Yea? Try to talk to one of them then."

Leon and Lonnie sat a short distance away from Lamar and Matthew. They ate their pickings in close quarters to one another, not speaking a word as they continued to peel and eat. *"Hey Lonnie! … … … Leon! … … … Ayy!"* Lamar said, trying to get their attention, but they ignored him completely and continued to eat.

"See, I told you!" Matthew shouted humorously. *"That's too funny,"* he said, nearly choking as he chuckled to himself.

"No, that's weird," Lamar replied abruptly.

Matthew suddenly paused. His face turned serious as he spit out the half-chewed orange. Then, he turned to Lamar and whispered, *"What if I call him by his nickname? Do you think he was say something then?"*

"Oh, I don't know. Go ahead. Try it. Go. Do it . . ."

With a serious expression, he replied, "Ok, watch." Matthew leaned forward, his hands between his knees as he held a half-peeled orange. He looked to his left, down towards Leon, who sat next to Lamar. Matthew's face started to brighten in color as he tried hard not to laugh. With a loud outburst, he blurted out, *"BUTTER-BALL!"*

At first, no one spoke. Both Matthew and Lamar stared at Leon, waiting for a response. But Matthew began to chuckle, causing Lamar to burst with laughter. He laughed loud and hard until he fell on his back, kicking his feet. Leon spat out his half-eaten orange and stood up. Then, without saying a word, he took a pitcher's stance and flung the remainder of his orange at Lamar. Shortly after being released, the orange split mid-air, spraying its juices back into Leon's eyes, causing him to cry out in pain.

Matthew starts to laugh even harder than before. He tugged on Lamar's feet and pointed to Leon. His face was bright red as he pointed and laughed till his eyes watered. He shouted, *"Stop it . . . stop it, please! This is too funny – hehehe yall making my stomach hurt!"*

Lonnie rushes over to aid his brother, wiping his eyes using his shirt. *"That's not funny, Matthew!"* shouted Lonnie.

"Yeah, it is!" he replied.

Lamar stood to his feet and pointed towards his house, *"Yall can use the water hose to wash his eyes out. But don't be long because my Granddaddy will come out."* Just after Lamar had finished speaking, they ran to the water hose without a second thought. Meanwhile, Lamar wiped his hands clean on his shirt and pants as he looked to the sky to watch the clouds float by.

A sudden breeze pushed the sun from behind the clouds causing Lamar to close his eyes and redirect his line of sight to the street. There he noticed a shiny object that glimmered gold in the distance. Curious about what it could be, Lamar slowly walked over towards the object. With each step, the object seemed to shine in a different color.

Once Lamar stood above it, another gust of wind uncovered the object in its entirety. Lamar picked it up and ran back over towards his friends. *"Look! Look at what I just found!"*

"I don't care," Leon said as he stood drenched with water. *"Yall play too much! Matthew AND Lonnie wet up all my clothes*

playing in the water. And YOU, Lonnie, already know how mamma be acting about our clothes!"

"Quit crying," Lamar replied. *"You will be dry way before you go in the house. Besides . . . Look at this!"* He added, showing everyone what he found.

"What is it?" Lonnie asked.

"A Boomerang," Lamar shouted, holding out his hand.

"Let me see it," Matthew said as he reached for the object.

Matthew looked it over and said, *"This isn't a Boomerang. Look. It's a funny-shaped metal stick. Boomerangs are plastic. And look at the words, I can't even read this, and I learned how to read a long time ago."*

"Well, throw it then," Lamar insisted. *"Let's see if it comes* back."

They all gathered in the street just feet beyond the driveway. Matthew cocked back his arm and flung the object as hard as he could, then shouted, *"Holy crap, that thing is light!"* The object soared through the sky further than any Frisbee the boys had played with before.

"See, I told you it was a Boomerang!" Lamar shouted, *"Look, it's coming back!"* Matthew jumped out of the way as the *Boomerang* sped in their direction. Everyone shouted at Lamar, *"Move!"* But he stood, fearless, in the *Boomerang*'s path. He quickly stretched out his hand, and the *Boomerang* smacked into his palm with tremendous speed, causing his hand to close rapidly.

"Holy shit!" shouted Lonnie.

"That was some superhero crap!" Leon added as Matthew stood with his mouth open. *"How in the hell did you do that?"* he asked.

Lamar replied, *"It . . . told me to catch it."* Lonnie rushed over, snatched the Boomerang from Lamar, and flung it into the air. The others watched as Lonnie ran into the grass across from Lamar's driveway to catch the Boomerang. He stood in a linebacker's stance, poised for the catch as his eyes locked onto the Boomerang. It made a sharp turn then bee-lined for Lonnie. He extended his hand out like Lamar did, but moments before, he would catch it. Lonnie's legs began to tremble as fear gripped his body. Then, just as the boomerang reached catching distance, he leaped out of the way.

The Boomerang crashed into the yard, impaling itself into the grass, flinging up dust upon impact. Lonnie shouted, *"Oh, heck nall! Did yall see that?!"*

Lamar, now agitated, charged over to the Boomerang and plucked it from the yard. *"Yall getting on my nerves! Look, it's a Boomerang – if you throw it hard-n-fast, it will come back hard-n-fast."* Lamar pointed at Matthew and said, *"Catch."* With a quick flick of his wrist, he tossed the Boomerang towards Matthew, who caught it with no problem. *"See? Do yall get it now? It's made of metal, but if you throw it softly, it won't hurt!"*

Matthew looked down at the Boomerang as the lettering began to glow. Then he shouted, "Lamar, go long!" Lamar took off running at top speed as Matthew hurled the Boomerang at him. Lamar turned and caught it, then shouted, *"Point! The first to five wins!"* He launched it back towards Matthew. He leaped into the air to catch the Boomerang shouting, *"Point!"* as he landed.

A Life Long Struggle

Matthew then tossed the Boomerang toward Lonnie. Again he poised himself to catch it, and again he fled, allowing Leon to intervene and nab the point. The game continued until Leon and Matthew both had four points while Lamar held the Boomerang.

Lamar yelled, "Last point! Go long!" Then he flung the Boomerang aimed at the center of them both. But, just as he released the object, time seemed to slow down. He watched as a shadow slithered along the ground and quickly entered Leon's body.

The Boomerang, once launched, flew in the intended direction until an ominous wind knocked it off course. As time began to flow normally, Lamar shouted, "Look out!" but before the boys could react, another gust of wind blew in the opposite direction sending the boomerang speeding towards Matthew.

Lamar quickly shouted out, *"Duck!"*

Suddenly Matthew slipped, enabling him to dodge the approaching Boomerang. Time slows once again as the Boomerang reaches Inches away from Leon's head. Just before it struck him, his body turned towards Lamar, and with a chilling grin, he mouthed something only he could hear. Then all at once, time sped back up, and the Boomerang crashed into Leon's skull, shooting blood into the air as his lifeless body tumbled to the ground.

No one moved. Blood ran from his head and down his neck. Lonnie screamed, "Leon!" and ran over to him, flipping him over and pressing his hands against his wound. Matthew quickly ran towards their house, banging on the door for help. Lonnie's shirt slowly turned red as his brother's blood continued to pour from his skull.

A Life Long Struggle

Amidst all the confusion, Lamar stood motionless and confused as a voice spoke to him. *"This is your fault. You found the Boomerang, you gave them the confidence to play with it, and you are the one who threw the Boomerang . . . Look at what YOU have done!"*

Lamar rushed over, tearing his shirt from his shoulders and planting it beneath Leon's head. But just as he tried to comfort Leon, Lonnie pushed him away, *"This is your fault! You and your damn toy! Get away from us!"* he shouted. Lamar stood to his feet, his heart heavy and his hands shaking. He thought to himself, *"So much blood . . . I told him to duck. I tried to warn him. It's not my fault...It's not my fault!"*

Leon's mother burst on the scene without warning. Still dazed by the ordeal, Lamar watched as Leon's parents wrapped him in bandages and carried him off. Again a voice spoke to him.

"He deserved to be hit. It's his fault he didn't duck. You told him to, didn't you?!"

Lonnie stood to his feet, covered in his brother's blood. He turned towards Lamar and punched him as hard as he could. Lamar stumbled back a few steps, his eyes burning bright as his face remained emotionless. Lonnie punched Lamar again, sending him falling to the ground as Lonnie continued to punch him as hard as he could. *"You did this to my brother! You did this! It's all your fault!"* shouted Lonnie as he continues to pummel Lamar. He didn't fight back at all. He just laid on the ground taking all that Lonnie dished out, up until Matthew tossed Lonnie aside.

"Get off of him. It's not his fault your brother is gonna die – he should have ducked like I did!" Matthew shouted with tears in his eyes.

A Life Long Struggle

Lonnie replied, *"Fuck both of yall!"* then ran off. Matthew turned to Lamar and helped him to his feet. His nose was busted, his mouth was bleeding, and his left eye was swollen. Before Matthew could speak, Lamar said, *"If he dies, it's my fault."*

Matthew replied, *"No it's not, just,"* Lamar interrupts, his face stale, battered, and emotionless.

"I'm going home Matt . . . See you later."

Filled with tattered emotions, Lamar turned and walked away. Matthew smiled devilishly and yelled out to Lamar, *"It will be ok. Surely he won't die! You'll see."* Then he turned and began his journey home. He smiled and laughed to himself as he rejoiced, *"Yes child, he shall not die . . . yet. There's far too much work to be done!"*

Internal Conflict

Mentally exhausted from the day's incident, Lamar walked home without uttering a word to anyone. His family watched as he walked sluggishly towards the bathroom, stripping himself along the way. He flung his socks and blood-stained clothes into a pile along the bathroom floor, causing the door to slam shut as he ran himself a warm bath. He slid in, submerging himself under the heat of the soothing water. His mind relaxed as he began to slip off into a world of bliss.

A sudden knock at the door shook him from his trance, *"Hey, are you alright in there,"* said someone at the door. But Lamar did not answer. He simply submersed himself deeper into the bath. Again there was a knock, *"Lamar . . . hey, it's me, Markie, can I come in"*. Before Lamar realized what was happening, Mark hovered above him and had already begun to speak rapidly.

"Everyone is talking about what happened today. Did you really hit Leon in the back of the head with a metal pipe?! He went to the hospital, and there was blood everywhere! Sim said he saw the whole thing! He said Leon was running away from you, then when you slung that pipe at him like a baseball and BAM got 'em,

right in the back of the head! Sooo, what did he do to make you so mad? You had to be really mad . . . I mean, really, really--"

Lamar interrupted Mark, *"I didn't tell you to come in here. I'm having a long day right now. So can you please just leave me alone, please? I'll tell you what happened later, but not now."*

"Are you ok," Mark asked? *"You didn't even yell at me for coming in here while you were taking a bath."* Lamar closed his eyes and said, *"I'm just not feeling it today . . . You knew how I'd react before you came in here . . . so whether I yell at you or not, the outcome would have been the same. That's something I've learned today . . . I've learned a lot today . . . and another thing I've learned is that I don't want to talk right now. So leave, and lock the door behind you."*

Shaken by what he just heard, Mark began to back-pedal away from Lamar slowly, *"You are different. I don't need you to tell me what happened. I know already."* Mark then turned and walked out of the bathroom, closing the door behind him.

Once Mark had gone, Lamar was again at peace. His mind drifted to a faraway land where his thoughts took form. He had found himself in a bright forest covered in a thick fog as a dark figure stood in front of him. Reaching out using its arms as if they were forming words, the creature spoke, *"Come now, child. No reason to trouble thy self with the concern of others. Live for thy self, and each moment ye shall prosper and gain knowledge years before thy time."* The creature vanished while its voice echoed throughout the forest, *"Go forth! Play! Enjoy thy self, for laughter and fun are no wrongdoings. Eat, drink and sleep as a child should."*

The voice dulled until there was silence. Lamar turned in all directions in search of the creature, only to see a child walking towards him in the distance. As the child walked closer, Lamar noticed that the child resembled himself. Before long, the two stood face to face as if he had looked upon a mirror. The child slowly reached out to touch Lamar's face as he spoke carefully, *"Discard the shackles of concern and worry, halt the war of mind and soul. Become one with thyself . . . become—"*

Just as the child was nearing Lamar's face, he suddenly stopped, his head looking upward as if something hovered above Lamar's head. The child smiled slightly, then stepped away. Lamar turned to look behind him, but there was nothing. Then turned back, and the child was gone. Only the figure stood in the distance. Lamar shouted, *"Who are you?!"* but before the creature could answer, Lamar was shaken back to reality by the icy hand of his mother. *"Oh my lord. Lamar, wake up! What are you trying to do to yourself? You are locked in here asleep, sitting in this boiling hot water! Are you out of your mind?"*

She stood Lamar to his feet and handed him a towel, *"You are done! Go on out of here,"* Vanessa shouted as she pointed at the door. Lamar stepped out of the tub and noticed the bathroom was thick with steam, just as the forest was thick with fog. Looking back at the tub, he saw steam rise from the water while his mother struggled to drain it without getting burned.

He then walked out of the bathroom and dressed himself in his room. Once dressed, he laid flat in the bed. His face pointed towards the ceiling.

"What's wrong honey?" Vanessa said as she walked into their room, drying her hands with a cloth. *"Simeon told me what happened as soon as I stepped foot in the house. Not only did he tell me what happened, but I could also clearly see today's events*

on your blood-soaked clothing. Honey, tell me what's troubling you."

Lamar leaned forward, his eyes filled with grief, *"It was an accident,"* he said softly. *"I didn't try to kill my friend."*

Vanessa then sat alongside him. She rubbed his back and spoke in a comforting tone, *"Aww, honey, is that what you think happened? Your friend will be ok – he's not going to die . . . he will need to get a few stitches, but he definitely won't die. And furthermore, it's not your fault. You—"*

Lamar interrupted her and said, *"I was the one who threw the Boomerang at him, I was the one who found it, and I was the one that pushed everyone to play with it even though they didn't want to. If it wasn't for me . . . then he wouldn't—"*

Vanessa jumped to her feet. She clapped her hands together, then snapped her fingers, *"I got it!"* she shouted. *"Your cousin Demetrius asked me to bring you over today. I heard he had just got a new game, and he wanted someone to play it with!"* Lamar's face brightened instantly.

"Really? What game did he get?"

"I don't know," Vanessa replied. *"Guess we will have to find out when we get there. You ready?"*

Lamar sprung to his feet, slipped on his shoes, then bolted for the front door. *"Come on mom,"* he shouted as he crossed the threshold of the doorway.

Curious about what new video game Demetrius had, Lamar completely forgot about the incident with Leon. Once they arrived, Lamar jumped out of the car just as quickly as he had got in. Then, without knocking, he flung open the door and charged into Demetrius's room. Meanwhile, Vanessa sat in the living room with her aunt, Demetrius's mother, to have a short exchange of words.

"Thank you Auntie, for allowing us to stop by on such short notice," Vanessa said in a humble melody.

"Oh, don't worry about it honey," her aunt replied. *"That's what family is for. I'm just happy you called ahead of time. Had you not, Lamar would have seen through our little plan."*

"Yes ma'am, he has grown a lot in these past few days. He looks at everything differently."

"Yeah. Helen told me about it."

"Auntie, do you know anything?" Vanessa said as she twiddled her thumbs. *"I know my mamma is hiding something from me . . . she just refuses to tell me anything!"*

After Vanessa finished speaking, her aunt sat deep in the chair and said, *"Vanessa, I would love to tell you, but it's not my place to mettle this time. Helen will tell you when she feels it's time. But for right now, just be a strong shoulder for that boy to lean on; because stormy days are coming his way. He growing up fast, so just be patient with him, and everything will work itself out."*

The two women sat at the table, drinking a fresh batch of tea as classical music played in the background. Vanessa sipped from her cup and stared at the tea leaves floating inside. *"Do you think it's my fault that he's changing so fast?"* she asked. *"I have sheltered him all his life . . . maybe that was wrong of me?"*

"Vanessa," her aunt replied, *"That's pish posh. We do our best with what little we have and that's all anyone can ask of us, or we ask of ourselves. Honey, there ain't no rule book to parenting, no how-to guide, just trial and error."* Vanessa stared back into her tea. She then took another sip and said, *"Auntie, My little boy is going through so much so fast, and all I can do is stand by and watch."*

"That's is the life of a parent," her aunt replied.

Vanessa placed her teacup on the table and stood to her feet, *"Is it okay if I leave him here for a bit, Auntie? I'd like to pick up something from the store."* Before Vanessa could get a reply, Lamar walked into the dining room.

"Mom, is it ok if I stay here for a little while longer?" Vanessa looked over at her aunt and replied, *"I don't mind if you stay, but that's not up to me."* Lamar immediately ran over towards the table and said, *"Auntie, can I stay here for a bit? I wanna play with Dee for a while."* She looked down at Lamar then said, *"Go ahead, yall just try not to be too loud back there."*

Lamar shouted out, *"Yes!"* as he pranced back in the room with Demetrius. He jumped on the bed and told Demetrius the good news, *"Yup, she said I could stay!"*

"I told you – I bet she said something like, Yall just don't make too much noise in there." Lamar flopped back on the bed kicking his feet and laughing,

"Yup, that's just how she sounds!" he shouted.

"Here, it's your turn," Demetrius handed the video game controller to Lamar. Fascinated by the new game, he sat focused on the television screen, unaware of his surroundings. Demetrius had slowly stood up to his feet and begun to gaze upon Lamar as if he had been hypnotized. Lamar continued to play the game until

he finally lost as Demetrius stood like a statue towering next to him the entire time. He turned to face Demetrius as he stood to the right of him and said, *"Why are you standing? Sit down and play with me."* Lamar handed the controller to Demetrius, but he looked down at the game controller with an emotionless glance. His eyes were glossed over as if they were frozen in place. His movements were short, quick, and random, similar to that of a squirrel.

Demetrius slowly reached out for the controller then paused. His head turned slightly as if he suddenly grew curious about something. Demetrius then retracted his hand and sat down next to Lamar on the bed, facing the television. *"You are really good at this game,"* Demetrius said in a strange tone, *"Play it again. I would like to see how to beat this level."* Lamar quickly pulled the controller back and restarted the game.

As Lamar redirected his attention to the video game, Demetrius began to talk aloud.

"This game reminds me of life. A constant struggle to achieve a pointless goal. You wander around, stepping on all those who get in your way in search of coin while desperately seeking what makes you happy. But alas, it seems to constantly be just out of reach."

Without pausing the game or batting an eye, Lamar said, "Demetrius, are you okay?"

"What is the purpose of this game?" Demetrius replied, *"Is it the satisfaction of completing a level or overcoming a challenge?"*

Lamar suddenly changed the tone of his voice, *"For real, stop talking,"* Lamar replied. *"I'm trying to concentrate."*

Demetrius spoke again, ignoring Lamar's previous request, *"Tell me child, if your purpose were sitting right next to you, in this very room . . . would you be as focused on reaching **that** goal as you are now with this video construct? Or would you bask in the work required to reach such a point?"*

Lamar paused the game. His eyes began to blaze as he turned to face Demetrius. But Demetrius was not who sat next to him. *"Who are you?"* Lamar asked.

"What do you mean?" Demetrius said with a slight smile. *"I am your cousin – Demetrius,"* he replied.

Lamar turned away, then un-paused the game and continued to play while he spoke aloud, *"You are not Demetrius, creature. I can see you for what you are despite the shell you wear."*

"Oh my," Demetrius replied as if he were surprised. *"This IS quite the surprise. It must be a side effect of the Voids or maybe a ploy of The Gatekeeper. Hmmm."* The creature then crossed his legs and propped his arm under his chin as if he were thinking intensely, *"And you don't fear what you see, child,"* the creature asked while it stared at Lamar intensely.

"No," Lamar replied without breaking his concentration. "For some reason, I am much calmer than I have ever been."

Stunned by his reply, the creature uncrossed his legs and sat forward on the edge of the bed, mimicking Lamar. He picked up the controller and said, *"Well, allow me to join you in this virtual adventure. We must keep up appearances if we are to . . . as you say, talk."* Lamar restarted the console and selected the two-player option. Growing more intrigued by Lamar's actions, the creature

said, *"You are indeed calm, child. Are you not concerned about what will happen to you after my curiosity has been satisfied?"*

Lamar sat comfortably on the edge of the bed and spoke confidently, "You are Nathaniel, am I right?"

"Yes. I am The Enigma, Nathaniel", he replied, holding the controller in his hands. Lamar starts the game by selecting the most challenging setting. They both leaned forward as they focused on the screen and began rapidly mashing the buttons. Lamar spoke first.

"Why are you here, Nathaniel?"

"As I said, I am curious . . . In fact, I grow more so by the second."

"As do I, Nathaniel. I have grown more in the past week than I have in my entire lifetime. Is that your doing?"

"So you have changed, child. You've become more aware . . . hmph! Now this will make you much more succulent. But I will not answer your questions—not before you answer mine. So tell me child, are you not concerned about what will happen to you after my curiosity has been satisfied?"

Lamar paused briefly, but instead of answering Nathaniel's question, he said, *"Can you permanently inhabit anyone, or is it only those that satisfy a certain condition?"* Nathaniel replied quickly, as if he had not heard Lamar's previous question.

"I truly dislike repeating myself, child," Nathaniel said, peering over at Lamar from the corner of his eye. But Lamar

appeared un-phased by Nathaniel's statement. Instead, he simply continued to speak.

"*My mother is a gentle person with a gentle soul. She has never struck me once. However, recently she has stepped out of character, striking me on multiple occasions. But when I looked upon her with* **these** *eyes, I didn't see my mother. Was that* **your** *doing, Nathaniel?*" Nathaniel paused, briefly forgetting his previous question.

"*Interesting . . .*" *he said with a slight nod.*

Lamar continued to speak as if he were thinking aloud, "*No. That couldn't have been you. This creature was different. I can only assume that you are unable to acquire a vessel from any of those who live in my house, for some unknown reason . . . which means there is a limit to your power.*" Nathaniel's curiosity peaked as he gripped the controller tightly, nearly crushing it as he continued to listen.

"*You asked me if I am worried about what may come of me after your curiosity is satisfied – I am not.*"

Nathaniel replied with a magnificent smile. "*Each day, you become more and more aware of your surroundings. You lose more and more of yourself and in its place . . . knowledge accumulates. You are shedding the coils of childhood faster than* **any** *that came before you. As you struggle with simplistic ideals, your naivety slips away. You will succumb to this world without incident.*"

"*And your presence now, is to ensure this information?*"

"*No. I am simply curious. I wonder . . . were you able to hear the conversation between myself and The Gatekeeper? No . . .*"

no . . . a better question, how much of our conversation did you hear, child?"

"Everything. I heard it all. And I am aware that The Gatekeeper has an agenda that is unknown to even you."

"Yes . . . I am unaware of his plot, but know this child. He and I are cut from one cloth, and we both will—"

Before Nathaniel could finish his sentence, Demetrius's mother walked into the doorway, "Are yall hungry?" she asked cheerfully. Both boys turned from the television screen, looked up at her, and said in unison, "No, we're ok." However, despite Lamar and Demetrius sitting on the bed, Lamar's aunt could only see Demetrius.

His cold eyes and pale face sent shivers down her spine as the cold air from the room brushed against her skin. Her hands began to tremble as her eyes started to water. She stared at the boys for a short moment, then she spoke. Her voice crackled, becoming thinner with each word, "Demetrius . . . honey . . . how are you feeling?" He smiled and said, "I'm okay mom, just having fun with Lamar playing video games." After hearing Demetrius's reply, her face twisted with grief. She covered her mouth with her hands as tears streamed down her face. Lamar then said, "Auntie, are you okay?" Without a single word, she turned and walked away.

"It seems I am not the only one that can see through your lies, Nathaniel," Lamar said after placing the controller on the floor.

"Oh no, child," Nathaniel replied. "It's wasn't me that frightened her."

A Life Long Struggle

"What do you mean by that?" Lamar asked as he quickly turned to Demetrius. *"There isn't anyone else in this room, so what else is there to see? Was it me? Was I the thing that scared her away?"* Demetrius, looking confused, replied, *"What?!"*

Lamar sat back on the bed, took a deep breath then replied, *"Never mind. I wasn't talking to you."* Suddenly Demetrius shouted, *"Holy crap, it's cold in here!"* Lamar looked to his feet as thick cold fog covered the floor. *"How are you not cold?!"* shouted Demetrius.

"I don't know. I feel warm. It's not cold in here to me."

"Bullshit," Demetrius said, pulling on Lamar's arm, *"Let's go outside. I don't want to play games in a freezing cold house."*

The two boys ran outside as Demetrius shouted, *"Mom, we are going outside to play for a bit. Be back soon!"* They sprung out the front door and ran to the backyard. The house sat on an acre of land, sharing a portion of the backyard with undeveloped bush. Lamar had never been in their backyard, but before he could take in the sight, Demetrius took his hand and shouted, "Let's play Batman!"

Lamar snatched his hand back and replied, *"That is so damn stupid. How can we possibly play Batman?"*

Without hesitation, Demetrius ran over to the shed that sat behind the house, walked in, and closed the door behind him. After a short while, Lamar walked towards the shed and sat a few feet from the entrance, waiting for Demetrius to emerge.

Suddenly Demetrius shouted, "Have no fear, *Batman is here!"* and flung open the door. He stood in the doorway, mimicking a heroic pose, his hands on his hips with his chest bulging outward as his chin tilted slightly. He wore a black long-sleeved shirt with a hand-drawn Batman emblem at its center. He had crafted a cape out of a torn bed sheet and utility belt made from an old bicycle inner tube.

Lamar burst into tears as he laughed until his stomach began to hurt. *"What is that!?"* he cried out. *"Are you supposed to be Batman now?"*

"Laugh now, but look!" Demetrius replied as he pulled out a grappling hook made from multiple deep-sea fisherman's hooks. Lamar's face brightened up.

"Let's use it to climb a tree," Lamar shouted as he leaped to his feet!

"No, Boy Wonder," Demetrius replied. *"We must catch Penguin before he reveals his dastardly plan to the innocent people."* Lamar looked at Demetrius peculiarly. He continued to hold his superhero's pose as he spoke again, *"Boy Wonder, I will meet you in the Bat Cave for preparations!"* He then turned, flung his cape heroically, and re-entered the shed.

Lamar felt a rush of energy surge through him. He charged in the shed, filled with excitement, ready for what Demetrius had planned next. Once inside, Lamar found that Demetrius had already created Boy Wonder's outfit for him. It was red with a hand-drawn R at its center, complete with a yellow cape and utility belt.

Lamar quickly undressed himself and put on the Boy Wonder outfit and utility belt. Eager to start their adventure, Lamar, as Boy Wonder shouted, *"Gee willikers Bat Man, Penguin is on the move again!"*

A Life Long Struggle

"*Let's go Boy Wonder,*" Demetrius replied in his Bat Man voice. "*It's time to put a stop to his evil plans.*" They sprung from the shed and began their adventure as Batman and Robin.

Their adventure led them deep into the brush, into ditches and murky water. They climbed trees and jumped from tables, all in pursuit of a good adventure. By day's end, the two heroes cornered Penguin near the south end of Demetrius's house. "*Give it up, Penguin! We have you cornered,*" shouted Demetrius!

Lamar fell to the ground as if he had suddenly been hit, "*Batman watch out,*" he shouted from below.

"*Jiminy crickets, Boy Wonder! He flew onto the roof of this building! Come on! We have 'em now!*"

Using their homemade grappling hooks, the two heroes scaled the side of the house until they finally reached the top of the roof. "*We have you now, Penguin!*" shouted Lamar, now in full character. Reaching into his utility belt, Lamar pulled out a short stick he had picked up that acted as a Bat-O-Ring. "*Take this Penguin,*" he shouted as he threw the stick, knocking Penguin off the roof!

Demetrius jumped out of character and shouted, "*Good guys, don't kill the bad guys!*"

Lamar replied, "*Well, the bad guys never die anyway! He's just lying down there. So now we just have to get down there and take him to jail. Watch!*" Lamar pulled a black garbage bag from his utility belt. He then slung the bag, filling it with air and expanding its size.

"*What are you gonna do with that?*" said Demetrius.

"I am going to be the first Robin that can fly."

"I don't want to play anymore. It's getting dark and—"

Lamar interrupted Demetrius and said, *"Well, we still have to get down somehow."* Demetrius starts to pat his pockets and says, *"I don't have a bag, so how will I get down?"* Lamar walked over to Demetrius and handed him the garbage bag.

"Here, use this."

"How will you get down if I take your bag?"

"It's not a bag . . . it's a parachute!" Lamar replied. *"Besides, if you use my parachute, then I want to use your grappling hook."*

There was a brief moment of silence, then Demetrius said, *"How will you get down using it?"* Lamar pointed at the powerlines, *"I will swing from there. We are already on the roof . . . and those cables are close enough to us . . . I'm sure I can swing down like Batman and Robin on the TV show."*

"OK," replied Demetrius as he took the bag from Lamar.

They both walked to the edge of the roof and looked down. *"Oh my God, this is high,"* said Demetrius.

"Just go! Don't think about it . . . just do it!" replied Lamar. Demetrius held the bag in his hand firmly, his palms shaking.

He began to count aloud as his heart pounded in his chest, *"I'm going to jump on the count of three,"* he said as he looked back at Lamar.

"I'm right behind you, Batman," Lamar said as he readied the grappling hook for his turn.

A Life Long Struggle

Demetrious took a deep breath and started to count, *"One . . . two . . . . THREE!"* Demetrius Leaped from the roof, holding the garbage bag over his head like a parachute. Midway through his descent, the bag filled with air, decreasing the speed of his fall. He crashed into the dirt like a pebble but stood to his feet unharmed. *"That was AWESOME!"* Demetrius shouted. *"It's your turn now!!"*

Lamar looked down at Demetrius while he started to twirl the grappling hook just like Batman would. Using all his might, Lamar flung the grappling hook onto the cabling and pulled as hard as he could. The hook wrapped around the cable several times before it secured itself. Lamar tugged at the hook once more to ensure it could hold his weight. Then he shouted, *"I'm going on the count of three!"* He took a deep breath and muttered to himself, *"Lord, please watch over me. I don't want to hurt anyone else. If I am truly a bad person, then show me here and now."* Lamar looked down towards Demetrius once more before he began his count. *" One . . . Two . . . Three!"*

He jumped from the rooftop holding the grappling hook tight as he swung away from the house. However, he didn't think about how to get down completely. He began to panic as the hook swung him back towards the rooftop. Lamar quickly started to release himself from the rope in an effort to reach the ground safely.

However, his efforts were in vain, as a loud snapping noise signaled the electrical line had popped. A flash of light followed by a surge of electricity flowed from the snapped cable, down the grappling hook, and directly into Lamar's body. The sudden shock of current hurled Lamar away from the house and into a small patch of brush. His body smoked as his flesh was electrified. He was covered with burns from head to toe. His clothing melted away, taking much of his exterior tissue along with them. Lamar laid on his back motionless as the smell of burned skin filled the night air.

The entire street was suddenly engulfed by darkness as Nathaniel appeared before Lamar's body. He lay helpless, unable to speak or move a single finger. *"What have you done, child? To submit one's self to such pain . . . such sorrow . . . I have come for you, child. Ready thy self."*

Lamar tried to escape, but he was unable to move. He could only think to himself, *"You cannot have me yet, Nathaniel. I have not succumbed to the world yet."* With that single thought, The Gatekeeper appeared from Lamar's body and spoke in a fury, "You shall **not** have THIS child!"

Thunder and Lightning: Nathaniel Attacks

Nathaniel dashed towards The Gatekeeper without hesitation. He shouted, *"I will not be the child's protector this time, Gatekeeper! I shall not hold back. If the child dies due to your carelessness, so be it."* He crashed into The Gatekeeper, pushing him away from Lamar's body. *"I shall push you to your limit, Gatekeeper,"* Nathaniel shouted as he suddenly turned toward Lamar. Using his tail like a whip, Nathaniel attempted to crush Lamar. To his surprise, The Gatekeeper made no effort to stop his attack. Just as his tail was moments away from sealing Lamar's fate, The Gatekeeper shouted,

"Do not confuse my actions with affection. *I do not care for this child."*

Then The Gatekeeper delivered a solid blow to Nathaniel's midsection causing him to levitate from the ground, stopping his attack. *"He is under my protection, and you shall not have him!"* Again The Gatekeeper shouted as he delivered a second blow, which sent Nathaniel flying up into the sky.

A Life Long Struggle

Lamar watched helplessly as the two creatures battled over his soul. They danced in the sky above the clouds lighting up the night sky with each clash. Flashes of lightning lit the clouds, followed by the crackle of thunder as if he laid in the midst of a thunderstorm. *"I must stand, I must stand up,"* Lamar thought to himself. He lay with his arms and legs stretched apart, his body completely numb and scorched from the electric line.

The entire neighborhood was now blanketed in complete darkness. Lamar cried out, *"Someone help me! Somebody . . . anybody . . . please help me!"* But no matter how hard he shouted for help, no one could hear. Tears formed in the corners of his eyes as his heart sunk into his chest.

His mind rambled as he thought to himself, *"This might be it—my final moments. Just when my eyes had finally opened up to this world,"* His built-up tears slowly fell from his face. *"I can see the many colors and hear the many sounds. I had been dormant for so long . . . unable to truly feel, to truly understand this world of ours. Only to find myself here, lying flat on my back, watching the battle for my life unfold in front of my eyes. Floating, riding this wave as a bystander . . . a passenger of my own existence. Things were just gettin' good. Hmph, I guess this is my fate."*

Lamar closed his eyes and took a deep breath. He listened to the battle that waged above him as the night air brushed against his face. He opened his eyes and turned to his left hand. *"I can't feel anything. Not even the pain from my burned flesh,"* he thought to himself. Then, beyond his feet, he saw a shadow in the distance. He tried to shout out, *"Hey . . . you there! Can you hear me…?"* But the figure didn't move.

A Life Long Struggle

"Why can't he hear me?" Lamar thought to himself. Suddenly, His eyes widened as he realized that no one could hear him. The electricity had scorched his throat, making it difficult for him to speak clearly. Once he realized this, Lamar struggled to speak in any way he could. He made high pitch squeals and screeches, desperately trying to be heard. But despite his efforts, his groans didn't reach the figure in the distance. So he struggled and thrashed about in efforts to draw attention to himself, flailing his body like a dying worm on the heated pavement. But the figure remained motionless.

Lamar's heart began to race in his chest as he thought to himself, *"Who is this person, and why can't they see me . . . Is this a trick of some sort, or is someone really there?!"* His thoughts paused as he looked over at the figure in the distance. *"Or could it be . . . Demetrius! Oh no, I had forgotten he was with me."* Lamar's struggle intensified as he started to thrash about violently. *"No! What if he sees Nathaniel? . . . or The Gatekeeper? No, I can't allow that to happen. I must reach him before they notice he is there."*

Suddenly The Gatekeeper came crashing to the ground, like lightning against steal, launching Lamar into the air. His body flopping around aimlessly like a ragdoll before slamming against the side of the house. He sat in an upright position, his head bleeding, and his vision blurred from the impact. The Gatekeeper stood to his feet as Nathaniel smashed into him full force, creating a shockwave that crackled like thunder and shook the earth. The Gatekeeper, able to fend off the attack with ease, pushed Nathaniel backward as dust clouded the air.

Lamar reached up to wipe the dust from his eyes as the two creatures vanished from his sight. *"I can move my arms!?"* Lamar thought to himself. Still unable to talk, Lamar tried to stand to his feet, but his legs would not respond. *"I must get to him, somehow,"* Lamar thought. He scanned the area in search of Demetrius, but he could not find him. His heart pounding in his chest, he suddenly relived the moment where The Gatekeeper crashed to the ground, flinging him against the house. But this time, The Gatekeeper didn't just land in the yard alone. Lamar envisioned the creature crushing Demetrius. Still images flashed through his mind slowly. First the fall, then the impact and bitter scene of a loved one being killed all flashed before him.

"No! That's not what happened! He is okay. I'm sure of it," Lamar thought to himself. Fear and sadness filled every inch of his being as he flung himself to the ground. He reached out, digging his fingers deep into the dirt. *"I will find him -- I will find him,"* he thought as he dragged himself along the ground. He struggled through the pain of each pull while using his face and chin as leverage. Just as he neared the spot where The Gatekeeper had landed, a brilliant flash of light lit the night's sky, and then there was silence.

Lamar stopped moving abruptly. He looked upward and thought, "Is *it over? Did The Gatekeeper win?"* As possibilities ran through his mind, they were met with a cool and comforting breeze that seemed to soothe him completely. He took a deep breath and continued to drag himself closer to the hole where The Gatekeeper had landed. Time seemed to slow down as the distance to the hole increased. The closer he got to his destination, the further it appeared to be. But Lamar continued until he neared the top of the hole. He grabbed a hand full of dirt and pulled himself to the top. He smiled as the sensation of satisfaction gripped him, only to remember what Nathaniel had said earlier, *"This game reminds me of life. A constant struggle to achieve a pointless goal. You wander around, stepping on all those who get in your way in search of coin while desperately seeking what makes you happy. But alas, it seems to constantly be just out of reach."*

As that thought coursed through Lamar's mind, thunder roared across the night air, shaking the leaves from the trees and causing Lamar to fall flat on his face. His struggle subsided, and his determination faded. *"What am I doing? I'm in the middle of a battle between two godlike creatures. I'm just a child. I'm not supposed to be here . . . I'm only eight years old – what can I possibly do?"* Lamar thought to himself. Suddenly, a voice in the distance replied.

"Nothing. You can do nothing." Lamar's eyes bulged open in fear. His body began to tremble as something landed softly, just inches from where he lay.

"Come now, child. Have you given up already? Surely you have more fight in you than that." Lamar pulled his hands closer to his body, slowly pushing himself upward. His face lifted from the dirt as he peered to his left. His eyes locked onto the face of Nathaniel just inches away from his own. *"Have you forgotten what I've told you, child?"* Without hesitation, Lamar reached out and slapped Nathaniel as hard as he could. Then clenched his eyes shut and desperately tried to escape. He tossed and turned, flinging up dirt and dust as he drug his body along the ground.

"Foolish child," Nathaniel said as he placed his hand near his cheek. He watched curiously as Lamar struggled to escape. *"There is no place for you to go, child. There is nothing you can do to escape me . . . why struggle. You grow more and more intelligent with each passing moment. I'm sure you have already come to this conclusion."* Nathaniel then followed Lamar while walking on all

fours as a cat would. His tail swayed with each step as he watched Lamar struggle to escape, dragging himself along the ground.

Nathaniel listened to Lamar's thoughts and fears until he spoke aloud, *"Enough! I tire of this game of cat and mouse. The time has come! Submit thy life, or I shall tear it from you!"* Nathaniel stood to his feet, grabbed Lamar by his legs with his tail, and held him upside down.

"Have you not caused enough pain?" Nathaniel said, pulling Lamar closer to him. *"Your mother is unable to sleep because of you. Your friends can't play a single game with you without someone getting hurt. You have single-handedly killed Leon, and now look at what you have done to Demetrius!"* Nathaniel grabbed Lamar by the shoulder and held him upright, pointing him in the direction of The Gatekeeper's crater. *"Look there, child. Look closely. Now tell me, what do you see?"* Lamar's eyes opened wide as he looked upon the hole. It was filled with blood, like a bowl of spilled tomato sauce. *"Look closer!"* Nathaniel shouted.

Lamar locked his eyes shut. His body trembled as he shrieked out, "No! It's not real! IT'S NOT REAL!" Lamar cocked his hand back and struck Nathaniel once more. Lamar's hand crashed into Nathaniel's face as a bug would a car windshield. Nathaniel remained still and silent, just before back-handing Lamar into the crater with immense power. His body skipping along the ground just before falling to the bottom of the crater. He plowed into the far corner of the hole in an upright position. His legs stretched out below him as if he had been sitting in a reclining chair.

He sat forward, then slowly opened his eyes. He was unable to move, and his body turned numb from Nathaniel's attack. However, his attention was quickly redirected once he realized where he had landed. He sat in a valley of blood and shattered limbs. He could see fingers, arms, and legs scattered about. *Demetrius's* torso lay torn apart, as if it had exploded, just below his feet.

Lamar's heart stopped, his vision blurred, and his stomach erupted as he vomited until there was nothing left. He felt empty inside. His hands trembled, his body covered in dirt, blood, and vomit. He screamed till he bled from his mouth. *"No, no, no, no, no! This is not happening! This is not happening!"* Lamar shouted. He stammered to his feet, forcing his body to move, pulling himself up using the crater walls. His legs were as noodles. They wobbled and trembled, barely able to hold his weight.

Lamar called out to Nathaniel, "Get your ass down here, creature!" Nathaniel replied while standing above Lamar at the crater's entrance,

"My...my, aren't we perky all of a sudden!?"

"Why have you done this, creature? Why have you killed Demetrius?"

"I have done no such thing. You may be naive, but you aren't stupid or blind. You saw what happen with your own eyes . . . so come to terms with what you have done."

"Me?! I have done nothing. This is your fault creat—"

"No Child! This all happened because of you! You chose to keep me a secret. You chose to speak with me while I inhabited Demetrius's body. You chose to play out until nightfall—just as you chose to Kill Leon! You alone cause those you love to suffer. Accept it! This— all of it – is your doing!"

"Liar!"

Nathaniel vanished from the top of the crater and reappeared in front of Lamar. He positioned himself face to face with Lamar, mere centimeters away from each other. Lamar could feel the air around him cool as Nathaniel faced him directly.

"I never lie," Nathaniel replied. *"What more do you need? Who else needs to suffer by your hands before you come to terms with the truth of this world?"* Nathaniel said while he scooped Lamar up using his paddle-like tail. *"Pain does not affect you, nor does the suffering of others. You are immune to sorrow. Even now, you stand among the crushed body of a dear family member, and you cannot shed a single honest tear. You are more of a beast than I, child."*

"You are right," replied Lamar. *"I cannot feel pain anymore, and I can't sympathize with the pain of others whether I caused it or not. I have changed. But I am no beast. I've learned how to care for the well-being of those I love. I have learned to harbor the burden that others cannot, to stand strong when others feel weak. I am strong for the sake of others, and you will never have me. I will fight you till death call for me and then some. My soul won't rest until you cease to be. And should you try to merge with me, I shall be the one to consume you! I will not quit! I will never give up, so you can just go to He—."*

Nathaniel drives his hand completely thru Lamar's chest. *"Now that's more like it,"* said Nathaniel as he slowly pushed his arm deeper into Lamar's chest. *"This is no fairy tale, child. False bravado and encouraging words cannot change this situation. But by all means, try. Struggle until all hope vanishes. Then and only then shall you see this world as it is! Now tell me, what do you think*

A Life Long Struggle

of this world now?" Nathaniel snatched his hand from Lamar's chest, "*No one in this world can save you. No one can harbor your burden, no one can see this reality that you live in, and no one can protect you from what is. Knowing this, tell me child . . . tell me just how colorful this world is now.*"

Lamar struggled to remain standing after Nathaniel had torn a hole in his chest. He watched as massive amounts of blood poured from his body onto Nathaniel's tail. His legs still shaking and barely able to breathe, Lamar opened his mouth to speak, but no words could form. He could only think. His mind hazy, his breath grew shallow as his vision blurred. He thought audibly to Nathaniel, "*I shall carry the burden of all those I hold dear. I shall endure all hardships that are bestowed upon me. And most importantly, you shall never harm anyone I care for ever again.*"

As Lamar's subconscious faded, his eyes turned crimson as Nathaniel let out a horrifying screech. Lamar's eyes grew heavy as he slowly fell to his knees. Nathaniel's tail quickly slid from up under Lamar and coiled up around Nathaniel as he appeared to be in great pain.

Lamar felt himself begin to sway back and forth as the cold night air showered his face. His feet dangled as his entire body fell numb once again. His head hung low, his chin to his chest as he heard a voice speak to him, "*Rest now child, I shall protect and guide you from now on.*" This voice resonated in Lamar's mind. Using his last ounce of strength, Lamar opened his eyes slightly, peering down where Nathaniel had skewered him. He noticed something had filled the hole in his chest. He took hold of it and followed it with his eyes, slowly losing consciousness with each passing second.

A Life Long Struggle

Unable to remain awake much longer, Lamar thrust his head upward, forcing himself into the upright position. His eyes widened – his heart stopped. And a single thought festered in his mind, for in front of him stood his greatest opponent, Nathaniel, and behind him, The Gatekeeper.

"Damn you, Gatekeeper!!" Nathaniel cried out in agony, causing Lamar's eardrums to burst. Lamar's head fell down to his chest. His hands dangled at his sides. He struggled to keep his eyes open as his sight slowly started to vanish. His thoughts drifted as a single image blurred his mind.

It clouded his thoughts until he could no longer feel the pain of The Gatekeeper's tail as it thrashed him about. His mind could only focus on what he saw. He couldn't hear the shriek of Nathaniel's voice, nor could he taste the blood that dripped from his mouth. He had lost all motor skills. Even the foul stench of his burned flesh turned odorless. His vision faded completely, and in its place sat a still picture -- the image, where his life ended.

He hung suspended in mid-air, his torso burst open as The Gatekeeper's tail passed through his body and pierced Nathaniel's chest.

Lamar drifted into the darkness, his eyes growing heavier with each passing second. He could finally see the cold truth of his reality. He was bound in-between The Gatekeeper and Nathaniel and could only watch as they fought for his soul. His eyes closed softly as the image faded into the abyss, and there was silence once more.

A Life Long Struggle

LAMAR AND NATHANIEL

A New Struggle Begins

Contents

Loss

"It is time! Awaken from your slumber and begin anew."

Lamar's eyes sprang open, his heart pounding from within his chest. He quickly sat up and reached for his chest, pulling up his shirt then placing his hand on his bare skin. "What the hell, man! Did all of that just happen, or was that a dream?! *Where am I? Think Lamar . . . think! Oh yeah! I'm at Auntie's house. And . . . we were . . . playing Batman and then I . . . . . . Demetrius! Where is Demetrius?!"* Lamar rose to his feet and shouted, *"Demetrius, where are you! Come out!"* No one responded. Again he shouted out for Demetrius, but again there was no answer. *"The hole, where's the hole…."* Lamar turned around in circles, desperately trying to map out his location. He thought to himself, *"I remember climbing on the house with the grappling hook. I gave Demetrius the parachute, and then I used the hook to swing from the powerline. Man, was that stupid. That's how I got electrocuted."* Lamar then turned west, facing the neighboring house. *"I must have fallen over there,"* he thought. He then walked over to where his body was once before, *"If I was here then . . ."* Lamar looked north of his position, *"There! Over there, that's where I saw him."* Lamar then ran in the direction where The Gatekeeper landed.

A New Struggle Begins

"Where is the hole . . . where is *Demetrius? What is going on here!!"*

A voice in the distance shouts, *"Quiet down, what are you yelling about?"* Lamar quickly turned around, holding his breath. He muttered, *"Demetrius . . . is that you?".* As the distant figure walked closer, Lamar's face brightened with happiness and relief as he shouted, *"It is you!"* He ran over to Demetrius and tackled him to the ground. His face covered in tears, Lamar cried out, *"I thought you were dead! I saw you get crushed by The Gatekeeper. I saw bits and pieces of your body, and your blood was all over me! But you aren't dead . . . you aren't! You are alive, and it was just a dream!"*

"What? Slow down. What do you mean? Did you dream I was dead or something? And who in the world is Gatekeeper?"

"No, it wasn't a dream. It was real!"

"How could it be real when I'm standing right here, in front of you, ALIVE."

"Maybe. "

"Maybe it was just a dream. Besides this Gatekeeper person, as long as I've known you, which is your whole life, by the way, I've never heard you mention anybody named Gatekeeper or knowing anybody that keeps gates."

"The Gatekeeper isn't even human. I just say he is because it's easier to identify the creature as such."

"Who are you right now? 'Identify as such,' where did this vocabulary come from?"

"I've always talked like this…."

A New Struggle Begins

"No, you have NOT. That shock to the head must have really done it to you. You were out for like ten seconds, and now you are some sort of crazy teacher person. Look around you Lamar! This is the real world! You are at my mamma's house, we played Batman, and you got electrocuted. Look around you. All of this is real, and I am alive!"

"But Demetrius, it was real. I felt everything. The smell of my burned skin, the taste of blood in my mouth, I felt every inch of pain when The Gatekeeper's tail ran straight through my body . . . I felt it all."

"Listen. Never tell anyone else that shit. You sound crazy."

"But..."

"No buts. Seriously. Tighten up and fast because my momma on the way."

"What!"

"Yeah. You caused a blackout! Look! All the lights are out, and you were electrocuted! I thought you were dead – so I ran. As soon as I saw you fly with sparks coming from your body, that's was it. I had to tell someone! So I did."

"No! If she asks me what happened . . . what do I say?"

"Tell the truth, just not that crazy shit."

"No, I don't want anybody to get involved. What if Nathaniel . . . or The Gatekeeper . . . what if what happened to you happen to someone else?!"

"Dude, it was a dream! Calm down. It wasn't real. You were knocked out for a few minutes at best. There's no way ANY of what you say could have happened."

A New Struggle Begins

As their conversation reached its climax, Demetrius's mother comes running from around the corner carrying an arm full of towels and bandages. She shouts out, *"Demetrius! Where is Lamar? Is he okay?!"* Lamar quickly turned to Demetrius and said, *"I have to go. I'm sorry man, but it's for the best,"* then ran towards the brush. He forced himself through the bushes, crashing into broken tree branches and tumbling over old logs and grounded vines.

His mind in disarray, Lamar continued running aimlessly through the brush as his mind recapped the events that led to The Gatekeeper's appearance. *"Just what is Nathaniel? Where did The Gatekeeper come from? And why are they after me!? Is this real . . . or am I imagining things? Maybe if I just think back to when this all started, maybe I can figure this mess out. Think! When did I meet Nathaniel, and what is he?"*

Lamar's thoughts continued, distracting him further away from reality. His body functioned on autopilot, Bobbing and weaving past trees and darting under and jumping over tree branches. *"Nathaniel doesn't seem to like The Gatekeeper. That much is obvious, but why does The Gatekeeper hate Nathaniel? I must be missing something. What is it that I'm overlooking? Damn it Lamar, think!"*

Lamar started to run faster and faster as his thoughts pushed him forward. Now completely unaware of his surroundings and deep in thought, he jumped over a small hole and reached for a tree limb to swing from, not noticing that the limb he reached for and the hole he jumped over were both unreal. Lamar extended his hand to grab hold of the branch, only to crash into a massive Oak tree, knocking him unconscious. He laid on his back with his arms and legs spread apart as blood slowly leaked from his forehead.

A New Struggle Begins

"*You're such a careless child,*" said The Gatekeeper, as he stood in front of Lamar's unconscious body. Blood from his forehead began to trickle down his face and collect near his left eye. Seeing this, The Gatekeeper kneeled down and placed a finger on Lamar's head, wiping away the blood and healing his wounds. Looking at Lamar, The Gatekeeper continued to speak, "*Running away from your own problems... Only being able to stand and fight when the issue is not your own. Such a peculiar child indeed.*" The Gatekeeper sat next to Lamar, resting himself at the base of the tree. "*I know you are here, Nathaniel,*" said The Gatekeeper. "*I shall not leave this child's side while he is in such a fragile condition. Stay thyself at bay.*" Nathaniel's voice spoke from the distance,

"*Is that so?! Very uncharacteristic of you, Gatekeeper.*"

Looking down at Lamar, The Gatekeeper spoke to Nathaniel once more, "*Idle thyself elsewhere, lest fury shall rain from the heavens.*"

"I've had my day's fill." Nathaniel then replied, "*Do as you please, Gatekeeper,*" Nathaniel's presence slowly vanished as The Gatekeeper redirected his attention back to Lamar, extending his tail, hovering it above Lamar's body. "*Let us retrieve what was once lost,*" said The Gatekeeper as he stabbed Lamar in the chest with the needle-like tip of his tail. Lamar's body rose from the ground from shock on impact as The Gatekeeper's stinger dug into his flesh. His body twisted and turned about as if he was having a seizure. The Gatekeeper watched as Lamar's body flopped about, slowing thrusting his tail deeper into Lamar's chest.

After Lamar's body had stopped moving, The Gatekeeper spoke, "*I have unlocked all that you have lost and locked away. Face your fears and grow strong,*" The Gatekeeper's body began to change and take a new form, a human form. He lifted Lamar's

A New Struggle Begins

unconscious body and laid his head on his leg. The Gatekeeper then said, *"This is only the beginning. If you want to survive, you must become stronger. As strong as you once were."* The Gatekeeper then stroked Lamar's forehead lovingly, as his tail remained deep within his chest. "Let us rest together as we once did," said The Gatekeeper. *"I can still remember holding you in my arms when you were firstborn. You were filled with such life, such joy, such power. And Vanessa, she's so naive to bring you into this family without knowing her ancestry. Hmph. But nonetheless, you broke into this world wide-eyed, without a single tear. That's when I knew I'd be the one to protect you. But this is far too soon."*

The Gatekeeper began to relax his body on the tree trunk. His eyes grew heavy as the world of sleep called for him. *"Come, let us awaken the sleeping beast that dwells within you."* The Gatekeeper fell into a deep sleep while his second tail acted as a sentry for protection.

A sudden jolt of electricity and The Gatekeeper sprung forth. He had entered a shared dreamworld with Lamar, composed of all repressed and lost memories of their mind. The Gatekeeper scanned his surroundings then said, *"This looks just like the area where his body lay next to the tree. Good, these are Lamar's latest memories. Let us begin."*

Suddenly the night sky vanished, along with the trees, the grass, and all signs of life. An eerie silence slithered around The Gatekeeper. He stood still, motionless. *"WHO ARE YOU,"* said a voice from a distance, *"WHY ARE YOU HERE!?"* The Gatekeeper replied.

"I am but a lowly servant, here to help you find your way."

Again there was silence. "LIAR." The voice shouted.

A New Struggle Begins

With a gust of heat and wind, a massive figure appeared from the darkness and punched The Gatekeeper, sending him flying into the distance. The Gatekeeper slammed against the ground, rolling until he came to a complete stop. *"WHO ARE YOU?"* The voice asked again.

The Gatekeeper repeated himself, *"I am but a lowly servant, here to help you find your way."*

"LIAR!"

The voice yelled out once more. The Gatekeeper took a defensive stance and braced himself for another attack. Then from amidst the darkness, the figure kicked The Gatekeeper, knocking him into a distant tree and causing him to cough up blood. *"This is bad,"* thought The Gatekeeper, *"I didn't think he'd be this strong."* The ground started to shake rhythmically. The sound seemed to get closer and closer to The Gatekeeper. When the sound stopped, The Gatekeeper quickly braced himself, but he didn't have enough time. Before he could react, he saw a massive barefoot coming straight for him.

The giant foot kicked The Gatekeeper up into the air. Then a massive fist punched him back to the ground before vanishing into the darkness. It was as if he were being pummeled by a giant from the shadows.

The Gatekeeper's body lay twisted upon itself. Barely able to move, The Gatekeeper desperately tried to lay flat on his back. Continually coughing up blood, his bones crackled and broke with every movement he made. The Gatekeeper managed to straighten himself out and lay flat on his back just as the voice spoke to him again.

"WHO ARE YOU?"

A New Struggle Begins

"I am . . a lowly servant. Here to help you . . . find . . . your way."

"LIAR!"

The earth beneath The Gatekeeper rumbled. Then a dark cloud surrounded him with heat and murderous intent. Again the voice spoke.

"WHO ARE YOU!?"

"A lowly servant. Here to help you . . . find—"

"LIAR!!"

Again the ground beneath The Gatekeeper shook as a set of massive claws slammed along both sides of him. A large head slowly emerged from the darkness. Its diamond-shaped eyes glowed as it glared down at The Gatekeeper. Its Lion like snout grinned, displaying its razor-sharp teeth. It slowly leaned down towards The Gatekeeper until it was inches from The Gatekeeper's body, then it spoke once more.

"WHO ARE YOU?!"

The Gatekeeper looked deep within the creature's eyes and replied, *"I am . . . a lowly servant . . . . whom you know quite* well."

"WHY HAVE YOU COME!"

"I am here to help you find your way back. You were . . . lost."

"WEAK! YOU HAVE NO POWER HERE!"

"You are correct. I have no power in this world. But you cease to be outside of this world."

A New Struggle Begins

"SPEAK NOW OR DIE!"

"A small part of me lives within this body, as do you live within his mind. You were forgotten, lost. And without you, the body is hopeless."

"I REMEMBER...YOU TRIED TO...KILL ME!! CONSUME...ME!"

"Yes, and I shall do just that. But now, we face a more formidable opponent. Join me, and we—"

Before The Gatekeeper could finish talking, the creature vanished in a cloud of smoke. A star-filled sky appeared over The Gatekeeper as the smoke condensed into an adult version of Lamar. He stood before The Gatekeeper's mangled body and kicked him repeatedly.

"How dare you come here in that form, creature?!" shouted Lamar. *"Where are your wings, horns, and claws? Where is all that makes you evil, you piece of shit!"*

The Gatekeeper, still battered and bruised from Lamar's initial attacks, could not defend himself and squirmed with each kick delivered from Lamar.

"Okay, okay, I get it. So you're mad," shouted The Gatekeeper.

"Mad isn't nearly close to how I feel!"

"I am here because of you."

"Oh no. I have waited for the day to see you here. I hunger for your presence!"

The Gatekeeper replied, *"In due time but for now—"*

A New Struggle Begins

Lamar silenced The Gatekeeper by kicking him in the mouth, *"You want me to help you, right?"* Said Lamar as he ground his foot in The Gatekeeper's face and continued to speak. *"Truth be told, I am not lost. I cut myself from the body to come here. I saw what you did to my uncle. I watched him every day up until the bitter end, so I know. I know everything, Mr. so-called Gatekeeper. Now you come here asking for me to return?! Ha! How cliché is that!"* Lamar bent down and picked up The Gatekeeper by the neck. *"I am all that makes the human experience. I am the memories, the emotion, the power . . . I am the real Lamar, and not you nor Nathaniel will have my body. You want my help, then listen closely . . . . NEVER COME HERE AGAIN!"*

Lamar then flung The Gatekeeper from his mind and back into the real world. His tail dislodged from Lamar's body, causing them both to wake up simultaneously.

The Gatekeeper quickly retracts and conceals his tails and then leans against the tree to pretend as if he's still asleep. Lamar woke up slowly, teary-eyed and heavy. He wipes his face with his shirt and sits upright. *"Where am I?"* He thought to himself as he analyzed his surroundings. *"I was running from Auntie's, then . . . I . . . saw a hole . . . then."* Lamar turned to his left while in mid-thought and noticed a strange yet familiar man sitting next to him.

The stranger shrugged about, then slowly opened his eyes. He yawned and rubbed his face with his hands, all while stretching his arms and legs. *"Oh, you're awake,"* the stranger said.

"Do I know you, mister?"

The stranger's face suddenly grew very serious. *"Do you know ME, kid? Have a good look…."*

A New Struggle Begins

Lamar looked at the strange man until his eyes started to water, then said, *"Nope, never seen you before in my life."*

"Well, that's a shame." The stranger replied as he stood up and brushed himself off. Lamar watched for a short while and said, *"Mister. Are you homeless? Your clothing looks weird. It's all shiny, like it's brand new or something. And I know homeless people don't buy new stuff."*

The stranger smiled, and he said, *"My clothes are a part of me. That's why they look so clean. I take good care of them because I only have one set."*

"So, you are homeless."

The stranger looked down at Lamar and said, *"Well, if you must know, I'm lost. I have a home, but it's out of reach right now. So for the time being, I'm taking care of my friend's house."*

Lamar looked down at his feet. His expression changed dramatically. He kicked a few sticks, and he said, *"If you are watching the house for a friend . . . that means you don't really care about the house."*

The stranger took a few steps back then replied, *"A house is as important as its contents. If there is no value inside, then there is no need to have someone watch over it, right?"*

"Yea, I guess that's one way to look at it. But, truth be told, I have a lot on my mind, mister. I'm not a normal kid."

"Yea, I can guess that much. You're in the woods talking to a complete stranger. Aren't you scared?"

"I can tell when things aren't right. It's a feeling I get. Like, I know you aren't being honest, and I can tell you are hiding

something. But I can also tell you helped me somehow. I know you are familiar, and I know you mean me no harm."

"All of this from a feeling? You ARE a weird one."

"Mister, can I ask you a question?"

"Sure, why not. I guess I have time for small talk."

"Ok. Well. I feel lost. I don't know what to do about my friends. The first claims he's looking out for my best interest, while the other makes it clear he is only around because I have nice toys. I'm confused because no matter what I do, they are always there, and I don't know if either of them are my real friends."

"I see. Here's food for thought. Confusion means that the mind and body aren't working together. Try to connect your mental state with your physical state, and I'm sure this battle between Nathaniel and The Gatekeeper will resolve much faster when you are unified."

"What do you mean by unified, and how do you know who Nathaniel and The Gatekeeper are?"

Before Lamar could say more, a sudden gust of wind sent chills up Lamar's spine, causing him to let out a loud sneeze. His eyes shut, and before he knew it, the stranger was gone.

The Gatekeeper

It didn't take Lamar long to walk back home after his interaction with the strange man. He drifted as his mind seemed clearer, his body felt lighter, and although he could not understand it, he was different somehow.

Lamar sat up straight, his back firmly against the wall with his legs crossed and tucked beneath him. He now sat in his bedroom with his eyes locked on the formless shadow of Nathaniel. No words were said as Lamar tried to make sense of what the stranger spoke of. Lamar's face intensified, he clasped his hands together, and in a firm tone, he spoke aloud.

"Tell me all that you have to offer, and we shall see what is fact and what is not."

"Facts are but a human's term to justify one's simplicity. I speak truthfully. They are as distinguished from one another as I am from The Gatekeeper."

"Your tongue is as sharp as you are sly. Fact and truth are as similar as you are to The Gatekeeper: One can easily be misinterpreted for the other, and the fine line of separation is that of the intent."

A New Struggle Begins

"What a clever boy you are. I see you have changed yet again, might I ask – what did this acute alteration stem from?"

"You promised me knowledge of this world of man, had you not?"

"I have . . . Has the seed I planted grown to bear fruit?"

"I grow impatient, creature. You say you harbor knowledge of The Gatekeeper, and yet we sit idle, skipping over the topic at hand only to exchange words of none-value. Do you jest, or is this another illusion?"

"I see . . . . This switch of personality isn't skin deep now is it? A question for a later time . . . yes?"

Nathaniel then steps from the shadows onto the tile floor of Lamar's bedroom. His body remained intact. There was no alteration nor discoloration. His armor was as fierce as it was during their first encounter. His tail lay flat on the floor as he towered above the bed, nearly bursting through the ceiling.

"I am the Enigma Nathaniel. I shall not hide myself from you. Nor shall I harm you in any way on this night. Listen, child of man. As I tell you the long-forgotten story of The Gatekeeper."

With a wave of his hand, Nathaniel darkened the room. Lamar was alone as he entered a world of memories, Nathaniel's memories. As this new world shaped around him, Nathaniel spoke, "During my first battle with The Gatekeeper, I attempted to merge with him. This act of instinctive desperation led us to share a single moment of consciousness. An exchange of knowledge that seemed utterly useless until today."

The world shaped itself until Lamar could see people of the distant past. They spoke a language unknown and didn't resemble the textbook image of the first humans. In this world of the past, there were streets and avenues, houses, and landmarks.

The room that Lamar once sat in had vanished. His feet were bare as he stood toe-deep in fine dusty sand. Gusts of warm wind broke against his newly clothed body as the sun lit the day's sky. Lamar dug his feet in the warm sandy street, breathed in the pure air, and watched the bustle of people around him. He quickly realized that he now walked the unpaved roads alongside ancient man.

As his eyes wandered the vast landscape as he spoke aloud to himself, *"The streets are filled with people, the fields are ripe with fruits and tilled vegetables. No airplanes, no cars, or tall buildings for as far as the eye can see. Is this just a memory, or is this truly the past . . . I wonder."* As Lamar's curiosity grew, so did his child-like mentality. Without a moment's thought, he took off in the direction of the fields, stumbling over himself out of anticipation. *"I wonder if the grass is as soft as it is back home,"* Lamar thought. *"How does their fruit taste? Do they have oranges and apples? What games do the children play?"* His thoughts ran faster than he could form words. Before he could control himself, he had already dove in the grassy field, rolling and laughing about.

He quickly lost sight of the journey's purpose. He played and played until another child caught his eye. He sat on a stump near the edge of the field. His face was filled with tears, and his body covered with bruises. Lamar approached the child cautiously, growing more curious with each step. Just inches away from the odd child's back, Lamar reached out to touch the child. His fingers trembled as they were about to touch the strange child. Suddenly the child jerked away and quickly turned to face Lamar directly.

A New Struggle Begins

He jumped back, frightened, then quickly spoke, "How did you know I was behind you?!" The child didn't respond. He only stared fixated on Lamar. Lamar stuck out his hand as a smile covered his face. His teeth simmered as he spoke cheerfully, *"Hey, what's your name? My name is Lamar,"* but the child continued to stare.

Lamar slowly retracted his hand as he gazed upon the boy's face. He looked over the child's shoulder peculiarly, as if something were preventing the child from speaking. Lamar looked the child over but couldn't find anything that would prevent him from talking. Lamar tried again, *"Where are we? What is the name of this town?"* but the child did not reply. Instead, he continued to stare as his eyes followed Lamar's every movement.

Lamar paused. He looked deep into the strange child's eyes, then without warning, he slapped the child incredibly hard across the face.

"OUCH! Why would you do that?!" shouted the child as he held his face tightly.

Lamar smiled then replied, *"That's what my momma do for me when I start spacing out. Besides, you didn't answer any of my questions. You completely ignored me, so I bopped you one to wake you up."*

"That is not how you greet people!" shouted the child. He hopped from the stump, balled his fist, then punched Lamar in the stomach. Lamar's eyes bulged as he fell to his knees, holding himself in pain. *"Serves you right,"* said the odd child. Suddenly Lamar hopped to his feet as if the blow didn't hurt at all.

"Fooled ya, that didn't hurt me at all," Lamar shouted as he stood heroically.

A New Struggle Begins

"You are like me!" shouted the child. He grabbed hold of Lamar's hand and placed it near his chest, but Lamar quickly pulled his hand away.

"What!? You feel weird." Lamar said, holding his own hand.

"I knew it. You can feel my shell, can't you!"

"Shell? Don't be stupid. You don't have a shell."

"You're right, I don't have a shell, but you still felt it, didn't you?"

Lamar paused. He looked down at his hand and back up at this odd child, who stood in front of him smiling. His clothes were worn and tattered. His hair looked as if it had never been combed, and his body was covered with scars and scrapes. He wore no shoes of any kind, yet he appeared to be so happy. The child extended his hand and said, *"My name is Quake. Nice to meet you."*

Surprised by his rapid change in demeanor, Lamar took hold of Quake's hand and said, *"Nice to meet you too, but why did you say we are the same? Surely I'm not as odd as you."*

Quake released Lamar's hand, then looked to the sky, *"You and I are alike. I can see our similarities in your eyes, just as you can feel it on my skin. However, we are different from everyone else, which is why we met here today."* But before Lamar could reply, Nathaniel spoke to his mind, *"Do not reveal your intentions to this child. Let us not awaken The Gatekeeper."*

Quake then turned to Lamar as he pointed to a tree in the distance. Lamar, following Quake's finger with his eyes, gazed in amazement. Then, without a single word, Quake ran for the tree at full speed. He darted in the grassy plains and weaved through

A New Struggle Begins

thorn patches. He jumped over small holes, evading all hazards, as he flung dust from his bare feet. Just as Quake was moments from touching the trunk of the massive tree, Lamar's hand dashed out in front, touching the tree first.

"I win," Lamar shouted as he bent over, gasping for air. Quake stood over him with a slight smile. He looked as if he hadn't taken a single step. There was no sign of fatigue only that of joy. Lamar flopped over to rest at the base of the tree. He pushed his back against the tree and stretched his legs apart. *"How are you **not** tired?!"* Lamar asked as he placed his hands on top of his head. Quake paused for a moment, then sat down next to Lamar and replied, *"I don't get tired anymore. No matter how much I run and play . . . I never feel tired."*

"REALLY?!" Lamar said, lifting himself forward, *"What if you ran really, really fast?"*

Quake shook his head, *"No matter what, I don't feel tired."*

"Awesome!!" Lamar said in a rhythmic tone. *"That has to be some kinda superpower."*

"Like what?" Quake replied with an awkward expression.

Lamar jumped to his feet and began to gesture his arms in excitement, *"A superpower! Like . . . umm . . . Batman!"* Lamar began to jump around, punching and kicking as if someone were fighting him. He threw a series of punches and kicks, while he gallantly shouted out "BAM!" and "KA-BOOM!" as each strike landed. Lamar danced around, fighting the air until his face dripped with sweat. He turned back towards Quake and shouted, *"Batman! Get it now?"*

A New Struggle Begins

Quake had an expressionless face. His mouth partially opened as he sat at the base of the tree, watching Lamar fight an invisible man. He began to speak softly, but all that came out was laughter. Tears filled the corners of his eyes as he held his stomach and pointed at Lamar. *"I get it now!"* Quake shouted as he rolled over, laughing. Irritated by Quake's response, Lamar walked back towards the tree and sat down, *"It's not that funny,"* Lamar replied.

"I'm sorry Lamar," Quake said as he sat next to him. *"It's just . . . I have never had any friends, and you are the first person that I actually like. You're weird, but in a good way, you don't look at me with fear or hate in your eyes like everyone else. It feels good to be myself for once."* As Quake continued to talk, Lamar could feel a familiar presence loom around him. He looked over at Quake as Nathaniel spoke to his mind calmly, *"Pay close attention child."* Quake continued to talk, and the more he spoke, the more of his shell Lamar could see. *"Lamar, I've just met you, and yet I feel like I've known you for years."* Quake paused then spoke oddly, *"I have a secret that I've been waiting to tell someone . . . but . . . can I tell you?"*

Quake looked up at Lamar only to see his reflection in Lamar's crimson eyes. He saw his true self for the first time. His skin was completely covered in scales, similar to a snake's skin. They glistened in the sunlight displaying nearly every known color in vibrant detail, shifting with each move he made. Quake quickly turned his eyes downward only to be greeted with Lamar's kind words.

"Quake – we are alike, aren't we? Like brothers. I will never judge you or treat you badly, and if you want to tell me whatever it is you are going through, I'll listen." With Lamar's words echoing in his mind, Quake stood to his feet and began to tell Lamar about himself. He cleared his throat and spoke clearly,

A New Struggle Begins

"*It started not too long ago. I was sleeping in the field below the apple tree when I heard a loud thump like something had jumped from the tree and landed near me. I sprung to my feet and looked all around me, and what I saw froze me still.*" Lamar crossed his legs and focused on Quake. "*In front of me stood a creature that I'd never seen before. It looked like . . . some kind of beast! It stood on many legs and . . . had a snout of a leopard but skin like yours or mine. It saw me so . . . I ran as fast as I could. But I stumbled . . . over a small twig. I fell, scraping my hands and knees on the way down but before I could stand to my feet . . . the creature grabbed me and slung me against this tree, pinning me here.*" Quake walked in front of Lamar with his hand on his chest, "*The creature then said, 'Child, I hunger,' -- and I froze. I couldn't move, I couldn't breathe . . . I couldn't even scream! Then I suddenly woke up, like it was all a dream. But when I looked at my hands, I saw that my body had been changed. My hands were claws, my skin was hard as stone, and my body felt numb.*" Quake turned his back towards Lamar as he looked off in the opposite direction, "*All I could do was run, so I did. I ran all the way home nonstop. But I didn't notice how long I had been gone. It felt like only hours had passed . . . but I soon learned that I had been missing for days.*"

Quake paused and stared into the sky as the sun had already begun to set. Then, Lamar shouted out to him, "*Well, what happened next? Don't keep me waiting!*"

"*That was the night everything changed.*" Quake replied.

"*Damnit Quake, what happened?!*"

Just as Quake began to speak, there was a loud explosion in the distance. Lamar stood to his feet alongside Quake as they witnessed his city erupt in flames. "*What's going on?!*" Lamar shouted. Quake darted off towards the burning city without a moment's hesitation, "We must get to my house now! Come on Lamar, let's go!" Quake shouted.

Again the boys raced through the fields, but this time they were neck and neck; Jumping over ditches and weaving through thick brush as if everything had been rehearsed. As Lamar continued his journey onward, he felt a sense of familiarity. Running alongside this odd child seemed right. He knew where all the shortcuts were and where Quake would step before he planted his foot down. Before long, they stood in front of the flame engulfed city. Most of the civilians stood on the outskirts of the city, watching as their lives burned away before their eyes.

"*Mommy! . . . Daddy!*" Quake shouted as he pushed his way through the crowd. "*Lamar, I can't find them!*" Lamar replied, "*What do they look like? What are their names? I'll help you find--*" But before he could finish speaking, Quake had already gone into the flame-filled city. Lamar hesitated only to have Nathaniel speak to him once more.

"*You wish to know of The Gatekeeper, do you not? This is your chance. Go now Child, witness the truth for yourself. Follow him! Go. Now.*"

Lamar took a deep breath and marched forward. He entered the town's main street in search of Quake. The homes were built in perfect lines stretching along both sides of the street. Lamar shouted out for Quake, but he could not hear his reply over the roar of the flames and the crackle of burning wood. One by one, the houses toppled over, sending burning segments into the street. Although the city was engulfed in flames, mere feet away, Lamar remained calm. His mind was clear and shaped by an unfolding will to know more.

A New Struggle Begins

Lamar started to breeze by each house, checking to see if Quake was nearby. He had nearly searched every home when a familiar voice in the distance spoke to him, *"Lamar, over here. Help me."* Lamar turned to his left and darted down the street to the third house on the right. Quake stood in front of the house, his shirt nearly burned off and his hands and feet as dark as tar.

"What the hell Quake! You're all burned up! Let's go!" Lamar quickly grabbed Quake's hand only to have him snatch it back. Before Lamar could shout out in rage, he looked down into his hand and noticed that he held much of Quake's burned skin. He had been trying to get into the burning house by using only his bare hands, burning his flesh in the process. Lamar dropped the charred skin from his hand then gazed upon Quake as time began to slow down. Nathaniel suddenly appeared behind Lamar and said, *"Look child. Look at the devastation caused by this so-called fire."*

"I see the flames Nathaniel, no need to—" Before Lamar could finish, Nathaniel redirected Lamar's attention and spoke in a furious tone, *"No child! You look but do not see! Look here, and there . . . Look and tell me what do you really see?"* Lamar's eyes widened as he saw the many bodies that lay all around him. There were men, women, and even small children. All scattered about.

"Look closer, child. Where are the burns? Had they perished from the flames, they would be burned to a crisp. But not a single burn on them, all of this fire, and yet none of these bodies are burned. I wonder what could have done such a feat."

As soon as he finished speaking, Nathaniel vanished, and time continued normally.

"Lamar, help!"

A New Struggle Begins

Quake shouted as he struggled to lift a fallen tree from the entryway of his home. Lamar rushed over to help Quake but quickly noticed that his hands were smoking. *"Quake, let go of that tree! It's too hot!"* Lamar shouted as he watched Quake struggle. *"I know, but my family is trapped inside, and this is the only way out,"* Quake replied. *Damnit,* Lamar said as he rushed to Quake's aid. He pushed Quake out of the way and shouted, *"Do as I do."* Lamar crawled as close as he could to the fallen tree. He propped himself on his back and pressed his feet against the tree. He pushed with all his might forcing the tree to lift up slightly. Lamar's legs began to shake as the weight of the mighty tree pressed back upon him.

"Help me Quake!" Lamar shouted, but Quake began to walk backward as if he was suddenly afraid of something. Lamar pushed with all his might, worried that the tree might crush him. *"QUAAAKE,"* Lamar shouted. Before Lamar knew it, Quake had launched himself towards Lamar and slid under the fallen tree, snatching Lamar along with him. The tree collapsed onto itself, blocking the exit and trapping them inside the house. Shaken by what happened, Lamar took a moment to gather himself. However, he quickly snapped to attention when he heard Quake shout, *"Who are you?! . . . Let my father go!"*

Lamar quickly stood to his feet and dashed behind Quake. The house was filled with smoke, flames, and fallen debris. Lamar stood in the distance as he watched Quake shout out at a shadowed figure that held his father up by the neck. His mother laid on the floor as her belly bulged out.

The shadowed figure turned towards Quake and said, *"Hello, my child."*

An Age-Old Bind

Quake gazed upon the shadowed creature as his body trembled. He took a step forward as he attempted to speak, *"L-L Let him go,"* Quake demanded. The creature shifted his body slightly towards Quake and spoke once more, *"Tell me, my child, why have you come here?"* But Quake was too frightened to answer. He closed his eyes tightly, hoping that everything would somehow go back to normal. The creature then turned towards Quake's father, lifting him upward into the air as his feet hovered slightly above the floor. Lamar suddenly shouted, *"Snap out of it, Quake!"* but he was too afraid to listen. He stood consumed by fear, trembling in the presence of the creature.

Lamar dashed towards Quake as fast as he could, but instead of stopping, he grabbed him by the hand as if to anchor himself for some unknown reason. Quake's body jerked, causing him to quickly open his eyes just as Lamar's hand crashed into his face. *"WAKE UP!!"* shouted Lamar nearly falling to the floor after the impact. *"God-Damnit, that hurt!"* Quake cried as he held his face. *"What the hell, Quake! This is no time to be spacing out!"* Lamar shouted, stomping his feet. *"Your right."* Quake said as he planted his feet firmly on the floor, *"It's time to show off my power."* Lamar smiled and stood next to Quake, *"Damn straight. Now let's get him,"* Lamar said, readying himself for battle.

A New Struggle Begins

The shadowed creature began to squeeze Quake's father's throat, causing him to pass out. *"Let him go! NOW!"* Quake demanded. He spoke firmly, no longer in fear of the creature. But the creature did not flinch; he simply placed his thumb on Quake's father's chin and spoke aloud.

"Tell me, my child, why have you come?"

"I am Quake, son of Melfice and future ruler of this land. I have come to protect my family, and no one shall deny me."

The creature turned to face Quake directly, *"Are you now?"* he said as he lowered Melfice to the ground. *"Surely you do not intend to protect THIS man-beast,"* said the creature as it stepped from the shadows. *"Surely you do not mean to challenge my will,"* the creature said as it began to walk towards Quake, holding his father by the neck as his feet dragged along the floor. The creature continued to walk closer with its thumb firmly planted on Melfice's chin.

"I am not afraid of you, creature!" Quake shouted as he launched himself at the creature, only to be held back by Lamar. *"Let go of me!"* he said as he struggled to free himself from Lamar's grasp. However, Lamar did not respond. Instead, he stood frozen as his body trembled in fear. His eyes were dull and colorless as he gazed upon The Gatekeeper's true form. Although Quake could not see the creature through Lamar's eyes, he quickly realized the severity of their situation.

"Face me child, and tell me once more. Why are you here?"

Quake turned around slowly, his mouth dry and stale. His body rattled with fear as he gazed upon the creature face to face. He could not speak; he could not move. He only stared into the face of the mighty creature.

It had no eyes nor any other distinguishing features. It wore a smooth shell that was engraved in red markings. It had kneeled to Quake's eye level, almost human-like in appearance.

Then there was a brief moment of silence. The creature seemed to be interested in Quake as if he had already identified Quake's uniqueness. Then, the creature suddenly moved, pulling Melfice – Quakes father -- along the floor closer to Quake. The creature then rose to its feet as his opposite hand became razor-sharp claws. *"I shall ask you three questions, my child. Each shall represent a life within this room. If you lie or answer them incorrectly, I shall strip the life away."*

By the time the creature had finished speaking, he towered above Quake's pregnant mother. The creature held Melfice out in front, his body dangled before Quake and Lamar as he spoke aloud, *"Child, I am going to kill this man-beast and all of his offspring. Can you stop me?"* Quake stepped forward as if he were eager to reply, but Lamar spoke out,

"No."

However, Quake quickly amended his answer, *"Yes. I can, I must."* The creature then took a step closer as if intrigued by the response. *"Do you believe me to be a monster, my child?"* Again Lamar spoke first, causing Quake to respond in the same way,

"Yes you are a monster!" Lamar shouted out.

But again, Quake amended his statement, *"What I mean to say is . . . you are not a monster, but you are not human either."*

The creature took another step forward, *"My child, you are quite interesting, however—"* the creature then pressed his thumb against Melfice's chin, easily snapping his neck and tossing his lifeless body aside. *"You did not give a satisfying response."* The creature then turned toward his mother and gripped her firmly by the shoulder. Quake rushed over to her aid, tackling the creature in an effort to stop his onslaught.

"I answered your questions!" Quake shouted, *"I did not lie, nor did I not answer them incorrectly! Why are you doing this, STOP IT!"* The creature then pushed Quake onto the floor and placed his foot gently on top of him, just enough to pin him firmly to the floor. *"Calm thyself, my child. Be still. You are too eager to cast life away and more naive than ignorant. Look upon this place covered in fire, yet you do not burn, nor are you crushed by falling debris. All of this is my doing, and yet you are still unable to comprehend my power."* The creature reached over and picked Quake's mother up from the floor by one leg. As her unconscious body dangled overhead, the creature looked down towards Quake briefly, then savagely tore open his mother's belly and ripped the unborn child from her womb. Her lifeless body emptied itself onto the floor, drenching Quake in her blood while the creature held the infant by its umbilical cord.

Having just witnessed the death of his parents before his very eyes, Quake's body grew cold and numb as his eyes watered. Still images of her death echoed in his mind. He turned his head to shelter his gaze from the creature, only to see his father's corpse in the distance. He lay mangled in the corner of the room. His eyes bulged outward as he was forced to witness his family's murder. Quake locked his eyes shut, *"This isn't real! This has to be some sort of crazy dream! There's no way this is happening for real."* Quake felt a sudden rush of relief. He smiled, hoping that once he'd open his eyes, he'd be in his bed. *"Good morning!"* he shouted as he opened his eyes. But to his surprise, his situation had not changed. He let out a horrifying scream and began to thrash back n forth, trying to free himself. His efforts caused his mother's body the shake slightly, allowing a single drop of her blood to slip from the womb into his mouth.

"Blood?. . This is my mother's . . . blood."

Quake had not only been covered in his mother's blood but now some of it had entered his body. The bitter taste of his reality consumed him, and he slowly succumbed to grief.

Seeing that Quake had lost his will, the creature tossed his mother aside. Her body fluttered in the air just before landing on top of Melfice. It then released Quake from beneath his feet and watched him crawl desperately towards his parents. *"You cannot save them, my child."* the creature said, watching from above. However, Quake pressed on.

"Foolish boy."

Just as Quake reached his father's body, the creature lit them aflame with a snap of his fingers. The fire dazzled in blue and black light while Quake watched his parents quickly burn to ash within seconds.

"Let us continue," the creature held the infant up by the head as its body dangled above Quake, *"My child, tell me. How are you going to defeat one as powerful as I?"*

Quake stammered to his feet and placed both hands on his head, *"Why didn't you help me, Lamar?!"* Quake shouted as he wobbled around the room. With his thoughts cloudy and vision foggy, he continued to shout, *"I thought we were friends . . . I thought we were like brothers! But . . . but . . . you watched me struggle! You watch my parents get killed!. . You didn't even try to help me!"* The creature was baffled,

A New Struggle Begins

"That child, Lamar --- is no more than a figment of your imagination. Created by your will."

Quake stopped. He just stood in place and down at his hands, *"I have power?"* Quake said as he turned to face the creature. But before the creature could respond Lamar shouted, *"You have power, you always did! Do not allow that creature to control you or your family. Show him your power -- take his and make it your own!"*

Quake faced the creature and spoke aloud, but instead of responding to Lamar's outburst, he talked calmly to the creature, *"I shall defeat you, and you shall serve my bloodline as its guardian and protector . . ."* But before Quake could finish, the creature had crushed the skull of the newborn child and lunged himself at Quake forcing his hand through his chest.

"I shall do no such thing," the creature replied.

Quake quickly grabbed hold of the creature and shouted, ***"LAMAR, NOW!!"***

Lamar's body turned crimson red and lunged itself at the creature. Moving seemingly undetected by the creature, Lamar's body jumped into the air to deliver a devastating blow, but the creature dodged the attack and caught him using his free hand.

"I can see you now, child." The creature held Lamar firmly in his grasp and began to squeeze, *"Tell me boy, who, are you?"* Then, just before Lamar lost consciousness, Nathaniel pulled him from the past and back to his own time.

He sat with his legs crossed in a pool of sweat. His heart was pounding in his chest as Nathaniel stood before him.

A New Struggle Begins

"Now child, who shall you side with." Lamar sat in bed, speechless, as Nathaniel faded into the darkness.

Lamar had finally gazed upon the true face of The Gatekeeper but not without consequence. His body had aged two whole years. His bones were stronger, and he stood a bit taller, but because he had not lived those two years, he felt as if his life was shortened by two years in a matter of hours. Had Lamar the ability to see The Gatekeeper with his eyes in the present, he would surely die. Knowing this, Lamar was now terrified by The Gatekeeper. Lamar slowly stood to his feet only to fall to his knees. His body seemed unfamiliar. His bones and muscles had all increased slightly, and he wasn't yet accustomed to this sudden change. He stammered to the bathroom and looked at himself in the mirror.

"What the hell happened to Quake?" he thought to himself. *"Why did Nathaniel pull me from the past if all the events had taken place already? Something is not right."* He sat on the toilet to collect himself. He ran all of the past events through his mind trying to piece together what had happened to Quake.

Before he could reach a satisfying conclusion, his thoughts were interrupted by a knock at the door.

"Is anybody in there?"

"I am," Lamar replied, *"I'll be out in a minute."*

Lamar stood to his feet, flushed the toilet, and turned on the sink as if he were washing his hands. After a few seconds, he turned off the sink and proceeded to exit the bathroom, only to be greeted by his grandmother. She blocked him from exiting, pushing him back in the bathroom and closing the door.

A New Struggle Begins

"Have a seat," she said calmly while she held a pair of hair clippers. Lamar sat on the toilet in silence.

"Are you surprised to see me like this Granny?" Lamar asked. But Helen did not respond. Instead, she simply kissed him on top of his forehead.

"It is about time you learned of our family's past," Helen said as a single tear fell from her eyes.

"Just sit here and let me do the talking," Helen said as she wiped her face clean. She plugged the hair clippers into an electric socket, wrapped a towel around Lamar's neck to collect the fallen hair, and pulled an old bottle of blessing oil from a hidden compartment. She dabbed her finger in the oil and marked Lamar in the same place she had kissed him, then splashed a tiny bit around the bathroom at their feet. Helen paused, took a deep breath, and placed the oil bottle back into the hidden compartment. *"Now, let us begin,"* she said as she turned on the clippers and started to cut Lamar's hair.

"Our bloodline started with our ancestors, generations ago. His name was Melfice. He ruled over the kingdom of Leohde in a land far east of here. He was a great man, but his soul was corrupt. He conquered many lands through much bloodshed, until he met and married his wife, Efrin. She was a battered woman from lands unknown, but he loved her nonetheless. She would later have his child whom they named--"

"His name was Quake." Lamar said abruptly. Helen paused to glance down at Lamar. Her hand gripped the clippers tightly as she replied, "Yes, his name was Quake." She placed her hand gently on his shoulder and continued, *"Quake was a gentle boy, but despite his demeanor, he was feared and hated throughout the kingdom. You see, Quake wasn't a normal child. He seemed to have had an imaginary friend for nearly every occasion. Each day he would call his friend by a new name until the day his mother conceived a second child. He began to have horrifying nightmares of the future that caused the king to slaughter innocent townsmen. Melfice feared the child that his wife would soon give birth to, so he prayed in secret that his child be stillborn. He wished death to his second child but loved his wife. Thus, he could not simply kill her. However, Efrin soon found out about what Malfice had done. She tried to take her own life, along with everyone else's who lived in the kingdom. She had betrayed Malfice and incited a war with the neighboring kingdom. As a result, the entire land was burned to a cinder on the same night she was meant to give birth."*

Helen paused and stood in front of Lamar. She peered deep within his eyes and spoke seriously, *"A creature rose from the burned city, and it slaughtered all that wished harm upon the kingdom. This creature . . . this all-powerful entity bound itself to this family with the death of Malfice and Efrin. From their evils, this being has lived among our family as our protector but at a steep cost. He will protect us as he did generations ago, just as Malfice protected his land, but the creature also wishes for death just as Efrin did. It steals the soul from one child of each generation. Once selected, there is no heaven nor hell for that child, only oblivion. In return, our family will know no unbearable pain or sickness. We will all live a long life until the day comes that we choose to die."*

Helen took a step back and looked at Lamar with tears treading down her face. *"That damn creature took your uncle. Do not allow it to take you. It is bound to our family, thanks to Quake. Just before he was killed by the creature, he bound his soul to the creature's body, and they merged as one. Quake was able to revive his younger sibling but at the cost of his own life. Should you ever come face to face with that creature, do not trust him and show*

A New Struggle Begins

him no mercy." Helen took another step back and spoke one last time, *"Remember Lamar, this is an age-old binding. He cannot harm you if you don't allow it."* She then left the bathroom as Lamar sat alone to think of his fate.

Feeling defeated, Lamar stood up and brushed the hair from his face. He turned slowly and peered into the mirror, hoping that a miracle of some kind would reveal that everything had been a dream. He filled his hands with water, took a deep breath, closed his eyes, and splashed the collected water onto his face. He stood silent in front of the mirror with his eyes closed. He then placed both of his hands on the corners of the sink. He exhaled, slowly releasing all of his pent-up anxiety and calming his mind. Lamar opened his eyes and again peered into the mirror only to see himself as he was. No miracles, no fairy tales, just the life that stood before him.

"Interesting story," Nathaniel said suddenly as he interrupted Lamar's moment of self-analysis.

"Go away, Enigma. I am in no mood for your antics."

Lamar walked out of the bathroom leaving behind a floor filled with hair shavings. He slowly walked down the dark hallway into the kitchen in search of a broom and dustpan as Nathaniel continued to speak to his mind, *"Enigma? . . . No, I am Nathaniel, child. You know this to be true."* Lamar navigated through the pitch-black house as if he had built it himself. He entered the kitchen and took the broom and dustpan from their hiding place. *"Do not ignore me, child. I grow impatient and weary of your antics."* Lamar turned and walked back toward the bathroom, but Nathaniel stood in his path. *"There is much, much more I can show you, child. Do you desire to see what exactly became of Quake?"* Lamar stood still, his eyes low as if he were uninterested. He then took a step

A New Struggle Begins

forward toward Nathaniel, *"Tell me child, who will devour you first, I, Nathaniel, or The Gatekeeper?"* Lamar froze as the image of The Gatekeeper ripping through Quake passed through his mind.

Nathaniel vanished, then reappeared sitting in the living room. He sat in a human form, his legs spread outward as he slouched over with his hands clasped together. *"Come here, child. I have a proposal."*

Truce

Lamar gripped the handle of the broom tightly in his hand and spoke calmly but in an angered tone, *"Do you expect me to trust either of you? You are no better than The Gatekeeper. You have stripped me of much innocence, taken my childhood from me, and now you want me to side with you against The Gatekeeper?! I will not!"*

"Then, you shall die. Painfully," replied Nathaniel as he pointed to the sofa across from where he sat. *"Come here, child. Sit and listen. I shall not ask again."*

Angered by the possible truth behind Nathaniel's words, Lamar walked into the living room, leaving the broom and dustpan behind. He sat on the sofa across from Nathaniel, *"What is your proposal, creature?"*

"Call me Nathaniel, and I shall address you as Lamar." He said as he spoke. *"And as far as my proposal . . . a truce. A temporary cease-fire between you and I."* Lamar leaned forward, mimicking Nathaniel's posture. *"I would agree to such foolishness, but a cease-fire implies that both sides are at arms. And I have no power. Only The Gatekeeper aids me."* Nathaniel unlocked his hands, allowing one to fall between his legs as he gestured with the other, *"Such power resides within you, just outside your current*

A New Struggle Begins

consciousness. If the power that dwells within you should emerge before I can do away with The Gatekeeper . . . then both of our fates are sealed."

"Really?" Lamar replied with a slight smile. *"Tell me more about this hidden power you believe I possess."* Nathaniel stood to his feet and walked closer towards Lamar.

"Before I tell you anything else, you must agree to a truce. One stating that you cannot do harm to me nor can I you, as long as the contract is in place."

"Agreed," Lamar said as he too rose to his feet and extended his hand.

"Ohh no, it is not that simple," Nathaniel took the form that he fought The Gatekeeper in, then pulled a dagger from his chest and held it in front of Lamar. *"This dagger represents my half of our agreement. All that is left is your half."* Just as Lamar reached for the dagger, Nathaniel spoke one final time, *"You must shed blood onto the dagger willingly and speak your terms aloud. Once this is done, our truce shall be solidified, and we will no longer be able to harm one another directly . . . as long as the contract is in place, of course."*

Lamar reached for the dagger, removing it from Nathaniel's grasp. Once he held it in his hand, his body began to pulse as if he suddenly grew frail. Lamar dropped down to his knees as the dagger burrowed itself into his flesh. Once his strength returned, Lamar stood and said, *"When will the contract expire?"* But Nathaniel did not answer. Instead, he simply turned away and drifted back into the shadows. *"Wait!"* Lamar shouted. He lunged towards Nathaniel, only to collapse on the living room floor. Nathaniel's dagger had sapped away more strength than he'd realized. Lamar struggled to stand, but he could only muster

A New Struggle Begins

enough strength to pull himself onto the sofa, where he lay on his stomach with his left leg and left arm dangled from the sofa. *"A truce between me and Nathaniel . . . I must be crazy,"* Lamar muttered with his eyes barely open. *"I am a true fool,"* he said just as he passed out.

The next morning Lamar awoke to the sound of running water and the chime of pots and pans clashing together. Someone had started to cook breakfast, and the aroma of food filled the air. Lamar slowly sat upright on the sofa, pressing his back deep into the cushions. *"Good morning honey,"* Helen said, peeking from the kitchen. *"You must have been really exhausted last night. I saw you stretched out on the couch, so I decided to make you some breakfast."* Lamar took a deep breath and slid off the sofa onto the floor. He collected himself by pausing momentarily on his hands and knees, then slowly stood to his feet. Helen stood in the distance and watched Lamar struggle, but regardless of how badly she wanted to help, she chose to stand by and watch. Once he had stood up completely, Lamar cried out, *"I'm coming, Granny."*

He stammered to the dinner table, pulled out a chair and sat down. Helen walked back into the kitchen and prepared a plate for him. Before she could finish, the remaining family members bombarded the dinner table, all eager to eat. Helen stood surprised with her mouth slightly open. Vanessa walked over to Helen and smiled, *"I'll help you out mamma."* She placed her hand gently on Helen's back as she walked into the kitchen and prepared plates for everyone. Helen smiled, walked over towards Lamar, and placed his plate in front of him. *"Here you are honey, go on and eat up."*

Lamar smiled big, but his eyes hung low as he still displayed signs of extreme exhaustion. He lifted his spoon as if it took a great effort, but he continued to eat nonetheless. Tears rolled down his face as he took another bite, *"What have I done to deserve such a tragic life."* Lamar *thought as i*mages of The Gatekeeper snapping Malfice's neck flashed in his mind. *"He just slaughtered them, all of them . . . like they were nothing."* Lamar glanced up at his family. They sat at the table smiling and laughing with one another. He took yet another bite of his meal while continuing to think to himself, *"And Quake. I'm sure he was torn apart . . . even the baby was killed by The Gatekeeper's hands. Will the same happen to my family if I oppose The Gatekeeper? And what of Nathaniel?* Lamar again glanced up at his family, *"This food . . . this feeling. It feels . . . good. So good. I will not allow The Gatekeeper to do to my family what he had done to Quake's. He will not have them!"* Before Lamar could control himself, he had slammed his hand down onto the table causing everyone's plate to pop up slightly.

"I will not let you take them from me!" Lamar shouted aloud. His family stared at him in silence.

"I'm glad to see you are back among the living," Helen replied quickly. Lamar sat back down in his chair, embarrassed by his sudden outburst. *"And you have plenty of energy, I see."* Lamar had not noticed that he had regained all of his mobility and overflowed with energy, somehow. Not only did he feel energized, but he had also eaten all of his food and scraped his plate clean. *"Now that you've finished eating, go on outside and play for a bit. Matthew came over looking for you. He seemed worried, and friends shouldn't make each other worry."*

Vanessa looked at Helen with a perplexed expression as Lamar removed himself from the table and walked to his room to get dressed. Once Lamar had distanced himself from the dinner table, Vanessa questioned her mother, *"That was very uncharacteristic of you, Momma. To allow him to go play after all that has happened and to ignore the fact that he has grown sporadically overnight. Have you not noticed?"* Helen sat down at the table as if she were exhausted, with both legs side saddled. She pulled a hand towel from the rear pocket of her homemade dress. She flopped the cloth across her lap then slid back into the chair, "Vanessa, that boy of yours is growing up faster than we can imagine."

Vanessa folded her arms and replied with a stubborn expression, *"And what do you mean by that Mamma?"*

Helen replied sharply, *"Don't you snap ya neck at me Nessa,"* Helen stood to her feet and continued to speak, *"We gotta watch over that boy. I feel that there is much more to come."* Vanessa walked into the kitchen, prepared herself a plate of food, then sat at the table across from Helen. She prayed over her meal then opened her mouth to speak, but Simeon interrupted her.

"Nassa, is Lamar ok? He looks different." As soon as he finished his sentence, there was complete silence at the table. Amanda, Vanessa's older sister, blurted out, "Your son is extra weird. I heard yall talking about him the other night. Was he possessed by a demon or something?"

"What kind of crap is that to say?!" Simeon replied.

"Well, regardless of what we think, the proof is in Lamar himself. I ain't the only one that noticed how his eyes been changing, am I?" Amanda insisted in her usual snooty tone.

There was silence. No one wanted to speak up. Helen sat at the table with her head slightly bowed. *"Well, tell us the truth Vanessa,"* said Amanda. *"Is Lamar possessed by a demon?"* Vanessa slammed her hand on the table and shouted

"No! He is not possessed! Why would you even say something like that?" Amanda stood to her feet and shouted back at Vanessa.

A New Struggle Begins

"Don't you yell at me because you have a demon child. It's not my fault tha—" But before Amanda could finish speaking, Vanessa had punched her in her mouth. *"Shut up heffa!"* Vanessa shouted. However, Amanda was no pushover. She leaped across the table, tackling Vanessa to the floor. Vanessa kicked and punched at Amanda as she sat on top of her, *"Who you calling a heffa!"* Amanda shouted as she gripped Vanessa's hair and punched her mercilessly.

Helen stood up and walked away from the dinner table quietly and calmly. After Helen took her leave, Simeon stepped in and pulled Amanda away from Vanessa, but she continued to punch Amanda as Simeon dragged her away. Suddenly Vanessa felt something tug at her waist. *"Stop it! Stop hitting my momma, auntie!"* shouted Samantha as she struggled to hold on to Vanessa's waist.

In one swift motion, Vanessa turned towards Samantha and pushed her away, then landed another solid punch on Amanda. As she reached for another punch, Simeon's face shriveled up in fear. He dropped Amanda and jumped back quickly as a sharp pain stretched down Vanessa's back. Amanda struggled to get away from Vanessa by turning away and crawling on her knees as fast as she could, but a swift object flew past Vanessa and struck her in the back as well.

Again and again, Vanessa and Amanda were struck by a swift and unseen force. *"Yall too old to be acting like lil children,"* Helen said as she held a small and sturdy tree branch. She continued to beat Vanessa and Amanda until the both of them were in a state of submission. *"If yall gonna act like children, then I'll treat you like children!"* Helen shouted just as Mark entered the living room.

A New Struggle Begins

"What the hell is going on in here?!" Mark shouted as he snatched the branch from Helen. *"Damnit Helen, you too damn old to be out here doing this."* Mark then turned towards Vanessa and Amanda, *"Why the hell yall grown-ass women in here fightin like some damn school churen? Are yall trying to make ya mamma have a damn heart attack?"*

Amanda stood up, pointed at Vanessa and said, *"Daddy, she hit me first."*.

"Only because you called my son a demon baby!" Vanessa shouted.

"I don't give a shit who said what! Shit, I outta kick both ya assess myself for acting so damn stupid early in the god-damn morning . . . hell! Act like you got some damn sense, especially you, Manda. Always startin some damn trouble wit cha gossipin ass. Learn to keep ya damn mouth shut." Vanessa looked down at the floor and smiled as Mark scolded Amanda. *"Nessa, what's so damn funny? You just as guilty! Running round here fighting anybody that say some bad about Lamar. That's foolishness. You gon find ya ass fighting every damn day like a damn fool. The both of yall need to get ya shit together!"* Mark reached out and held Helen's hand but she swatted him away.

"I know how to ruise my children," Helen said as a tear slowly rolled down her face.

"Come on ni Helen. You know I didn't mean no harm. These some big ass girls now. Too big for all of this here."

Before Mark could say anything else, Lamar walked into the living room. He was fully dressed, shoes included. He paused, looked around at everyone, then continued to the front door. Without saying a word, he opened the door and exited the house while everyone stood in silence. Vanessa burst into tears and ran down the hall to her room, slamming the door behind her.

"Damnit to hell," Mark said as he turned to go after Vanessa.

"*Just leave her be,*" Helen replied as she motioned to Amanda to clean the kitchen.

"*It's too damn early for all this here. I'll be back later. I need a damn drank,*" Mark said as he walked back to his room. Simeon stood in the background as he watched the entire fiasco unfold. He slowly back peddled until he stood next to the back door. He reached for the doorknob for a clean escape, but his curiosity would not allow him to leave without asking some questions of his own, "*Momma . . . what's going on with Lamar?*"

Helen looked over at Simeon, smiled, then said, "*Nothing that you should concern yourself about.*"

Simeon gripped the doorknob tightly and spoke softly, "*It's happing all over again, isn't it?*" Helen turned away and began to walk down the hall towards Vanessa's room. As she entered her room, she heard the back door open and shut as Simeon left, taking Samantha along with him. Helen stood in the doorway as Vanessa laid in bed underneath the covers, sobbing. She sat next to Vanessa and rubbed her back gently. Vanessa removed the sheets from her face so that she could see her mother clearly. She wiped her tears away then spoke softly, "*Mamma, is Lamar a demon child?*" she asked with tears in her eyes.

Helen smiled, "*That boy of yours is a lot of things, but he is no demon child.*" Vanessa collected herself in the corner of the bed, pressing her back to the wall as the sheets remained wrapped around her lower body. "*Then tell me what exactly he is,*" Vanessa said, speaking more seriously. Helen repositioned herself to face Vanessa with one leg comfortably on the bed, *"Ok honey, I will tell you as much as you need to know. But, you must promise not to act recklessly."*

"I won't. Mamma, just tell me what's going on with my son."

Helen took a deep breath and began to tell Vanessa about their family's past. Meanwhile, Lamar searched for a functioning bicycle from their backyard. Instead of walking to Matthew's house, he thought it would be more fun if he rode his bicycle there instead. But to his surprise, his bicycle had a flat tire. However, that did not stop Lamar. Instead, he decided to look for a different bike. Before long Lamar uncovered Samantha's old bike, it was hidden behind his grandfather's shed and covered with a blue plastic pool covering. Her bike was bright pink in color with white and blue tassels that hung from the sides of the handlebars. He pulled the bicycle from behind the shed and pushed it into the front yard, where he washed it off with the water hose. He used his hands as a cleaning cloth to scrub the bicycle clean and sprayed it with water.

Once the bicycle was cleaned, Lamar used his shirt to dry off the seat, and then he tore the tassels from the handlebars. Satisfied with his work, he rode off down the street on his new bicycle. He sped down the street as fast as he could, speeding past Matthew's house and around the corner. The bicycle zoomed over the cracked street with ease. He darted into small holes and jumped small curbs as if he were a skilled cyclist. His mind was clear, and no thoughts troubled him as he rode along, taking in the sights along the way. Before he realized it, he had arrived at the park. His heart danced in his chest as he rode towards the swings. He hopped off his bicycle once he entered the sandy area around the swing set. With his mind at peace, he sat in the swing and gazed into the day's sky. Lamar seemed to have found a brief moment of peace while his mother had just been debriefed of his situation.

"*What do you mean by that?*" Vanessa said as fear gripped her mind. "*Are you telling me that my brother was taken . . . KILLED by some . . . . CREATURE! And that same thing is after my son?!*"

Helen quickly stood to her feet and closed the room door firmly shut. "*It is extremely important that no one else knows about this. Although this is a family ordeal . . . if everyone were to know, there's a chance that a repeat of what happened to Quake could happen to us!*"

Vanessa pulled her legs in closer, "*And what are we supposed to do? Pretend like this isn't happening?!*"

"*All we can do is help Lamar through it.*"

"*What do you mean, 'help him through it?' You just told me something is gonna rip the soul out of my child! And you want me to just stand by and do nothing?!*"

Helen leaned over towards Vanessa and held her by the shoulders firmly, "*Then you tell me what to do. Tell me how to fight a godly creature, which has been around longer than the land we live on. TELL ME! Tell me how to get MY son back!*"

While the conversation between Vanessa and Helen reached its climax, Lamar and Nathaniel were having a conversation of their own. Nathaniel appeared on the neighboring swing in the form of a small child.

"*Why the hesitation? Do you not want my help against The Gatekeeper?*" Nathaniel asked. Lamar glanced over at the small

A New Struggle Begins

child and replied, *"A part of me doesn't see The Gatekeeper as a threat."*

"You alone have looked upon the true face of The Gatekeeper, and you are still hesitant?"

Lamar stood to his feet, *"I am not hesitant, Nathaniel. It is as you said. You and he are cut from the same cloth."* Lamar walked over to his bicycle, picked it up from the sand, and brushed it off. *"I'm going to Matthew's house now. Do not follow me, Nathaniel."* Lamar hopped back onto his bicycle and rode off towards Matthew's house. He took a shorter route on the way back as he grew more eager to play with Matthew. Once he could see Matthew's house in the distance, he noticed his mother's car just a short distance away. Lamar pulled over and stopped on the edge of the street to speak with his mother.

She pulled up next to him and rolled down her window; both Vanessa and Helen were in the car. *"Me and ya mamma are going to the store,"* Helen said with a smile. *"It seems you will need some new clothes. We will be back shortly. Falisha is home if you need anything."* Lamar simply nodded and said *Okay,* as he rode away.

Lamar quickly rode to Matthew's house, jumped from his bicycle, and rushed to the door. But before he could knock, Matthew's uncle Rheal opened the door. *"Is Matthew home?"* Lamar asked excitedly.

"No," Rheal replied in a stale and unpleasant tone.

"Okay," Lamar said with his head slightly tilted downward. He picked up his bicycle and sat in the driveway as Nathaniel spoke to his mind. *"You really should finalize our truce, child. I will not protect you from The Gatekeeper should you deny my offer."*

A New Struggle Begins

Lamar ignored Nathaniel's advice and started to head home, but before he could get a few feet out of Matthew's driveway, he noticed an ominous car in the distance. It was an old brown station wagon. The car sat in front of Lamar's house and slowly crept up the street in his direction. Lamar looked around as an unpleasant feeling coursed through his body. Lamar spoke aloud, *"I'm in no mood for your games, Nathaniel."*

"OH no child, this is not my doing. I am nowhere near you – as requested." Lamar got off his bike and began to walk home alongside it. The car crept closer and suddenly revved its engine as if it was preparing for a race. Lamar stopped. His hands trembled, and his body shook, but he never took his eyes off of the car. Again the car revved its engine. But this time, Lamar took off running and jumped onto his bike.

The car sped in Lamar's direction with a burst of burning rubber and a cloud of smoke behind it. Lamar jumped into the gutter to evade the speeding vehicle. However, the car swerved in his direction, jumping into the gutter with Lamar and smashing into his bike, sending Lamar crashing over the hood and onto the pavement. The car struck a neighboring fence and mailbox post, stopping it in its tracks.

Lamar laid in the street, and blood poured from his body onto the pavement. He was light-headed and could barely breathe. The sun gleaned across his face as a voice spoke aloud to him,

"Get up Lamar! Get up! He is backing up now! GET UP! OR YOU WILL BE CRUSHED!"

Tragic Accident

Without warning, the car's back wheels began to spin and screech, tossing up dirt and dust in the process. Lamar smacked himself across his face to restore his blurred vision. His eyes swayed back and forth as once foggy images grew clear. The sound of the car's spinning tires forced him to act quickly. He wobbled himself to his feet, twisting and turning until he stood upright. Lamar turned with his back facing the car and took a quick step, only to tumble straight to the pavement. He let out a painful shout as he fell. Pain surged throughout his body, but he could not pinpoint the exact area the pain stemmed from.

Lamar could feel the hair on his neck stand as if they were preparing for death. Time seemed to slow down. Lamar's movements were sluggish and staggered as he flipped himself over. He watched as the car freed itself and sped backward in his direction. Lamar reached behind him and pulled his body as hard as he could to avoid the speeding car, but there was nowhere he could go. He sat still and watched as the bumper of the car approached his face.

"There is no way I'm going to live through this," Lamar thought to himself. But instead of bracing himself for the inevitable impact, he watched helplessly as his life ended before his eyes.

A New Struggle Begins

The car crashed into Lamar's face, knocking his body down flat and crushing his nose on impact. It continued to drive in reverse, dragging Lamar's body along for the ride. His legs were crushed at the knees, exposing bone and all interior matter. His body skidded under the car like a speed bump, crushing his chest and causing his innards to burst from his stomach. His body tumbled as it was. The car continued to drag him along, leaving a trail of blood in the street. Lamar's eyes remained wide open as he witnessed his demise. He felt his bones break while the cold taste of iron rose from his blood-filled throat. He could feel the blood drain from his body as he was dragged about. The pain was so great that Lamar could not cry out. He could only watch as tears fell from his face.

Then, the car stopped.

Lamar could not breathe. He could not talk, nor could he feel pain, but for some reason, he still struggled to live. He lifted his battered and broken left arm into the air from under the car as if to signal for help, but just as he reached out, the car started driving forward slowly. The left tire crept towards his face inch by inch, but Lamar continued to reach out for help until the very end. The car's back tire slowly crawled up Lamar's head until the weight of the car pressed down on him. Lamar's hand fell flat to the ground as he felt the pressure of the car upon his head. He could hear sounds of cracking bones as his skull began to bend and break. His eyes bulged outward, nearly popping from their sockets. Lamar's hands lie flat on the pavement gripping the street as if it were made of sand. His vision faded into darkness as a popping sound like a newly opened champagne bottle echoed in his ears.

"What have you done, child?" Nathaniel said as he spoke to Lamar's mind. *"If you wished for death, you need only to ask, and I, Nathaniel, would have acted swiftly. But to willingly choose death*

By the hands of another is the same as choosing The Gatekeeper over me."

"*I am not that child,*" said Lamar as he stood to his feet in the darkness. "*I am he that dwells within that child. You cannot fool me with your mind games and parlor tricks, Nathaniel.*" Lamar waved his hand, and the world around him rewound itself until he and Nathaniel stood side by side. "*This is the current reality,*" Lamar said as he looked downward at the much younger version of himself.

"*It seems that you are the true Lamar, the one Gatekeeper protects,*" Nathaniel said as he examined the adult version of Lamar. "*You are not real, are you, child? Just a manifestation of his subconscious soul.*"

Lamar bent down towards his younger self and spoke aloud to Nathaniel, "*I am more real than this shell, and in this domain, I am **far** more powerful than you.*" Lamar stood up, his eyes still locked on his youthful self, "*I advise you not to address me as a child.*"

"*Let us test your theory, child,*" said Nathaniel as he readied himself.

"*Let us not,*" Lamar said as he walked towards Nathaniel. "*But a demonstration should suffice. I shall reach into that child and pull the dagger from him and stab you five times. If you are truly stronger, then stop me.*"

Lamar turned and reached for the dagger buried within the child's chest, but Nathaniel grabbed hold of his free hand and smashed Lamar with his tail. But to his surprise, Lamar was unphased by his attack and had already grabbed the dagger.

A New Struggle Begins

"You are indeed strong, child," said Nathaniel as he chuckled aloud.

Lamar quickly pulled the burrowed dagger from the child's chest and, with a flip of his wrist, held Nathaniel up in the air. *"I shall not repeat myself,"* Lamar said as he thrusted the dagger into Nathaniel's chest with each word. *"I. AM. NOT. A. CHILD."* Lamar then released Nathaniel from his grasp and landed a powerful punch in his mid-section and another to his face that sent him crashing to the ground.

"Do you believe me now, Nathaniel?" Lamar asked as he held the blade in his hand.

"You do possess some power," Nathaniel said as he arose from the crater, *"But explain thyself, manifested one."*

Lamar kneeled down and reached out for Nathaniel's hand, *"It is just as I claim. I am stronger than you are in this moment, and this place is not the real world. This place . . . all that you see is my doing."*

Nathaniel ignored Lamar's gesture of kindness and arose from the crater on his own. He firmly planted himself at Lamar's side as his tail lay at his feet. *"So this is the power that Gatekeeper wanted for himself."*

Lamar took a step forward and knelt down to the child's eye level and said, *"No, this is the power he has stolen for generations."*

"Stolen, you say?"

"Do not play coy with me, Nathaniel. The time for enlightenment through misdeeds has passed. As I said before, I am not this child, and you cannot fool me."

A New Struggle Begins

Nathaniel's curiosity peeked as he hovered above Lamar, *"Tell me manifested one, how much do you know?"*

Lamar placed his right hand gently on the child's shoulder and held the dagger tightly in the other. *"I know everything,"* he said as he slammed the blade into the child's chest. *"I know what really happened to Quake, I know the half-truths you spout to this child. I know why Leon nearly bled to death and hell, I even know how to kill you."*

Nathaniel's body began to grow cold as if he were readying for battle, *"Should I be worried, manifested one?"*

Lamar stood to his feet and smiled. *"Do not worry. If I wanted you dead, I would have killed you already."*

"You are starting to annoy me chil—" but before he could finish speaking, Lamar interrupted.

*"I am no use to you here, in this form, so if we **are** to kill The Gatekeeper, we must work together."* Nathaniel paused, then tilted his head slightly as if he were amused.

"Yess. Please, continue."

Lamar opened his hands and looked deep into them, *"In my present state, I am just a thought that resides within this child. Although I am all-powerful in this domain, in this world of dreams, I am also the most vulnerable."* Lamar looked directly at Nathaniel, his face serious and expressionless, *"In order to merge with this child, you would have to defeat me and forcefully take this body. Whether it be you or The Gatekeeper, I would be the last opponent you'd face."*

"So what do you propose," Nathaniel said as he walked over to the time frozen car. *"Should I cause this vehicle to veer off*

A New Struggle Begins

course without further damaging the child . . . or should I create a divine miracle and allow the child to escape unscathed? Nathaniel placed his hand on the car and turned around to face Lamar, *"Tell me, what is your agenda?"*

Lamar smiled, *"Now, where's the fun in that?"* He crouched beside the child and placed one hand on his head, *"All you need to do is watch, from within this vessel. I will allow you to occupy this space without being detected by The Gatekeeper. I shall then summon him to my side, and drag him here where WE shall do away with him together. However, this arrangement is temporary, and you will have no control over this vessel. You'll be like an esteemed guest in my home. Should you try anything, I will remove you, like a shoe would a cockroach."*

Lamar continued to speak, but Nathaniel remained silent.

"I will not need your help until The Gatekeeper is here. Then and only then can he become aware of your presence."

Nathaniel gripped the bumper of the car and climbed on top of the trunk, perching himself there with his tail draped across the side of the car, *"You are just a thought, a manifested will of a child. Tell me, how are you going to accomplish such feats?"*

Lamar replied, *"Like this."* He plunged himself into the child, taking over his body. Nathaniel watched as Lamar stood to his feet after joining with the child, *"Such a clever one you are."* Nathaniel said as he watched Lamar carefully.

*"Clever? No. Do not forget, I was once a part of this child. This is my vessel, **my** body. However, I am not the lump of flesh that you see now, so address me as his soul, the true Lamar."*

A New Struggle Begins

Nathaniel's body began to revert to his enigma state as he spoke to Lamar, *"Show me the path that you desire, let us begin . . . Lamar"*.

Nathaniel then unfroze time and watched the events unfold from within Lamar's mind. Once time had begun again, Lamar, now with his soul in control, managed to avoid the oncoming car but not without further damage. He was able to throw his torso from harm's way by lunging backward using his hands as propellers. The car zoomed past his head, torso, waist, and knees only to land smack in the center of his lower leg. He was able to avoid the brunt of the impact, but the car ran over one of his legs, snapping it in two. Lamar let out a horrifying shout that caught the attention of the driver. He slammed on breaks, and as the car swerved to a complete stop, then peered out the rearview mirror. Lamar was lying on the pavement in agony, holding his broken leg as blood spewed onto the street. The driver panicked. He quickly put the car in drive, and then sped off, never to be seen again.

After being brutally run over, Lamar's body was in a state of severe shock. He drug himself into a neighboring patch of grass and passed out. *"What are you doing, Lamar?"* Nathaniel said, speaking to Lamar from the depths of his mind. *"Is **this** your plan?"*

"Shut up, Nathaniel," Lamar replied. *"I'm working on it."*

"If you die, I will have you."

"If I die, all you will have is death. The Gatekeeper will see to that."

"Get up! I will not have you die before I have my chance!"

A New Struggle Begins

"You speak as if you cannot see . . . my leg is broken, I have internal bleeding and not to mention nearly half of my blood has painted the street!"

"I care not for your excuses, child!"

Lamar's eyes sprung open, "I am not a child!" he shouted as he struggled to sit up. He stammered to his knees as blood poured from his mouth and leg.

"Look there!" Nathaniel said. "Just ahead! The bicycle, get it." Without hesitation, Lamar closed his eyes and allowed Nathaniel to guide him towards the bicycle. He scooted and dragged himself along, leaving a trail of blood behind him. "I must reach the bicycle," Lamar thought to himself. "If I can get the bicycle, then I can get home. And if I can get home, I can get help."

Lamar began to feel a growing sensation within his mind, "Calm yourself, Nathaniel," Lamar said telepathically. "Do not give us away,"

"If you die, this is all for naught. I will intervene if I must!"

"You shall do no such thing!"

"Who is here to stop me?! You— The Gatekeeper?!" Lamar remained silent as he continued to reach for the bicycle. "Where is he? Where is this almighty protector of yours? You are on the brink of death, and he is nowhere to be found!"

"Shut up," Lamar shouted aloud.

"I shall do no such thing! Call upon him! Call him – your protector!"

"That is not how it works, damnit!"

A New Struggle Begins

Nathaniel's frustration intensified, *"I shall wait no longer!"* Just as Nathaniel was about to reveal himself to help Lamar until someone shouted out, *"There he is, oh my God. HURRY! Call 911!"* It was Rheal. He had seen the last few moments, he and his wife rushed to Lamar's aid. Rheal stopped Lamar from crawling, *"I'm here . . . be still,"* he said as he tore off his shirt and wrapped it around Lamar's broken Leg. "IT HURTS, IT HURTS!" Lamar shouted out as Rheal tried to stop the bleeding. *"Just hang in there,"* he replied.

Rheal picked up Lamar just as his wife pulled up next to them in her car. She cried out, *"Put him in."* Rheal quickly and carefully placed Lamar across the back seat, and his wife drove him home. Moments later, Rheal jumped out of the car and banged on the door of Lamar's house.

Lamar had begun to breathe short and shallow breaths. His heart rate was on a steady decline, and his vision was nearly absent. Rheal rushed back to the car with Falisha, Lamar's aunt, at his side.

He opened the door to the back seat and picked up Lamar. The torn shirt he had used to stop the bleeding fell from Lamar's leg allowing blood to pour out. Falisha screamed out in fear, *"Oh my lord! Get him in the house! Now!"*

She ran in front of Rheal, held the door open, and then sprinted to the sofa where Rheal laid his body down. Without thinking, Falisha instructed Rheal to find the ambulance and direct them to the house. She then wrapped Lamar's broken leg with clear wrap to stop the bleeding, propped his head up with pillows, and quickly scraped together some spider silk and Aloe vera. Once the clear wrap was completely saturated with blood, she pulled up a chair near Lamar's broken leg, sat down, and collected herself.

A New Struggle Begins

Her face flooded with tears as she held a pair of scissors and began to pray.

"*Oh lord, I have never seen this much blood,*" she said as she cut the wrap from Lamar's leg. "*Please guide me so I don't cause my nephew to die.*" Blood burst from the sealed wound. "*Guide me and steady my hand that I may relieve his pain.*" She wiped away the blood and packed the silk in the wound and around the protruding bone. "*Clear his mind that he may be at ease and keep him safe from further harm.*" She cut away the remaining wrapping and replaced it with clean cloths. "Protect his body, mind, and soul and allow him to endure." Falisha stood to her feet as tears streamed down her face, "*I have done all that I can, Lord. It's your turn now.*"

A sudden burst of energy flooded the house as the paramedics entered the home with Helen at the helm. Falisha burst into tears. "*Thank God!*" she shouted as she embraced Helen.

The paramedics rushed past them to analyze the situation. The first paramedic placed an oxygen mask over Lamar's nose to provide ample oxygen to his lungs. The second checked his pulse to ensure he had a strong heartbeat, while the third unwrapped his leg to assess the damage. The paramedic was able to pull the silk from the wound and successfully unwrap the leg without causing significant bleeding. After a few seconds, they determined that Lamar's broken bone needed to be re-positioned before moving him safely.

The third paramedic turned to Helen and Falisha and said, "*His leg has been broken almost perfectly in half. We must set the bone before we move his body to ensure there will be no further damage. Please step back and don't interfere.*"

A New Struggle Begins

The paramedics braced Lamar's body and quickly snapped his leg, opening up the wound. Lamar shouted out in agony as his body began to sweat profusely. He grabbed the closest medic and bit his arm, all while struggling to escape. The second medic held Lamar's legs and arms by laying his body partially on top of Lamar, restraining him. The last then forced the bone from Lamar's broken leg back in place. He gripped Lamar's ankle and knee cap then quickly jerked them together, causing the center bone to snap in place. Lamar screamed out in pain, then abruptly passed out.

The third medic ordered the second medic to check for a pulse, but when he did, his face turned cold. He looked back at the third medic and shook his head in disapproval. After seeing the medic's response and Lamar lying motionless, Falisha lunged herself at Lamar only to be stopped by the second medic. She kicked and screamed, demanding that they do something.

"He's dying! One of you do something! Help him! Help my nephew PLEASE!"

The third medic shouted, "CPR! Perform CPR quickly...Do it now!" The first medic began to breathe into Lamar's mouth and pressed on his chest in an effort to revive him. Again and again, the medic tried to revive Lamar, breath after breath after breath.

Helen stood watch as a familiar presence loomed within the room in the midst of the chaos. It hovered as a mist of smoke over Lamar's body and spoke so that only Helen could hear, "The fate of this child shall be decided on this day."

Enter Gatekeeper

After hearing the voice from the ominous cloud, Helen's heart sped up. She began to sweat profusely and clenched her chest as if she could not breathe. Her legs grew weak, and she collapsed to the floor with her eyes still locked on the cloud that hovered above Lamar. Falisha turned to her mother and rushed to her aid.

"Momma, what's wrong?" Falisha asked, holding Helen in her arms. But Helen couldn't speak. Her body trembled with fear as she held out her arm and pointed slowly in Lamar's direction. Falisha turned in the direction that Helen pointed and said, *"He's going to be ok, mom. Lamar is strong. He will pull through. All we have to do is believe and have faith."* Helen's eyes widened as Falisha spoke. It was clear that she was the only person that could see the cloud hovering above Lamar's lifeless body.

Helen bowed her head, closed her eyes, and took a deep breath, all in an effort to calm herself down. She then lifted her head to gaze upon Lamar once more.

The cloud that once loomed over him had now blanketed his body from head to toe, molding itself around him, *"Calm thyself elder mother, no harm shall come to his child."*

A New Struggle Begins

"Who . . . what are you?" Helen replied.

"I have been known by many names, but you may know me as the one who took your son away."

Helen's eyes widened as her heart grew heavy. She held Falisha, leaning on her as a crutch while she struggled to stand to her feet. *"It was you who took my son away!"* Helen blurted out towards Lamar's lifeless body. *"You killed him, and now you want my grandson!"*

Falisha held Helen tightly, hugging her as tears fell from her face, *"Mamma, calm down. Lamar will pull through."*

"Girl, let me go!" Helen shouted. *"He's going to kill Lamar if we don't stop him. He's gonna die just like your brother!"*

Helen's outburst caused the medics to lose focus, *"Ma'am, we are doing the best we can. Please calm down and let us do our job."*

Helen broke free from Falisha's grasp and stumbled over to Lamar. She reached out to place her hand on his head but was stopped by the first medic. He held her arm tightly to stop her advance, *"Calm down ma'am. If you cannot contain yourself, your grandson will die for sure."*

Although the medic spoke directly to Helen, her eyes remained locked on the creature. *"Ma'am, are you ok?"* the medic asked as he gazed into her eyes. But Helen did not respond; she simply stared into space. Helen appeared to have calmed down, allowing Falisha to help her to the nearby chair.

"Mamma, are you ok?" Falisha asked with a puzzled expression. Helen remained in a daze, her eyes locked on Lamar as

A New Struggle Begins

if they had had an intense conversation. She suddenly spoke aloud, *"Please don't take him from us, creature."*

"Mom, who are you talking to?" Falisha asked. Helen's eyes suddenly shifted towards Falisha then back at Lamar, causing Falisha to step back, stumbling over herself. She remained silent as Helen spoke in a whisper to the mysterious creature.

"Elder one, why do you detest me so?"

"You took my son from me."

"I did no such thing. This family is special in ways you cannot fathom, and your son was no exception."

"I know the monster that you are, I've heard the stories, seen what you call help, and you are no savior."

"You have only heard the lies humans have told. Humans that are not of this family."

"Then why do you kill us? If we are the family you speak so highly of, then why?"

"There are many things that are still unknown to you, elder. I do not kill this family. Look. Even now, I have healed this child. His internal injuries are gone, his blood loss restored, and—"

"And yet he does not wake. You have only aided him as means to an end, one that only suits you!"

There was a long pause. The Gatekeeper did not reply to Helen's previous statement; he simply remained silent. *"He's breathing, he's breathing!"* shouted one of the medics, *"Good, now let's put him on the stretcher and get him to the hospital."*

A New Struggle Begins

Two of the medics rushed to the ambulance to retrieve an adjustable stretcher, while the third remained behind to monitor Lamar's vitals.

"*Speak!*" Helen blurted out. "*Tell me why my grandson hasn't woken up yet!*"

The medic quickly turned around to face Helen with his right hand placed firmly on his chest, "*Oh my God, you scared me!*" The medic said with a frightened expression, "*I am convinced that your grandson will be fine.*" Although the medic continued to speak, Helen continued to stare in Lamar's direction. "*We have stabilized him and stopped the bleeding. Unfortunately, there isn't much else we can do from here, so we will need to take him to the hospital right away.*"

"*Which hospital are you taking him to?*" Falisha asked. She stood closer to Helen. "*We responded to the emergency call by our dispatch from Gifford Memorial Hospital, being that we were the closest ambulance to this area. But this city is smack dab in between our hospital in Gifford and your neighboring city Samaria. We can go to either, but if you prefer one to the other, it's fine.*"

"*Let's go to the one in Gifford. It's a little closer, and that's the hospital we, as a family, trust the most.*"

"*That's a great idea. It's good to have some degree of familiarity when dealing with stressful situations like this.*"

Just as the medic and Falisha agreed to take Lamar to Gifford Memorial Hospital, the other medics burst into the living room with the stretcher in hand. "*Alright, let's get him on and out to the hospital as fast as we can.*"

"*WAIT!*" shouted Helen, with her eyes still locked on Lamar. "*Something is not right. The creature has healed Lamar, and*

A New Struggle Begins

yet he isn't awake. *Something is wrong."* The medics all looked at one another with puzzled expressions.

"Ma'am are you okay?" one of the medics asked. Suddenly Falisha screamed out, *"His eyes are open!"*

Lamar's eyes were wide open as a sinister grin coated his face. *"Hello everyone,"* Lamar said as he sat up on the sofa with his legs stretched outward. The medics stood in the background, confused by what was unfolding in front of them.

"Hi there. We need you to lay back down. We don't want you to hurt yourself more than you already are."

Lamar looked at the medic who spoke to him and replied, *"Don't you worry yourself, little man. You should be more concerned about your own well-being."*

Lamar then turned himself to face Helen, "Hey Granny. How have you been?" But before she could reply, the cloud that once coated Lamar spoke from the corner of the room. It had freed itself from Lamar's body and gathered in the corner of the Living room.

"Caution, elder mother, this child isn't the Lamar you are familiar with."

"Quiet, Gatekeeper!" Lamar suddenly blurted out in a menacing tone, causing the medics to flee to the opposite side of the room where they stood next to Helen and Falisha. *"You are the source of this family's adversities, the very root of our misfortune. How dare you give caution to anyone!?"*

Falisha and the medics watched as Helen continued to stare at Lamar while sitting comfortably on the sofa as if he had not been hit by a car. *"Something is not quite right with this family,"* said one of the medics, *"It's time to go."*

It was common for the medics not to reveal their anxieties to the general public, but that practice soon faded once Helen began to speak.

"Lamar, is that you?" Helen asked cautiously.

"Yes, I am Lamar. The real Lamar."

"Are you my grandson, or aren't you? No need to play coy with me, child."

Lamar smiled and proceeded to speak, but the medics took action. *"Now, Brandon! Go! Run for the door!"* shouted the first medic to the second. Brandon bolted for the door, pushing through Helen and Falisha along the way. *"Susan! Jack! Follow me!"* Shouted Brandon as he neared the door. Helen had been forced to the floor by the fleeing medics, nearly breaking her fragile bones as they trampled over her fingers and legs.

"How dare you!" shouted The Gatekeeper. However, the medics could not see or hear The Gatekeeper's threats. Instead, they grabbed the door handle and swung it open as they made their escape, only to slam into an invisible barrier.

"You shall not escape my wrath!" shouted The Gatekeeper. *"Let us not repeat history Gatekeeper,"* Lamar replied in a humorous tone. *"Keep them trapped.....here. They shall be of use to me soon."*

Lamar stood to his feet as his broken leg began to heal within the bandages. He walked over to Helen and helped her up, placing her in the nearby chair. *"What the hell is going on here!?"* Brandon shouted. Susan began to scream and point at Lamar, *"He's walking! Oh my God, he's walking with a broken leg! He's a devil! We have to get out of here!"*

Lamar turned to face the panicking medics and walked back over to the sofa, where he laid back down. *"Oh no, I'm no the devil. I'm far more terrifying."*

The cloud-like creature began to take form slowly, vanishing from Helen's sight. *"Where did you go, my guardian?"* Helen said as she regained her composure.

"You cannot see me in this form. Only when I answer your prayers am I visible to you. Lamar and others like him are the only humans that can look upon me."

As Helen spoke aloud to the vanishing creature, the medics began to plot a second escape plan. Susan let out a high-pitched scream, causing everyone in the home to look in her direction while Brandon dashed over and took Helen as a hostage. He pulled a knife from a compartment on his med-pack and placed it to her neck. *"Everyone get the fuck back, or she dies."* Falisha, who stood just inches from Helen, lifted up her arms as if she were under arrest, *"Oh my lord,"* she shouted.

"Susan! Jack! Get your asses over here! It's time to get the hell out of here!" Susan and Jack ran for the other door across from the dining room. *"The damn door is locked,"* Susan shouted.

"What the fuck is going on here?! You bastards better let us go, RIGHT NOW!" Brandon shouted as he pressed the knife against Helen's neck, piercing her skin. Helen's face tensed up with pain as she remained silent.

Without further hesitation, The Gatekeeper stepped in, *"This foolishness must end now."* With a wave of his hand, The

A New Struggle Begins

Gatekeeper stopped time and readied himself to slaughter all of the medics, but to his surprise, Lamar intervened.

"Don't act so rash, Gatekeeper. That's a human trait."

The Gatekeeper paused, turned towards Lamar, then spoke calmly, *"So you are not alone I see."*

"Not quite. I harbor an old friend of yours, but before we dismiss the pleasantries, let us watch this event unfold. I'm curious to see a glimpse of this family in action."

"This family?"

"Have you forgotten Gatekeeper? I have not inhabited this body for some time now. And the bonds that this vessel shares with this family are not my own."

The Gatekeeper then sat next to Lamar, curious about what will happen next. *"I am eager to see how today's events will unfold. You and Nathaniel working side by side is quite unusual."*

The Gatekeeper unfroze time as the knife pierced Helen's neck deeper. *"I'm not playing with you guys. I will kill this old lady,"* shouted Brandon. Suddenly Helen closed her eyes and relaxed her body, allowing Brandon to hold her up. *"Hey, Granny! Don't you pass out on me here! HEY!!"* Brandon lost focus of the knife and struggled to stand while holding himself and Helen's weight. As soon as his attention had become diverted, Falisha took a firm step forward and shouted,

"HEY, BRANDON!"

As he turned to look at Falisha, she landed a massive punch to the center of his face that caused him to drop the knife and

A New Struggle Begins

release Helen from his grasp. Once freed, Helen opened her eyes, then turned and kicked him in his crotch as hard as she could.

Brandon fell to his knees, holding himself, but before anyone else could react to what had just happened, Lamar stepped in to deliver the final blow, A swift and powerful front kick to the face.

"Hell yeah! That felt good! Who else wants some?!" Lamar shouted, jumping around in circles.

"No one," The Gatekeeper replied as he had already refrozen time and stood behind Lamar.

"What? Damnit Gatekeeper, you're a party poop—"

Before Lamar could finish speaking, The Gatekeeper grabbed him by his neck and said aloud, *"You have satisfied your curiosity. Now it's my turn."*

Lamar pulled the dagger from within himself and gripped The Gatekeeper by the head, *"Yes, let us satisfy our hunger, NOW!"* Lamar smiled sinisterly as he stabbed himself with the dagger. The Gatekeeper reached for Lamar's hand, but the blade had vanished, leaving a gaping hole in Lamar's stomach.

"You foolish child . . . what have you done?"

"You shall soon find out first hand, my glorious protector. Now let the battle for my soul begin."

Nathaniel VS The Gatekeeper

"Come forth, he who dwells within the generations—the devourer of souls and keeper of time. Burn away the flesh and consume the mind. Merge us as one, an everlasting bind."

The Gatekeeper flung Lamar onto the couch effortlessly. He turned and faced him as his body altered, taking on the form he used to combat Nathaniel. His massive tail lay at his feet as he poised himself in front of Lamar.

"You have triggered events that I have fought for generations to conceal. I am very disappointed."

"Disappointed! You have no right to be disappointed. You have taken the souls of countless people. Countless! And you are disappointed because I chose to fight back!?"

"No. I am disappointed because you will lose."

The Gatekeeper lodged his tail into Lamar's head, *"You want to merge with me prematurely then endure every second of it."* The Gatekeeper's second tail slithered along the floor as Lamar cried out in agony. *"This time, it won't be a dream. If you die here . . . then you die."* The Gatekeeper's second tail struck Lamar in the stomach, precisely where Nathaniel's dagger had pierced his flesh. Lamar's body began to quiver. Thick foam spewed from his mouth as his eyes rolled to the back of his head. His heart stopped, and his struggles ceased. He sat motionless on the sofa, nearly dead, as The Gatekeeper spoke aloud, *"Calm be thy mind. Calm be thy spirit. Calm be thy soul that I may enter it."*

Once he'd finished speaking, The Gatekeeper dislodged his second tail from Lamar's stomach and spoke to the vessel directly, *"I am coming for you."*

Lamar's lifeless corpse replied as the foam fell from its mouth, *"Preparations have been made. Come Gatekeeper, we all await your arrival."*

The Gatekeeper's body began to glow vibrant crimson. He turned to look upon the time frozen family once more; then, by using his tail as a bridge, The Gatekeeper merged himself with Lamar's body entering his soul through Lamar's corpse.

Once inside, The Gatekeeper didn't recognize the vast space. It was entirely different from his previous visit. There were no signs of life, just an empty, desolate, and spacious plain.

"Gatekeeper! Welcome!" The voice resonated from behind him, but before The Gatekeeper could fully turn to face the voice's source, he was brutally attacked. *"Oh, this feels good,"* the voice said as it continued its onslaught with a flurry of strikes, knocking The Gatekeeper to the floor of the dimension. *"This is too good to be true. The mighty Gatekeeper reduced to a mere punching bag."* The Gatekeeper struggled to stand to his feet. He used his tail as a crutch, leaning back onto it while searching his surroundings for his attacker.

"I have not come here for you, creature. I am here for the boy. Return him."

"There is no captor here, Gatekeeper."

A New Struggle Begins

"Do not speak as though you retain all knowledge. You are as foolish as an infant."

"Ohh, am I now?"

The Gatekeeper stood to his feet just before the voice struck again, but this time The Gatekeeper was able to fend off the attack by capturing his attacker with his tail.

"There you are, Nathaniel."

"The child is mine, Gatekeeper."

"SILENCE!" shouted The Gatekeeper. *"You imbecile, he is far beyond your grasp!"*

Nathaniel's wings sprouted from his back, allowing him to break free from The Gatekeeper's clutches. *"You are not as strong here as you are in the real world, Gatekeeper."*

"I am still far more powerful than you, Enigma."

"Oh no, Gatekeeper. Not at all."

After escaping from The Gatekeeper's grasp, Nathaniel landed a few feet in front of The Gatekeeper with his wings spread out full length. *"I am the stronger one here,"* Nathaniel said joyously.

"I shall enjoy watching Nathaniel strip the life from you." As Nathaniel retracted his wings, Lamar stepped forward, but this was not the child from before. It was his soul incarnate, *"I am all-powerful in this domain, and by my decree, you shall die."*

The Gatekeeper quickly readied himself, his armor brightened, and he posed for battle. Lamar raised his arm and pointed at The Gatekeeper, *"Kill him."*

A New Struggle Begins

Without hesitation, Nathaniel lunged at The Gatekeeper, but before he could strike, The Gatekeeper vanished. Nathaniel quickly grounded himself and let out a powerful aura as hundreds of spike-like appendages spewed out from his body in all directions, skewering The Gatekeeper multiple times. Despite his wounds, The Gatekeeper landed a devastating blow on Nathaniel with his tail, causing him to retract his appendages and pummeling him to the floor. The Gatekeeper then flew up into the sky and crashed down unto Nathaniel. *"I will make sure you cease to be this time, Enigma,"* The Gatekeeper then kicked Nathaniel in the stomach mercilessly, tearing away his exoskeleton. *"This will be our last battle, Nathaniel The Enig...."*

Before The Gatekeeper could finish speaking or deliver the final blow, Lamar stepped into the fight and back-handed The Gatekeeper sending him flying off into the distance. Lamar then kneeled down and began to heal Nathaniel, *"The Gatekeeper did not lose any strength once he entered this domain; he is simply more cautious here."*

"Do not toy with me boy," Nathaniel said as Lamar healed his wounds. *"I know he has lost much of his strength. I can sense it."*

Lamar placed his hand gently on top of Nathaniel's chest and pushed Nathaniel deeper into the floor with his incredible power, *"No. You don't sense his loss of power. What you feel is...."*

Lamar quickly turned around only to meet The Gatekeeper's fist. He had punched Lamar in the stomach knocking him off into the distance as his tail wrapped around Nathaniel, lifting him into the air then smashing him into the floor once more. Again and again, and yet again. The Gatekeeper repeatedly tossed

A New Struggle Begins

Nathaniel around with his tail like a ragdoll. *"Do you see the difference in our power, Nathaniel?"*

Before Nathaniel could speak, Lamar rejoined the fight. He landed a solid kick to The Gatekeeper's blind spot, nearly severing his head from his body. Worried that the next blow from Lamar would be his last, The Gatekeeper flung Nathaniel at Lamar, using him as a temporary shield while his wings sprouted from his back, encasing himself in armor like a bat.

Lamar's lust for vengeance pushed him forward. He grabbed Nathaniel by the wings and flung him back towards The Gatekeeper so that he could serve as a useful distraction. Once The Gatekeeper had encased himself, Nathaniel's armor collided with The Gatekeeper's, enabling Lamar to approach from The Gatekeeper's blindside once more. Just as their bodies collided, Lamar sped behind The Gatekeeper and tore open a hole in his armor, but The Gatekeeper's second tail burst through his armored wing and stabbed Lamar in the shoulder.

Lamar tumbled to the floor as The Gatekeeper uncased himself and took to the sky above, *"You are fast Gatekeeper, but this is my domain. There is no place you can go that I cannot."* Lamar sprouted angelic wings from his back and took to the sky after The Gatekeeper while Nathaniel watched helplessly from below, his body battered and beaten.

"Just what is going on here? I am Nathaniel, The Enigma! How can I be defeated so easily?" Nathaniel stammered to his feet, *"The Gatekeeper is supposed to be much weaker here...I know he is much weaker! I can feel it!"* Nathaniel continued to watch their fight as The Gatekeeper struggled to keep up with Lamar. *"This creature, this child . . . is he truly human?"* Nathaniel stepped forward as he intended to join the fight, but another presence

A New Struggle Begins

called out to him. Nathaniel paused, looked around, then took to the sky to rejoin the battle. He sprouted two sphere-shaped appendages as he flew towards Lamar and The Gatekeeper. Nathaniel flung his appendages towards both of them, stopping their battle cold. His first appendage struck Lamar in the center of his chest then quickly changed its shape to mimic a rope. Next, the appendage wrapped itself around Lamar's upper body, binding his arms to his torso and locking his legs together, constricting his movements.

With his wings free, Lamar watched helplessly as the second appendage struck The Gatekeeper. But instead of unraveling itself like a rope, it spread across his body like a rapidly growing mold, thickening and hardening as it spread across his body. The Gatekeeper struggled to remove the substance, but it had quickly entangled him.

"Out of my way, boy! The Gatekeeper is mine!"

Nathaniel flew past Lamar and smashed into The Gatekeeper dragging him into the domain floor. Restricted by Nathaniel's appendages, The Gatekeeper could only endure the fall. He braced himself for the bone-shattering impact. Just as they neared the bottom of the domain, The Gatekeeper spoke, *"That creature is using you."* Before Nathaniel could fully grasp what The Gatekeeper had said, they collided with the domain floor with enough power to devastate a country.

The Gatekeeper let out a fearsome and painful roar, one that frightened Nathaniel. The impact from their collision left a massive crater, a mile in diameter and over a mile deep.

The Gatekeeper lay stretched out in agony at the bottom of the pit. His body was dismembered, and his armored exoskeleton was nearly completely destroyed.

A New Struggle Begins

Nathaniel stood on the top of the crater's entrance staring down at The Gatekeeper. *"That was a swift change of events,"* Lamar said as he slowly descended behind Nathaniel. *"Not even I could inflict such pain on the mighty Gatekeeper,"* Nathaniel remained silent as he continued to watch The Gatekeeper from above. *"Don't tell me you are afraid of him...was that the first time you heard his true voice?"*

Nathaniel replied, *"Silence creature. I've come to understand that you are not what you claim."* He then retracted his wings and recalled the appendage that bound Lamar.

"I could have broken free at any time had I wanted to," Lamar said as he walked towards Nathaniel and stood at his side.

"I know," Nathaniel replied.

"The current Gatekeeper is as strong as I. He could have freed himself in an instant had he wanted."

"I know."

"I wonder. Why do you think he would allow you to cause him such pain knowing he cannot heal himself here? In this place, he is the most vulnerable, yet he allowed himself to sustain such injury. Well nevertheless, this only accelerates my plan to—"

"Silence boy, he is moving." Nathaniel jumped down into the crater as Lamar shouted from its edge, *"Careful Nathaniel, the real fight is about to begin,"* but Nathaniel was fixated on The Gatekeeper so much that he didn't hear Lamar's warning. The Gatekeeper let out yet another furious roar that stopped Nathaniel cold. His body trembled with fear as he watched The Gatekeeper in shock.

A New Struggle Begins

"I shall obliterate you all!" shouted The Gatekeeper as he thrashed about in pain. He struggled to his feet then let out a massive burst of energy. His chest exploded as an abundance of light expelled from within him. He began to tear away at himself, ripping off his armor plating as his innards fell to the floor. His tail stretched up above his head, then crashed down onto the floor of the crater shattering its casing. Again The Gatekeeper let out a roar, but it was more concentrated than before. His body shimmered brighter than any known color, then suddenly dulled.

There was silence in the domain. No one spoke a word.

The Gatekeeper lifted his head and turned to face Nathaniel as his armor flaked away. Lamar quickly shouted at Nathaniel, *"He's coming! Brace yourself!"*

The Gatekeeper's body exploded with enough force to destroy a small planet. Lamar flew towards Nathaniel, grabbed him by his face, and attempted to sling him across the dimension as fast as he could, but The Gatekeeper was much faster. He out sped the shock wave of his own explosion and caught Nathaniel before Lamar could throw him. Moving faster than light itself, The Gatekeeper plunged his hand through Nathaniel's chest and slapped Lamar back into the oncoming shock wave from the blast.

The Gatekeeper floated mid-air over the explosion with Nathaniel's corpse in his hand. His body radiated in a brilliance of colors as his tail hung below his feet. *"You cannot win. This creature called Nathaniel is no more."*

Enter Powerful One

Once the dust from the explosion had settled, Lamar stood at its epicenter unharmed. He brushed the dust from his shoulders then vanished only to reappear in front of The Gatekeeper. *"What will you do now, Gatekeeper? I am no fool. Creatures like yourself cannot be killed in such a primitive way. No physical attack of any kind can kill . . . your kind. So what will you do with Nathaniel?"* Lamar waited for The Gatekeeper to reply, but he remained silent. *"I have an idea,"* Lamar said with a smile, *"Give him to me."*

Lamar reached out for Nathaniel's corpse, but The Gatekeeper did not budge. *"Give me that damned creature Gatekeeper!"* Lamar shouted as he tried to snatch Nathaniel from The Gatekeeper's clutches, only to be smacked away by The Gatekeeper's massive tail. *"What will you do with him then, Gatekeeper? He cannot be killed . . . and I will **not** allow you to leave this domain with him."*

The Gatekeeper remained silent. He ripped his hand from Nathaniel's chest and wrapped his tail around his lifeless body. The Gatekeeper's back softened, resembling beach sand, as he attached Nathaniel's body to his own. The Gatekeeper never took his eyes off of Lamar. He waited to see how he would react to his actions.

A New Struggle Begins

"Are you serious, Gatekeeper?" Lamar said as he laughed aloud. *"Do you really want to kill Nathaniel so much that you'd revert back to the way you were before!?"* Lamar continued to laugh, but The Gatekeeper did not respond; he remained poised while his tail slightly swung back and forth. *"I don't care why you've suddenly had a change of heart . . . . After generations of killing, generations of my family falling prey to you, and now you have a change of heart! FUCK THAT!"* Lamar's voice began to deepen as his body began to change back to the way it was during their first encounter. His face stretched as his bones broke and reformed in the shape of a ferocious lion. His chest blistered with muscle as his hands sprouted forth claws. A lion's mane covered his neck, back, and midsections, and a thick devilish tail sprouted from his spine. He resembled a lion-like man-beast with fangs and retractable claws. His skin was gray and mottled with black, while his mane was black and white with grey frosted tips.

"Gatekeeper, the last time we met, I warned you to never come here again. Yet here you stand before me once more." Lamar's rage boiled over as he grew in size, but The Gatekeeper did not flinch. *"You puny piece of shit!"* shouted Lamar as he readied himself for an attack. To his surprise, The Gatekeeper started to descend to the domain's floor without protecting himself. This simple gesture calmed Lamar's rage and piqued his curiosity.

Lamar followed The Gatekeeper to the floor of the domain, towering over him 100 fold. Lamar touched down moments after The Gatekeeper causing the entire space to rumble below his feet. He watched The Gatekeeper intensely as he began to speak, *"Calm the fire that burns within you, my child,"* said The Gatekeeper in a saddened tone. *"There is no need to hurry. This shall be our last exchange."* Lamar remained silent as he listened closely to what The Gatekeeper had to say. *"I have fought many souls, devoured many souls, and never have I met a soul like yours. You cannot beat me child, but you are welcome to try. However, allow me to bestow the gift of knowledge."*

Without warning, Lamar felt immense pain branch from his stomach and stretch throughout his body, but The Gatekeeper displayed no signs of motion, *"What did you do to me, you despicable creature?"* Lamar shouted as he fell to his knees, causing the entire domain to shake violently.

"I struck you, my child," The Gatekeeper replied.

"Son of a –ugh! I didn't even see you move!" Lamar shouted as he held his gut with his left hand and braced himself with the other.

"It is not fatal . . . only about five . . . no . . . less than five percent of my true ability." The Gatekeeper took a step forward and kicked Lamar, causing him to fall backwards onto his back. *"I wish to tell you my story,"* he said as he leaped onto Lamar's chest, planting his feet firmly into Lamar's body. *"You shall be the first to hear my story without human lies."*

"I don't care for your life story, Gatekeeper!" shouted Lamar as he reached out his hand, *"I already know **what** you are, and your life's story won't change **anything** you've already done!"* Just as Lamar's hand neared The Gatekeeper's chest, it was swatted away, and The Gatekeeper plunged his tail directly into the base of Lamar's head. Lamar shouted out in pain as he tried to snatch out the tail. However, his movement suddenly grew heavy and sluggish as The Gatekeeper emitted his own gravitational field that paralyzed Lamar, stopping his movement cold.

"Be still child, and learn. See my past that was. See me for what I am."

A New Struggle Begins

The force emitted by The Gatekeeper was so great that Lamar couldn't speak or blink his eyes. He laid flat on the floor, helpless as The Gatekeeper had the upper hand. *"Let us begin by tearing away the lies that Nathaniel placed into your mind."*

Lamar began to see flashes of his ancestral past. He saw himself play with Quake day in and day out. He watched himself and Quake embark on multiple adventures, overcoming every obstacle that stood before them. *"Do you understand, child? You and Quake had known each other far before Nathaniel brought you to the past."* Although Lamar could not speak, his thoughts could reach The Gatekeeper, so he spoke aloud through his thoughts.

"I cannot be fooled with these childish mind games."

"Oh no child, this is no trick. What you see is true. These are your memories."

Lamar's eyes closed and reopened as he entered his past. He stood on the edge of the village just before it was set aflame. He marveled at the beauty of the land. *"Go. Find Quake and see how I came to be."* Lamar took a single step forward, and day suddenly turned to night. *"Go. Find him."* Without further hesitation, Lamar ran towards Quake's home, but it seemed different. It was decorated in gold and silver, and the door was decorated with flower petals and honey. The windows were marked in red dye as the ground was saturated with sacrificial blood. *"What is this place, Gatekeeper? What lies are you manifesting here?"*

"This is no lie child, but truth. This place where you thought Quake had lived is, in fact, the ritual chamber."

"What?!"

A New Struggle Begins

"Go. Enter, and see for yourself."

Lamar walked towards the door but couldn't open it. There wasn't a handle or knob to grasp hold of. He stared at the door, and with each passing moment, he felt more and more familiar with the structure and its entryway. Lamar reached out with both hands and placed them in a hidden slot parallel to the door's edge. His finger slid into the hidden compartment, and he pushed the door open with ease.

"What?! How . . . what did I just do?!"

"It seems that you have been here before. Enter the chamber and witness my birth to this place."

Lamar entered the chamber, and to his surprise, it looked exactly as it did when Quake and his family were killed, with one exception. Quake's mother, Efrin, was kneeling on the floor with her head bowed and her arms stretched out wide. Her knees were planted firmly beneath her, and she wore decorative clothing that shimmered with each breath she took. She raised her head and pressed her hands to the sky, her earrings chimed, and her bracelets gleamed in the light as she spoke,

"You have given me all that I desire. A husband of vigor and pride, a land to call my own, and my beautiful firstborn, Quake. You have bestowed upon me wonders that stretch beyond the eye's sight and prosperity that is as vast as the deepest waters. Even now, I bare the fruits of your kindness, a second child to call my own. But I feel others do not understand your power . . . your benevolence. I ask you for one last request…."

Her head quickly shifted towards the doorway where Lamar stood. His heart sped up as he thought he had been caught,

A New Struggle Begins

"*Calm yourself child,*" said The Gatekeeper, "*Do not miss what happens next.*"

Suddenly Melfice stormed into the chamber and grabbed Efrin by the arm.

"*What have you done, Efrin?!*"

"*I have done nothing!*"

"*Nothing! You sit here in this chamber praying to some forsaken deity while your family, your son, is being frowned upon! Have you any idea the shame it brings to me . . . to this family?!*"

"*Quake lives because of my traditions and prayers!*"

"*Foolishness!*"

"*It is not foolish to have faith!*"

"*You will stop this madness now, or I will....*"

"*You will what, Melfice? Will you kill your wife to satisfy this bloodthirsty kingdom?!*"

"*This bloodthirsty kingdom is our home!*"

"*NO! It's your home, not mine. I don't belong here...I see how you all look at me. The way you and the others talk about me. My unborn child has shown me everything!*"

"*This is madness! First, it was Quake. Now it's your unborn child?! When will this end, Efrin? When our son cannot make any friends? Or when the kingdom revolts against me? This has to stop . . . for all of our sake.*"

A New Struggle Begins

Efrin raised her hand and quickly slapped Melfice across his face, *"I don't care what happens to these people. They can die for all I care."*

Before Melfice could react, the chamber floor shook as an explosion erupted from the distance, *"Did you hear that?"* Melfice asked.

"Don't change the subject...you know how hard it was for me to have children! You know my customs are foreign to this land, so why do you treat me like this!?"

"Quiet, Efrin!"

"I will not be silenced!"

Melfice forcibly closed Efrin's mouth with his hand and scanned the chamber quietly. He could hear footsteps and chanting from outside the chamber.

"Kill the wench and the king! Death to them both...."

"...Kill them, Kill them KILL THEM...."

Vast members of the kingdom stood outside the chamber, chanting for the death of their leaders. They had toppled over a massive tree and used it to block the entrance of the chamber. *"Death to the king and his wench!"* shouted one person. *"Burn them alive!"* shouted another.

Efrin pushed Melfice away and flung herself to the floor. She shouted in anger as tears fell from her face, *"Kill them all! Punish them for all eternity!"* Melfice grabbed Efrin by her feet then pulled her from her praying position, *"That is what got us into this mess!"*

A New Struggle Begins

"No, **you** are the reason we are here! Do not blame me for your kingdom's downfall!"

"You ungrateful bitch! I took you into my home, cared for you when no one else would. I fed you, clothed you, and this is how you repay me?!"

"You have done nothing for me! Everything you've ever done was to soothe your own grief. You killed families on your conquest for power. Ravaged women and treated the heads of kings' as spoils of war. Do not treat me as if you are favorable when it was you who slaughtered my land!"

"Stay your tongue, woman!"

"I will not!"

Efrin stood to her feet, pushed Melfice to the floor, and then reached for the sacrificial knife that lay on the mantel. Melfice rolled himself onto his stomach and pulled Efrin's feet from underneath her, causing her to collapse to the floor and knocking her unconscious. After watching her body fall to the floor, Melfice slowly stood to his feet and peered over at Efrin's body. The dagger that she had attempted to reach had found its way into her chest. Melfice's stood to his feet as his world had suddenly been turned upside down. His wife lay dead at his feet as the kingdom he spent his life building was tearing itself apart. His mind drifted in possibility for a while until he heard a voice from outside speak to him, "Bring us the head of Efrin, and we will know she has not tainted you, my king!" Then another voice spoke, "Yes my lord bring us her head!"

"But she is my wife," Melfice replied. "She is with child, of eight months. To kill her is to kill my unborn." Despite his attempts to reason with the angered mob, it would only fall onto deaf ears.

A New Struggle Begins

"If you cannot bring us her head, then you should die with her!"

"No!" shouted Melfice. He ran over to Efrin's body and pulled the dagger from her chest, causing her to enter an early labor. Without second-guessing his options, he slammed the dagger into Efrin's neck in an attempt to cut off her head, but the blade didn't pierce her flesh. Efrin's eyes opened, and she gazed upon her would-be murderer and said calmly, *"Kill them all, my Lord."*

Melfice franticly pushed Efrin's body away from him and shouted, *"Help! She isn't human! She isn't human!"* He rushed towards the door, pleading for his freedom but was met with fire. The Villagers had set the chamber ablaze and refused to release either of them.

As the small chamber filled with smoke, Melfice could see a figure in the distance take form. It stepped into the chamber from the shadows and walked directly towards Efrin's body. It peered down at her and let out a mighty roar that killed all the villagers who stood outside the chamber. The creature then turned towards Melfice and spoke clearly to his mind, *"You despicable creature."*

Melfice shouted out for help, but no one answered. The creature then moved across the room and stood in front of Melfice in an instant. It grabbed him by the neck and tore open a hole in the ceiling of the chamber.

"You shall watch as your kingdom burns to ash."

The mysterious creature then levitated until he held Melfice over the roof of the chamber. ***"Burn,"*** the creature said as he held Melfice out in front of him. Fire began to erupt from beneath the streets, burning all that had been built. The screams of fleeing women and children and the aroma of burning flesh filled the air.

"Show me no more!" Lamar suddenly shouted, interrupting The Gatekeeper's memory.

"Oh no child, there is more, much more."

"I don't need to see more, I get it. You were brought to this world because Efrin wished it so."

"I am no conjured-up manifestation of man's will. I am much more than that."

"Spit it out then! What do you wish for me to know?!"

Although Lamar and The Gatekeeper spoke back and forth to each other, the memory continued. The Gatekeeper had burned the kingdom to the ground and lowered himself and Melfice back down into the chamber where he intended to kill him. *"Look there child,"* The Gatekeeper said as Quake stood his ground against the mysterious creature. *"Nathaniel had shown you this part with a little tampering, but watch."* Just as the creature killed the unborn child Quake charged forward to attack the creature, only to be overpowered. *"You shall witness this first hand,"* said The Gatekeeper as he slung Lamar into the creatures grasp, inserting him directly into his memory.

Lamar was now trapped inside The Gatekeeper's memory, forced to live it out as if he were there. *"You are quite strong child,"* said the creature as he held Quake by the neck. *"To have manifested a soul from generations to come, takes immense power. And you disembodied soul, what are you called?"*

"Don't listen to him, Lamar! He is a bad guy, and us good guys don't talk to bad guys."

A New Struggle Begins

"Silence, child. Or do you want me to kill your friend too?"

"I will kill you if you hurt my friend!"

"Oh really. Your mother and father lay dead at your feet. I've even crushed the skull of your unborn sibling in my bare hand, and you dare to threaten me? Pitiful."

The creature tightened its grip around Lamar's neck, making him unable to breathe, *"Let us put this to the test. Should you somehow free yourself and save your friend, I shall let you live, but if he dies, then your time on this plain shall end as well."*

Quaked reached out and held the creature's arm in an attempt to forcefully make The Gatekeeper release Lamar but he wasn't strong enough. He struggled and struggled as Lamar gasped for air. Quake clawed and scratched at the creature, kicking his feet and flailing himself about, doing anything to loosen The Gatekeeper's grip. Lamar's body dangled as he slowly began to lose consciousness. His struggles began to subside as Quake watched with tears in his eyes, *"Stop it! You are killing him!"* Quake shouted. But the creature continued to squeeze tighter and tighter until a slight popping sound echoed from Lamar's body. His hands slowly fell and hung to his side as his feet dangled lifelessly below.

Quake suddenly cried out in sorrow as he watched his best friend be killed in front of his eyes! *"Damn you creature!"* Quake said as a menacing aura sped from his body. His voice deepened, and his eyes turned cold, *"I shall devour you . . . I shall devour EVERYTHING!"*

Quake tore off the creature's arm and absorbed it within himself. He fell onto the floor like a cat then stood to his feet. His body began to mature almost instantly. He grew in size as fangs and claws replaced his teeth and fingers. His arms stretched to the

A New Struggle Begins

length of his body, and dark scaled wings sprouted forth from his back. *"Come creature. Let me kill you,"* Quake said just before he vanished. The creature held up Lamar's body and said, *"Have you forgotten? I still have your friend, boy!"* Quake then reappeared, completely transformed. He severed the creature's arm and pulled Lamar from his clutches. Quake kneeled down to the floor, staring at Lamar as if he were a lost treasure. He then placed his claw-like finger on top of Lamar's head and breathed life into his soul while he transferred much of his power into his being.

But the creature had not been defeated. It stood and watched Quake. Once he had let down his guard completely, the creature plunged his massive tail through Quake's back. But Quake didn't flinch. He revived Lamar then spoke to him calmly, *"I will watch over you and our family for all time."* Quake then released all of his power at once, tearing his soul from his body and merging it with the creature, and causing an explosion the obliterated that entire kingdom.

Before the memory was concluded, The Gatekeeper felt an ominous presence loom all around him within the domain. He quickly ended the shared memory, tearing his tail from Lamar's body, as he flew off towards the sky. He distanced himself from Lamar and hovered above him, *"So, you have finally decided to show yourself,"* said The Gatekeeper. *"Come, let us put an end to this struggle."*

Out for Blood: Nathaniel's Truce

Lamar let out a horrifying roar as he clenched his head with both hands.

"What have you done, GATEKEEPER?"

Lamar's massive body rocked back and forth as he screamed out in agony. He began tearing away at himself, pulling out chunks of his flesh. *"Get out! Get out! I wish to be free of you!"* Lamar shouted as he continued to rip away at himself. Blood spewed from his body as he began to rapidly shrink in size. *"I will strip you from me and be reborn!"* The Gatekeeper watched as Lamar fought with himself. While he struggled to maintain his physical state, The Gatekeeper spoke to him from above.

"Come forth child. Let us be reunited."

"Shut up, you bastard!" Lamar replied. *"You are fooling no one!"*

"Silence! I am not speaking to you, boy."

Lamar thrust himself up and flopped onto his knees as he looked up towards The Gatekeeper, *"You damned creature! You will never leave my domain alive!"* Lamar then launched himself into the air as blood burst from his body.

A New Struggle Begins

"Such a foolish child."

The Gatekeeper glanced down in disgust, and with one single swing of his tail, he sent Lamar crashing back down to the domain's floor. Lamar's massive body caused the domain to shake upon impact while a bloody mist filled the air, obstructing Lamar from The Gatekeeper's sight. The Gatekeeper watched as the figure within the blood-soaked mist began to shrink in size and slowly disappear from sight.

"You think you have won, do you? Your attempt to separate us has failed. I don't need him anymore!"

The red mist began to settle, and a figure stood at its center. *"Look upon me, creature. See your failure. See your demise."* The Gatekeeper then peered down and focused his attention on the figure as the mist cleared. To his surprise, Lamar was unharmed. *"Are you surprised, Gatekeeper? You thought he'd emerge from my body, didn't you? Ha, not a chance! I felt his power begin to manifest its own will, so I tore him from me—piece by piece. Your beloved child is scattered along the floor as pieces of my flesh, never to unify, never to become whole again! But wait, there's more!"*

As Lamar continued to speak, the dust settled, and The Gatekeeper could see him clearly, but what he saw caused him to vanish and re-appear before Lamar.

"Don't be so rash Gatekeeper," Lamar said as he appeared before him. *"Let us not forget; I am the arbiter of this domain."*

*"I am no one's fool. I am aware of the extent of your power in **this place**. You are the soul of the vessel, its right-full owner, and this domain is an extension of your being. But do not overestimate yourself. You control this domain and only **this domain**."*

A New Struggle Begins

"Aren't we talkative today?"

Lamar knelt down and reached for Nathaniel, whom he had freed from The Gatekeeper moments before he had been swatted down to the domain's floor. He reached out slowly, then stopped abruptly.

"With all your alleged power, I'm curious . . . why do you hesitate? Surely you could have subdued me by now or even escaped from my domain, but you haven't done either? Why is that? Why allow so many opportunities to pass by?"

The Gatekeeper remained silent, but Lamar quickly recognized something was off. He shoved his left arm through the hole in Nathaniel's chest and stood to his feet with Nathaniel's body dragging on the floor. *"There **is** something you're not telling me, isn't there? Something that's keeping you on edge, what is it?"* Lamar began to walk circles around The Gatekeeper as he continued to speak, *"Are you afraid of this corpse? Of Nathaniel? You yourself acknowledged that he cannot die, and you have already demonstrated that you are superior to him. So why the hesitation? Are you worried that I will overpower you, or is it that you can't finish me off because I remind you of little Quake. Or must I submit before you can kill me? WHAT IS YOUR REASONING, GATEKEEPER!? TELL ME!!"*

Just as Lamar's temper began to overflow, a familiar presence filled the domain once more. The chunks of flesh that were scattered along the floor of the domain had all collected in the distance and were trying to merge together. Seeing this The Gatekeeper rushed over to the mash of flesh and took a defensive stance in front of the mass. *"So this is what you are after,"* shouted Lamar. *"You wanted the child, the fake?!"*

A New Struggle Begins

"Oh no, child. You misunderstood his purpose, our purpose."

Lamar, startled by the sudden voice, looked down at his left arm and noticed that Nathaniel had risen. *"There are two parts to every soul, my child. Two parts that forever battle for dominance over the vessel."* Nathaniel stood to his feet as his tall wrapped around Lamar and pulled him closer.

"Release me, Nathaniel or I shall—"

"You shall what?!"

"I shall kill you."

*"You hold no power here...and you **never** did."*

Nathaniel pulled Lamar in tighter until he could no longer move. Nathaniel gazed into Lamar's eyes as they stood face to face. Lamar could feel the icy shell of Nathaniel press against his flesh.

"You cannot harm me! We have a truce! I've already used the dagger that binds us under oath!"

"Ha, Silly boy. That dagger doesn't prevent me from harming you. It was the catalyst for our merger!"

Nathaniel's body grew cold as he suddenly changed form. His cold and expressionless face opened to reveal a mouth equipped with razor-sharp teeth.

Wings sprouted from his back and wrapped around Lamar until only his head was visible. Lamar couldn't move a single inch. It was as if he had been constricted by a snake. Nathaniel stood behind Lamar as he cried out for help.

A New Struggle Begins

"Help me, Gatekeeper! Help me, and I shall help you destroy Nathaniel!"

But instead of a reply from The Gatekeeper, Nathaniel spoke with his newly formed mouth. *"There is no need to struggle; he shall not aid you, my child. Although each vessel is inhabited by two souls, we can only devour one. You have struggled to become the dominant will of this vessel, so I shall devour you and absorb the other. It is as I promised, or have you forgotten?"*

Lamar looked up at Nathaniel as tears flooded his face and fear filled his heart. He watched as Nathaniel's mouth stretched wide open. He could see the countless number of teeth. He could smell the putrid aroma of death as his body grew cold. Nathaniel paused with his mouth open as massive horns sprouted from his head. Lamar, unable to move or speak, closed his eyes as Nathaniel's final words resonated within his mind, *"Your eyes shall open to the world around you; a true judge of your own existence and no longer bound to the bliss of ignorance. Remain immune to this world of human nature and you shall live abundantly, but should you succumb to this world's chaos, I shall devour you whole."*

Nathaniel then closed his mouth tightly, crushing Lamar's skull as blood poured onto the floor. The Gatekeeper watched from the distance, readying himself for what was to come.

Nathaniel continued to eat away at Lamar's head while his body merged into Nathaniel's being. He then retracted his wings and released the frozen remains of Lamar. His body shattered as it collapsed to the domain floor. *"Now as for you, Gatekeeper. Finish off the other one so that we can*

put an end to our petty squabble. You get the soul you desperately wanted, and I'll have the vessel."

"I will not."

"Of course, you won't."

Nathaniel then charged at The Gatekeeper without restraint, *"There is no need to hold back now. It's just you and me, Gatekeeper."* The two creatures took to the sky, as Nathaniel fought without restraint. *"Is this all that you can muster, Gatekeeper?"* shouted Nathaniel as he knocked him to the floor, *"You must do better if you want that precious soul of yours to go unharmed."* The Gatekeeper recovered from Nathaniel's blow and landed softly. With cat-like reflexes, he then ran in the direction of Nathaniel and jumped into the air, swatting the approaching Enigma again with his tail. Again, Nathaniel was sent crashing to the domain's floor, mere feet away from the coagulating flesh.

Without further hesitation, Nathaniel reached out for the formless mass only to be greeted with a foot to his face from The Gatekeeper.

"Do not touch him!" shouted The Gatekeeper.

"Don't test me Gatekeeper!" shouted Nathaniel as he tackled The Gatekeeper and flung him to the floor by his tail.

*"I do as I please! Now be still that I may **obliterate you!**"*

Power Struggle

"You are strong Nathaniel, but not strong enough!"

"I've gained more than just strength by consuming that pathetic creature!"

The Gatekeeper wrapped his tail around Nathaniel's neck and lifted him slightly, then, with a mighty thrust, slung him to the floor.

"I do not care."

"Oh, but you should."

Nathaniel quickly rolled over and stood to his feet. His movements lacked the distinctiveness of an inhuman creature. He seemed more centered, more focused.

"Enigma, speak. I wish to know all that you've acquired."

"A soul becomes stronger over time as it matures, but not due to the passage of time or accumulated information . . . it's the conviction of the souls. The two souls battle within the vessel until one defeats the other and devours it just as I have. And the two souls become one, ripe and ready to be plucked from the tree of life! But I have only consumed one of the two, only half . . . but this half was very informative."

A New Struggle Begins

The Gatekeeper quickly interrupted Nathaniel, *"Imprisonment for a millennia could not prepare me for your endless dribble. Speak words of importance or do not speak at all."*

"Hmph, well then," Nathaniel vanished from The Gatekeeper's sight and abruptly appeared in front of him as he delivered a powerful blow to his mid-section. The Gatekeeper stumbled backward, but Nathaniel quickly gripped his head and flung him to the floor. *"Listen close, Gatekeeper."* Nathaniel then squatted down towards the floor and spoke rhythmically,

"What am I . . . new, different, unique? Far too long misunderstood by looks and speech."

The Gatekeeper sprung to his feet and posed himself in front of Nathaniel, *"Where did you learn that poem, creature?"*

"Now, now . . . calm thy self, Gatekeeper. No need for harsh words. Feel free to call me Nathaniel. That is my name after all. And I shall address you by yours—"

The Gatekeeper did not wait for Nathaniel to finish speaking. He lunged himself towards Nathaniel with the intent to kill. The Gatekeeper took full form. His wings sprung from his back as he dug his tail into Nathaniel's leg. *"You shall perish here, on this day!"* shouted The Gatekeeper. Without total mobility, Nathaniel was unable to dodge The Gatekeeper's next attack. As The Gatekeeper readied himself to punch yet another hole through Nathaniel; Nathaniel shouted

"MA-NIP-YA-LUTE!"

A New Struggle Begins

The Gatekeeper froze. His body didn't move an inch. Noticing this, Nathaniel quickly took to the sky in efforts to avoid the impending attack.

"You could have concluded this skirmish had you not had that ridiculous flaw. How pathetic."

"That will not work twice."

"There is no need. I have more than enough power to defeat you, Gatekeeper. No, I shall address you as Manipyalute. Come."

The Gatekeeper vanished and appeared before Nathaniel, *"Manipyalute, was once worshiped by many. Refrain from using that name."*

"I am the Enigma Nathaniel. None shall command me."

Nathaniel then charged at The Gatekeeper at full force, causing the domain to tremble with each attack. Meanwhile, on the ground below, the lump of flesh began to take shape. It waddled back and forth as it slowly gained consciousness. Without any limbs to aid it, the mass of flesh fell to the floor and splattered into a puddle. It reached upward, desperately trying to construct some form. But each attempt failed as its limbs would break off and fall back into itself. Although the lump of mass could not yet speak, it continued to press onward as one single thought coursed throughout its being.

A New Struggle Begins

Suddenly a massive shockwave from the distant battle struck the lump of flesh and caused it to clot. Its exterior hardened rapidly, turning the once pool of flesh into a hardened mound of flesh. With its newly acquired exterior, the mound slithered along the floor in search of the source of the shockwave.

Meanwhile, the battle between Nathaniel and The Gatekeeper continued.

"You are a fool, Manipyalute. To protect this child, a single soul, is a fool's errand."

Despite Nathaniel's efforts, The Gatekeeper would not yield. He continued to attack Nathaniel without speaking a single word. But Nathaniel would not stop. He continued to speak aloud to The Gatekeeper as he fended off his advances.

"I will not be denied, Manipyalute! I will have this vessel!"

Nathaniel then stopped fighting back, allowing The Gatekeeper to land a solid attack to his mid-section. Nathaniel counter-attacked by wrapping The Gatekeeper up with his tail.

"Now, let us put this struggle to an end," Nathaniel said as he clasped his hands together over his head. *"I have you now, Manipyalute,"* he shouted as his fists crashed down onto The Gatekeeper, sending him crashing to the domain floor.

A New Struggle Begins

The Gatekeeper's body collided with the domain floor, releasing a wave of energy upon impact. But Nathaniel wasn't finished. Instead, he dove into the crater left by The Gatekeeper, striking him again and sending out another powerful surge of energy upon impact.

"This is where I end your existence," said Nathaniel as he stood on top of The Gatekeeper with his foot dug deep into his chest.

"Come Manipyalute, oblivion awaits."

Nathaniel reached down and grabbed The Gatekeeper by his head and held him out in front of him. *"I, Nathaniel the Enigma, claim this vessel as mine and mine alone."* Nathaniel then wrapped his tail around The Gatekeeper as he pulled him closer to his body. The weakened Gatekeeper began to struggle slightly as his tail swayed back and forth on the floor. *"Do not struggle, Manipyalute. You have lost our wager, and now it is time for you to face your demise."* Nathaniel's wings wrapped around The Gatekeeper as his horns once again sprouted from his head. The Gatekeeper suddenly stopped moving, causing Nathaniel to pause momentarily. *"What are you up to, Manipyalute?"* asked Nathaniel. But before The Gatekeeper could answer, Nathaniel could feel the presence of something familiar approaching fast.

Without releasing The Gatekeeper from his grasp, Nathaniel turned to face the approaching force. He could see a misconstrued creature approaching them in the distance. It ran on six legs and left a trail of thick ooze behind it. Nathaniel's curiosity peeked as the creature finally stood before him. Its body was comprised of Lamar's discarded flesh and the living tissue that Nathaniel tore from his being. It swayed back and forth as its sticky body oozed onto the floor. It had no hands or legs nor any remnants of previous limbs.

"Look at this monstrosity, Manipyalute. It looks like you will have an audience as I consume you. And once I'm finished with you, I shall devour this pathetic remnant of a soul."

Nathaniel redirected his attention towards The Gatekeeper. He began to release his energy in attempts to freeze The Gatekeeper and drain the life force from his body, as he did with Lamar. The Gatekeeper let out a horrifying howl as he smashed his tail down onto the domain floor. Nathaniel's mouth stretched over The Gatekeeper's head as his tail continually crashed down on the floor. Each impact was louder than the last until he caused the lump of flesh to react. Once he had gained the attention of the creature, The Gatekeeper hovered his tail over Nathaniel's head, causing the lump of flesh to climb up Nathaniel's back and onto his head.

Nathaniel quickly crunched down on The Gatekeeper's head and bit through his tail and part of his face. The Gatekeeper then slapped the unformed creature to the floor with his tail causing it to become more aggressive. The creature latched itself onto both Nathaniel and Gatekeeper and began tearing at them both.

A New Struggle Begins

Nathaniel released The Gatekeeper from his grasp, flinging him into the distance as he captured the formless blob.

"You little shit! I will consume you here and now!"

Nathaniel opened up his mouth and bit into the mass of flesh, but before he could rip into it completely, The Gatekeeper tackled him to the floor, distancing him from the mass of flesh. Nathaniel dug his feet into the floor and slammed the wounded Gatekeeper to the ground.

"Just what are you after *Manipyalute*," Nathaniel shouted. *"You claim you want to protect this child and his soul, yet you allow me to consume half of him,"* Nathaniel then kicked The Gatekeeper in his stomach, *"Then you use that pathetic half-soul to free yourself from me. How dare you insult me?!"*

Nathaniel stepped away from The Gatekeeper and readied himself for the approaching creature. But instead of the bumbling and partially constructed mass of flesh from earlier, Nathaniel faced a figure that rivaled his size and stood firmly as a human would.

"My, my, what do we have here? The little monstrosity has grown."

The creature stood in front of Nathaniel as he walked circles around him, inspecting his every movement. *"Creature, can you speak?"* Nathaniel asked as he continued to walk around the creature. *"Do you know who you are or where you are?"*

A New Struggle Begins

There was a brief moment of silence, then Nathaniel attacked the creature. To his surprise, the creature countered his advance. Nathaniel swung his tail at the creature like a hammer. But this time, the creature quickly darted towards Nathaniel. It was able to dodge the brunt of Nathaniel's attack, stumbling just before grabbing Nathaniel by his neck.

"Lit...tle....mon...stros...i...ty," muttered the creature as he lifted Nathaniel from the floor.

"Monstrosity?! You dare call me a monstrosity," Nathaniel thrust his tail into the floor and wrapped his legs around the creature's arm. He then used his tail like a powerful rudder to twist himself rapidly, severing the creature's arm from his body. However, the creature seemed un-phased by Nathaniel's actions and quickly reached out to grab him once more. But Nathaniel was much faster. Still holding the creature's severed arm, Nathaniel used it as a bat and bashed the creature sending it slamming to the domain's floor. Nathaniel then tossed the severed limb aside and kicked the mass of formed flesh a short distance away.

"Just what is this creature?" Nathaniel asked as he readied himself for the creature's counter-attack.

"That is the form a soul takes once it has lost its way. You consumed its better half before they could unify, and this is the result." The Gatekeeper sat on the floor and crossed his legs, *"You will not survive this battle, Nathaniel the Enigma."*

Rebirth

"I am Nathaniel! No incomplete being will ever overwhelm me. If this creature desires to be whole, then I shall reunite it within my being."

Nathaniel rushed carelessly towards the creature without a moment's hesitation. He began to thrash the creature about violently, tearing off slight pieces of its flesh with each attack.

"It is unfortunate that Nathaniel has to suffer such a fate. Had he first consumed that lump of flesh, the younger version of Lamar, he might have uncovered the origin of his birth. Hmph. He and I are of the same, so it is only natural that he would seek out this child long after he had been expunged from my being. I have awaited countless generations for this battle to unfold, and soon I shall be whole again. I have played the weaker long enough. This battle is at its climax – once the souls are whole, I shall consume the victor."

Before The Gatekeeper could finalize his thoughts, Nathaniel flung the creature at his feet. The creature looked battered and beaten. It oozed blood as its movements slowed to a crawl. The Gatekeeper gazed upon the seemingly defeated creature as if he were saddened. Suddenly, Nathaniel crashed down onto the creature, crushing its would-be-spine. Nathaniel dug his feet deep into the creature until they burst through its stomach, splattering The Gatekeeper with its entrails.

Without further hesitation, Nathaniel prepared to consume the creature as he stood within its gut. He kneeled down closer to the creature as his wing and tail hovered overhead, creating a dome. Nathaniel then began to drain the life force from the creature as an icy mist began to freeze the creature's body. The Gatekeeper's tail slammed against the floor, causing Nathaniel to pause briefly and look up at The Gatekeeper. He had turned his back to Nathaniel, and his tail lay flat, circling his body.

The Gatekeeper then looked over his shoulder and spoke proudly, *"Next we meet, we shall be whole again."* Just as The Gatekeeper finished speaking, the creature's body liquefied and wrapped itself around Nathaniel's body. Nathaniel quickly stood to his feet and struggled to fight off the creature, but it was much too late. The creature's body was as elastic as a melted rubber band and had already begun to harden around Nathaniel. He fought desperately, clawing at the creature in an attempt to free himself.

Just as the creature had nearly cocooned Nathaniel, his hand burst through the creature's flesh and began tearing into the creature, freeing his head.

"I will not be defeated! I am Nathaniel, the Enigma!"

Nathaniel let out a sudden burst of energy in an attempt to free himself from the creature. To his surprise, the creature not only endured his blast but absorbed the power through its hardened exterior. Hundreds of spikes now coated the creature, and it began to glow with the same energy Nathaniel had just released. With a single blast, the spikes covering its newly formed shell forcefully receded inward, stabbing Nathaniel and oozing into his being upon entry.

A New Struggle Begins

Nathaniel's struggle subsided as the creature slowly began to devour him. *"You clever, clever creature,"* Nathaniel said to The Gatekeeper as his body was being engulfed by the lump of flesh. *"This was your plan all along."* Just as Nathaniel finished speaking, the blob of flesh consumed him entirely.

The Gatekeeper stood to his feet and faced the cocooned creature, *"Now let us see what soul emerges."* The Gatekeeper watched with anticipation. He had long healed from Nathaniel's attacks and now waited for the birth of a complete and new soul.

Suddenly the shell of the cocooned creature dulled and began to crack. The Gatekeeper quickly lifted his tail unto the air and slammed it down upon the cocoon in efforts to kill whatever that would emerge. But before his tail could collide with the cocoon, a hand burst from the shell and caught his tail, stopping his attack. However, The Gatekeeper took one step forward and delivered a powerful kick that shattered the cocoon. He retracted his tail as he witnessed this newly vested soul stop his second attack as well. He took a step back as the soul took its first step in the domain.

"Who are you?" asked The Gatekeeper.

"Lamar," it replied as it examined itself.

"You are not Nathaniel?"

"I am also the one called Nathaniel, and I am aware of your mischief, Manipyalute. And I thank you. Had it not been for you, I may not have matured, and you would have devoured me like the others."

"Indeed."

A New Struggle Begins

"For generations, you have protected this family's bloodline, awaiting my return. Waiting for my souls to unify. In this world of calamity and disorder, you are quite stubborn."

"My intentions have changed over the generations."

"Then tell me, what are your intentions now? What more could you desire? One who has been worshiped as a god and has devoured countless souls. As the protector of an ancient bloodline and deity, what more is there?"

The Gatekeeper held out his hand with his palm facing upward, *"I intend to make you whole,"* then The Gatekeeper squeezed his hand shut as he spoke directly, *"And then devour your soul at its peak when it's most ripe."*

Moved by The Gatekeeper's determination, the now unified, subconscious soul of Lamar stepped slightly forward and spoke calmly,

"I am whole. So what is your delay?"

"Are you eager to meet your demise?"

"I am no fool. I know that you cannot forcefully consume me . . . not while I am whole. The proof of this is Nathaniel's doing. He merged with a portion of my soul but failed and was taken over by my other half. Furthermore, a human soul takes time to ripen. One must endure struggles, hardships, and accumulate a pool of knowledge."

"Yes. Now you know my intention."

"Hmph! You will continue as Gatekeeper until I have experienced the world of man."

A New Struggle Begins

"You shall ripen through the world's chaos and endure many hardships. I will prolong your life, and you shall not die until I deem it so."

Lamar suddenly lunged himself at The Gatekeeper, punching a massive hole through his chest, *"And if I choose to defy you?"*

The Gatekeeper looked into Lamar's eyes as he stood baring Lamar's arm in his chest, *"That would be foolish,"* The Gatekeeper replied. Then with little effort, The Gatekeeper expelled Lamar from his chest using only his backhand.

"Do not confuse me with Nathaniel. The laws of this domain do not apply to me. I have played fetch long enough. It is time for you to be reborn."

Lamar gathered himself and shrugged off The Gatekeeper's attack. He placed a hand on his face where The Gatekeeper struck him and smiled.

"That hurt . . . that truly hurt," but before Lamar could react further, his vision began to fade. A sharp pain like none he had felt before coursed throughout his body. His eyes bulged as he collapsed to his knees. He gripped his stomach as The Gatekeeper stood over him.

"This is but a glimpse of my power. Remember this feeling as you traverse back."

"You . . . . . BA...STARD!"

"There is much you have yet to learn, much you have yet to feel, and even more that you must endure."

A New Struggle Begins

The Gatekeeper picked up Lamar by his neck and struck him once more, *"This is the first step of our journey. With this pain, you shall be reborn."*

Lamar felt powerless as his body dangled before The Gatekeeper. His strength drained as his vision faded. The Gatekeeper's voice echoed in his mind as his vision went blank.

"I shall protect you from harm as an extension of myself. Gifted to you is a portion of my power. Use it and grow strong; endure and grow wise; age and become a part of me.

Now AWAKEN!"

Acknowledgments

I could not have asked for a better team!

Bogdan Lucut .... Illustrator (Nathaniel)

Brian Matthew .... Illustrator (Front Cover)

Dave Branch ....Illustrator (Lamar)

Debbie Bowen .... Illustrator (The Gatekeeper)

Sarah Howard .... Senior Editor

Thank you for all of your hard work.

In loving memory of

Helen Drisdom

(July 5, 1945 – April 2, 2013)

www.ingramcontent.com/pod-product-compliance
Lightning Source LLC
Chambersburg PA
CBHW071859020726
47502CB00003B/812